STARGÅTE
SG·1™

A MATTER OF HONOR

BOOK ONE OF TWO

SALLY MALCOLM

FANDEMONIUM BOOKS

An original publication of Fandemonium Ltd, produced under license from MGM Consumer Products.

Fandemonium Books
PO Box 795A
Surbiton
Surrey KT5 8YB
United Kingdom
Visit our website: www.stargatenovels.com

STARGÅTE
SG·1.

METRO-GOLDWYN-MAYER Presents
RICHARD DEAN ANDERSON
in
STARGATE SG-1™
AMANDA TAPPING CHRISTOPHER JUDGE DON S. DAVIS
and MICHAEL SHANKS as Daniel Jackson
Executive Producers ROBERT C. COOPER MICHAEL GREENBURG RICHARD DEAN
ANDERSON
Developed for Television by BRAD WRIGHT & JONATHAN GLASSNER

WWW.MGM.COM

ISBN: 1-978-9547343-2-9 Printed in the USA

For Jessica and Ben,
with love.

Many thanks to

Sabine, TL and their red pens.

Erika and Linz,
for always keeping the glass half-full.

Marcy,
for the idea I twisted out of all recognition.

And Tom,
who made it happen.

CHAPTER ONE

The winter sun didn't linger on the low gray wall; its flat marbled surface absorbed the light as easily as the names of the dead.

From the mountains a cold wind whipped down through the Academy cemetery, tugging at the black coats and sharp-lined uniforms of the men and women who gathered solemnly before the memorial. Standing toward the back of the small group of mourners, Colonel Jack O'Neill felt the icy breeze stir the short hairs at the nape of his neck. He shivered, but not from the cold; he felt as though they were burying the living. Again.

The minute's silence was broken by the soothing tones of Chaplain Captain William Zaremski. "We shall remember them," he promised, and Jack found his eyes fixed on the paper fluttering wildly in the man's hands as he read the names. "Lieutenant Jessica McLeod, Lieutenant Jonathan Reed, Captain Roger J. Watts, Major Henry Boyd."

Henry Boyd. O'Neill's mental image of the man – smart, eager and ready for command – was shattered by the stifled sob of the woman standing not ten feet in front of him. Heather, Boyd's wife – his young wife. Even now, five years later, her pale skin was smooth and supple. At her side stood a young girl, staring at the Memorial Wall with serious eyes. She couldn't be more than nine, Jack guessed. Old enough to know she should be sad, but too young to remember much about her father. He looked away, back at the small plaque on the wall. Killed in action, it read. And they might as well be dead, although he knew they might not be. Not yet. But it was coming, a slow, rending death that would be over in seconds and yet would last an eternity. It was enough to send a shiver down his spine colder than any mountain breeze.

After the chaplain had finished speaking, a lone bugler sounded Taps. The mournful notes were snatched by the wind and fell flat. They weren't dead yet. Five years on and they were still dying. His thoughts drifted and he wondered how long it would take for them to–

"Colonel O'Neill?" The voice startled him. He glanced around to see the group breaking up and Heather Boyd standing before him. She was barely thirty, he guessed, blond and gray-eyed. But seeing her up close he realized that her face bore the weight of loss; there was something of himself in her shadowed eyes, damp with tears. "Thank you for coming," she said. "Henry would have been honored. He respected you a great deal."

Jack winced at the irony. "No. I'm honored. Really." And so far from deserving her thanks it wasn't funny. He'd all but sent the man to his death, and then cut off his only way home. The guilt nagged at him, a familiar pain, reminding him of something buried deep. Something he didn't want to contemplate.

Heather glanced over at her daughter, who stood with a silver-haired woman – her grandmother? They were reading the plaque carefully and, as he watched, the girl reached out and touched one of the names.

"I don't know how much she remembers him," Heather said quietly. "Sometimes I think she deliberately tries to forget. She was only four when it happened."

O'Neill cleared the emotion from his throat with a quiet cough. "She looks like a good kid." His words, as always, felt heavy and inadequate.

Heather smiled and nodded, her lips a thin line of restraint. "She has Henry's eyes." She took a step closer. "Colonel O'Neill, would you walk me back to the car?"

Uneasy this close to so much overt emotion, the cowardly part of him wanted to run. He ignored it and swiped the formal dress uniform cap from his head. Even he could tell the damn thing made him look unapproachable. "Sure," he said, running a hand through his hair. Probably didn't help much. "So, how've you been–"

"How did it happen?" Heather kept her eyes facing forward as the wind tugged at her blond hair and her black shoes tapped out a steady rhythm on the frozen path. "I've been trying for five years to get some answers, but you know the military. All they'll say is he was 'killed in action on a covert mission.'" She paused, and in a soft voice added, "I know you were there, Colonel. You know how he died."

O'Neill sucked in a cold breath. It was an impossible question to answer. What the hell was he supposed to say? Your husband traveled through something called a Stargate to a planet in a binary system, just in time to see one of its twin suns implode and become a black hole. Timing sucks, huh? The gravitational field created by the black hole contracted time to the point at which it became impossible for him to reopen the Stargate for more than a second. And so I'm afraid your husband and his team are trapped there, slowly being ripped apart by extreme gravitational forces. Oh, and by the way, when he was trying to get home I slammed the door in his face to stop the black hole from sucking the whole damn planet through the 'gate!

Great answer, O'Neill.

Fact was, she'd never believe the truth, even if it weren't bound and gagged with Top Secret red tape. He glanced at her as they walked, knowledge hanging heavily around his shoulders. She wasn't looking at him and slowly her head sank. "I understand about national security," she said, tears rounding the edges of her words, "but he was my *husband*. Don't I have some right to know how he–" She shook her head angrily and swiped at her eyes.

"I wish I could, Heather. I'm sorry."

Anger sharpened her tone. "He's *dead*," she hissed, keeping her voice low enough not to be heard by her daughter. "What difference does it make?"

O'Neill shook his head, torn. The truth was impossible to tell, and in this case maybe better not heard. How do you tell a woman that her husband is still fleeing in terror, that to him mere minutes have passed since he first tried to get home? His voice was gruff when he spoke again. "It's not that easy."

"Nothing in the military ever is."

She had a point there. "Look, if there's anything I can do–"

"You can tell me how my husband died!" she insisted. "At least tell me *where* he died! Can't you even do that? Make it so that he didn't just leave home one morning and disappear from the face of the Earth. Give me something to tell my daughter, Colonel!"

O'Neill looked out across the green field full of headstones; an entire Air Force of dead men and women. "He died far away," he said quietly. "He died trying to save his team." He turned back to her. "I'm sorry, I wish there was more I could do."

"Do you?" There was a challenge in the words, mirrored in her disbelieving eyes. It drilled right through him.

"I–"

She cut off his excuses with a flick of her head, stopped walking and held out a hand toward her daughter. "Hey, Lucy," she said, with the determined smile parents reserve for the protection of their children. "You ready for that pizza and ice cream?"

Lucy nodded, glancing suspiciously at O'Neill as her eyes brushed over his starched uniform. "Can we see a movie after, Mom?"

Heather took her hand, drawing her closer. "Sure, why not? It's our special day, right?" Over the child's head her accusatory eyes met Jack's. "Thanks for your *help*, Colonel."

He flinched. "If you ever need anything–"

"I'll be sure to call the Society of Military Widows." With that she turned on her heel and walked away, leaving O'Neill alone with his memories and regrets. *I wish there was more I could do...*

And suddenly he was back there, in the control room, staring at the frozen, terrified face of Henry Boyd on the monitor and waiting to destroy, forever, his only chance of getting home. But he hadn't been alone in that room, someone else had been with him waiting to set the self-destruct: Colonel Frank Cromwell – a man he'd learned to hate over the weeks and months of his imprisonment in Iraq.

"We used to be friends, Jack." Cromwell's words surprised and aggravated him. But they were the truth. They had been friends, the best. Brothers-in-arms. A team.

"Yep," was all he said, and he refused to say more.

"I was sick to my stomach when I found out you were still alive," Cromwell pressed, butting valiantly against O'Neill's intransigence. "I wanted to go back for you."

He couldn't hear this, not now. "Why don't we just do this and get the hell out of here, all right?"

Cromwell wouldn't let it rest. Maybe he considered this his deathbed confession. "Someone dropped a dime on the incursion. You got hit, you went down. I made a judgment call to save the rest of the team."

O'Neill scowled. "And I saw you take off!" He didn't believe in

absolution; he believed in duty and loyalty to the end. He remem-
bered the helicopter, his lifeline, spiraling up into the hot, blue sky
as the thud of booted feet and gunfire rose behind him on a wave
of terror. He swallowed, diverting the remembered fear into anger.
"And then I saw four months of my life disappear in some stinking
Iraqi prison."

"I thought you were dead."

"You thought wrong!" He stopped, slamming down hard on his
anger. It was a distraction, a danger, especially now. They had a
job to do. "What do you want? You want me to forgive you, is that
it?"

"Yeah, I guess I do." Cromwell said it quietly, humbly. It wasn't
enough. Not nearly enough.

"Well, that's tough," O'Neill retorted. "What happened to
'nobody gets left behind'?"

Cromwell glanced over his shoulder at the frozen image of
Henry Boyd's face on the monitor. "Well, what about him?"

Guilt hammered like a fist into O'Neill's gut, but he buried the
pain instantly. He had no choice, there was no other way. "That's
an entirely different scenario."

"That is the exact same damn thing, Jack."

The exact same damn thing.

He shivered in the cold winter air as the truth slid home, unsettling as snow in summertime. He'd left him behind. He'd left
Henry Boyd and his team behind.

And nobody gets left behind.

Cheyenne Mountain had been cast into shadow. Daylight fled
before a premature evening, dark beneath a brooding sky heavy
with snow. A storm was brewing.

Deep beneath the mountain, at the very heart of a military command that didn't officially exist, General George Hammond felt
the weight of foreboding pressing down hard on his shoulders. The
threat he faced didn't come from anything as innocent as storm
clouds, however; it came from the kind of politicking and Machia-
vellian double-dealing that tied his guts into queasy knots and left
a distinctly foul taste in his mouth.

Sitting at his desk, fingers laced across his ample belly, he stared at the report in front of him and considered his options. In truth they were limited. When the politicians said jump he had no choice but to ask how high. Although – and the thought drew a smile across his lips – the politicians hadn't actually stipulated *who* was going to be jumping. The Devil, and in this case the angels, were in the detail.

A brisk rap on the door drew him from his musing. It opened before he had time to answer and a familiar face peered inside. "You rang, sir?"

Hammond rose to his feet. "Come in, Colonel. How was the service this morning?"

O'Neill stepped into his office with a shrug that hid everything. "Fine, sir."

With a nod, Hammond acknowledged the subject was closed. Jack O'Neill was a man who liked his emotional privacy and the general certainly had no desire to intrude. Instead he picked up the report he'd been studying, coming around to the front of his desk. The colonel watched him carefully, suspicious eyes fixed on the bland manila cover.

"Trouble, sir?"

With a heavy sigh, he handed the report over. "Senator Kinsey will be paying us a visit."

O'Neill scowled, opened the report and started reading. After a moment his brow knitted in confusion. "This is SG-2's initial report on P4X-481." He looked up. "This is why Kinsey's here?"

"Apparently so," Hammond replied. "SG-9 was scheduled to return to the planet this week, to open trade negotiations with the local people – the Kinahhi. But Senator Kinsey wants to send his own man instead. He's on his way from the Pentagon as we speak."

The colonel was silent for a moment, dropping the report back onto the desk in disgust. "We can't let Kinsey's mook run around out there." He paused for a beat. "Can we?"

"On that we have little choice, Colonel. I wish we did."

O'Neill blew out an angry sigh. "What does he want? What the hell does Kinsey care about '481?"

"That I don't know," Hammond admitted, picking up the folder and handing it back to him. "Which is why SG-1 will be escorting him."

"Us? Sir, is that wise…?"

"Jack, I need our best team on this. Heaven knows we have no reason to trust Kinsey or his people. I need to know what's going on. I need to know why he's so interested in P4X-481."

O'Neill nodded irritably and swallowed the rest of his objections. From the look on his face, they tasted sour. "Kinsey won't like it," he warned. "For some reason he doesn't like me." There was a pause. "It's a kinda mutual loathing thing, actually."

Hammond bit back a dry smile. "I'm aware of that, Colonel. Get your team together; briefing in one hour."

With a grim face O'Neill headed toward the door, rolling up the report and tapping it thoughtfully against his thigh. At the last moment he stopped and turned back, dark eyes meeting the general's with a serious look. "Sir?" he said, in a voice unusually somber. "You know – I've got a bad feeling about this."

Hammond nodded, his earlier foreboding returning. "Me too, son. Me too."

Dr Daniel Jackson shifted his pack awkwardly as he stood waiting in the 'gate room and wondered if bringing all four hundred pages of *The Cypro-Phoenician Pottery of the Iron Age (Culture and History of the Ancient Near East)* had been an indulgence too far. But, given that they'd be off-world for a week, he considered it worth the effort. He had to have something to pass the time in the evenings, other than listening to Jack O'Neill complaining. Something which he'd been doing non-stop for the past four hours.

"I'm just saying," Jack groused, on cue, from where he stood fidgeting on the foot of the ramp, "that it stinks. This whole thing stinks."

Daniel grimaced and squeezed out another drop of patience. "I'm not arguing with you, Jack," he pointed out, still trying to settle the heavy pack more comfortably on his shoulders. "All *I'm* saying is that since we have to baby-sit Ambassador Crawford, there's no use in carrying on about it."

There was a pause. And then, "I'm not 'carrying on about it', Daniel. I'm just making a point."

Behind them Teal'c shifted, the butt of his staff weapon thudding softly against the concrete floor. "I believe your point was well-made in the briefing, O'Neill. And in the corridor. And in the locker room. Several times."

Daniel turned and caught the Jaffa's eye. Teal'c rarely smiled, but that didn't mean his humor was lacking. "So," Daniel said into the irritable silence. "Where's Sam?"

"Briefing Kinsey's lapdog on 'gate travel." Jack glanced up at the control room and Daniel followed his line of sight. General Hammond was up there, his solid presence as reassuring as Cheyenne Mountain itself. Yet, even from this distance Daniel could see the uneasy set of the man's shoulders. There was a tension there that they all felt, and its source stood right next to the general – Senator Kinsey, possibly Stargate Command's most intractable enemy outside the ranks of the Goa'uld.

His crown of white hair lent the Senator a genial look that entirely belied his predatory nature; Kinsey was all about what he could get, and his eyes were constantly fixed on the prize. The prize, in his case, having less to do with the defense of planet Earth and everything to do with his presidential ambitions.

In front of the general and the Senator, Sam Carter sat talking earnestly to another man – Ambassador Bill Crawford, Daniel guessed. He was younger than Kinsey, his hair black and sleek. And although he was dressed in standard military battle dress uniform, he wore it with the sort of awkwardness Daniel remembered from his first days at the SGC. Crawford was a civilian, a diplomat and, in the immortal words of Jack O'Neill, 'Kinsey's creeping toady-spy.'

Daniel wondered how the ambassador would get along with the Kinahhi. He'd read SG-2's initial report, and by their account the Kinahhi were a reserved people, technologically advanced to a level slightly beyond Earth, but reticent about sharing their knowledge.

"What do you think he wants?" Daniel asked after a moment. "Kinsey, I mean. Why's he so interested in the Kinahhi? How does he think they're going to help him get into the White House?"

"So cynical, Daniel?" Jack jumped off the end of the ramp and glanced impatiently up at the control room.

"I've been learning from the best."

O'Neill gave a slight smile and glanced at his watch, tapping it theatrically and holding it up toward the control room for Sam to see. She must have had one eye on her team because she gave Jack a tight nod and rose to her feet, still talking to Crawford. He stood too, and Daniel was irrationally, and rather absurdly, pleased to see that the top of Crawford's sleek black hair came no higher than Sam's nose.

At his side Jack snorted. "Oh look, Mr. Big."

Daniel shook his head, determined not to be amused by such juvenile humor, and tried to pretend he hadn't been thinking the exact same thing. Fortunately, Teal'c came to his rescue.

"According to SG-2, the Kinahhi's security technology is most impressive," he said. "And the Tauri, I have noticed, desire to feel secure – however false that feeling may be. Kinsey surely knows this."

Daniel sobered and nodded. "The Kinahhi are also a little, um, paranoid. Right? I mean, they wouldn't even let SG-2 outside their Stargate complex." He paused for a moment, considering. "Mind you, we don't let aliens out of the SGC, so I guess you could say–"

"You don't think they'll share?" Jack cut right across his tangential thoughts.

"I guess it depends on whether we've got something they want."

In the control room, Sam was having a few final words with Hammond and the Senator, before ushering Crawford ahead of her toward the stairs. As she left, Hammond must have given the order because the 'gate started to spin.

"At last!" Jack muttered, stepping back and away from the splash-zone. He settled his weapon in front of him, and although he was ostensibly watching the Stargate, Daniel knew he also had one eye on the doors. The fifth chevron was already locked by the time they opened and Sam strode into the room, trailing Crawford behind her.

"Sir," she said as she took her weapon from the waiting airman, "this is Ambassador Bill Crawford. Ambassador, this is Colonel Jack O'Neill."

Jack turned until his back was to the 'gate and nodded slightly.

"Crawfish."

Unrevealing eyes glittered darkly in response. "It's Craw*ford*."

"Yes," Jack said vaguely, as if the word barely registered, letting his eyes wander up and down the man in a careful scrutiny. He looked like a weekend-warrior in his BDUs and over-sized helmet. Daniel repressed his amusement, but O'Neill didn't bother. "They found something in your size then?"

"Senator Kinsey has told me a lot about you and your team, Colonel." Crawford's voice was thin and nasal. It suited him. "I look forward to giving him a full report on your methods."

"You haven't written it already?"

The ambassador's lips compressed into a humorless smile and the silence stretched taut. Daniel rubbed at a sudden knot in the back of his neck and saw Sam's eyes flitting carefully between the two men. Like him, she smelled trouble.

Sergeant Davis broke the moment, his voice crackling over the PA system, "Chevron seven, locked."

Jack didn't move, holding Crawford's gaze. Waiting. Daniel stepped back in anticipation, but Jack was barely in the safe-zone. He always had to push it to the limit. And then, like an undersea volcano, the silver-blue event horizon mushroomed into the 'gate room, hitting an invisible wall mere inches from Jack's motionless head. Crawford yelped and stumbled backward in shock, his helmet flying free and clunking heavily onto the concrete floor.

"Holy crap!" he gasped, struggling for balance and composure as the wormhole sucked back in on itself and eventually came to rest, shimmering brightly inside the Stargate.

Daniel smiled; that just never got old.

Turning his back on Crawford's alarmed face, Jack settled his weapon firmly in his hands. "Let's go," he barked, striding up the ramp. "Carter, with me. Daniel, Teal'c – bring the newbie. And Crawford? Don't forget your hat."

Sam cast Daniel an amused look as she headed after O'Neill, leaving him with the ruffled, and now dangerously embarrassed, Ambassador Crawford. He was tempted to sigh at Jack's lack of people skills, but actually he knew the man too well. Jack O'Neill never did anything by accident.

Crawford flashed Daniel a baleful look as Teal'c handed him

his errant helmet, and he smoothed down his hair. "I see the Senator wasn't exaggerating."

Tugging his glasses off his nose, Daniel squinted up the ramp. "He's not so bad once you get to know him." *Unless,* he added silently, *you really piss him off.* He smiled and gestured toward the 'gate. "Shall we…?"

Crawford nodded and glanced up at the control room where Kinsey stood watching. The Senator's face was set and grim, much like Crawford's. With nothing more said, he turned and strode toward the event horizon; if he felt any anxiety, he didn't show it. Fearless, Daniel wondered, or afraid of seeming weak?

Settling his pack one last time, he followed the ambassador. "Gonna be a long week, Teal'c."

The Jaffa fell in at his side, casting him a look out of the corner of his eye. There was a glitter of humor there, but all he said was, "Indeed."

CHAPTER TWO

T he nerve-stretching, body-crushing sensation of being ripped
apart and reassembled in a fraction of a second left Sam Carter
with the usual bone-deep chills as she emerged from the Kinahhi
Stargate. She repressed a shiver and glanced around. The colonel
was already at the bottom of the three metal steps leading down
from the 'gate, and he stood eyeing the welcoming party with a
studied friendliness. She could tell by the way he was balanced
slightly forward onto the balls of his feet that he was far from
relaxed.

It was obvious why.

The Kinahhi Stargate was housed in a room not dissimilar
to the SGC. Tall, white walls rose up on either side, narrowing
toward a slim door at the apex of the triangle. The muzzle of a
large artillery weapon was pointed directly at the 'gate – and hence
at them – shielded by huge transparent plates behind which two
rows of armed men, uniformed in gray, stood vigilantly waiting.
Their weapons weren't raised, but they were just as relaxed as the
colonel.

Cautiously, Sam came to stand at her CO's side. "Friendly," she
observed quietly.

"And here I was expecting a red carpet and balloons."

She smiled slightly, but said no more.

O'Neill raised his hand and waved. "Hi! Good to meet you
guys. How're you doing?" There was a long hanging silence.
"Great. Glad to hear it."

Behind her a sudden scuffling noise, accompanied by gasp-
ing breaths, announced the arrival of Ambassador Crawford. He
retched and Sam winced; it was easy to forget that, despite adjusting the frequency dampeners, the first trip through the Stargate
could still be a disorienting experience. She vividly remembered
her own stomach-churning arrival on Abydos all those years ago
– and the colonel's obvious amusement at her discomfort. She
risked a sly glance in his direction; a lot had changed since then.
And a lot had stayed the same.

"I see they've put out the welcome mat," Daniel murmured, his quiet voice breaking into her thoughts. "I wonder if I should–"

Suddenly the door at the back of the Kinahhi 'gate room opened, admitting a woman and two men. The honor guard that followed marked them out as leaders. Tall and slender, they wore pale robes that hung from their narrow shoulders and arms, lending them a willowy grace that made Sam feel gauche and uncomfortable in her one-size-fits-all uniform. She shifted, irritated at herself, and turned her attention to the military escort.

There was no gold braid or brass buttons, but she recognized the flashes of red and blue as rank insignia on the gray, utilitarian uniforms; these men were obviously Kinahhi top brass. But she was surprised to see that they all bore some kind of sidearm. O'Neill tensed edgily, and she shared his unease.

The woman who led the delegation was poised and elegant, with dark skin and pale blue eyes that glittered like stars. Her face was thin and narrow beneath a cascade of silver hair, and she dominated the whole room, although Sam wasn't sure she inspired a whole lot of trust. She looked like she'd eat her own grandmother for breakfast if the Cheerios ran out.

Behind her came the two men, one elderly and the other young. As the ranks of waiting soldiers parted to let them pass, it was the younger man who arrested Sam's attention. She found herself caught and held by his eyes. They were an odd amber color, which wasn't unattractive, but she saw secrets and shadows in their depths that raised the hairs on the back of her neck. Glancing over at O'Neill she wondered if he'd noticed the silent exchange, but his attention was fixed on the Kinahhi leader. She had drawn to a halt before the Stargate and chose that moment to begin speaking.

"Representatives of the Tauri, I am Councilor Tamar Damaris, leader of the Security Council of Kinahhi. On behalf of the Council I bid you welcome in Peace and Freedom. It is our hope and desire that our talks will benefit both your people and our own in the war against those who would do us harm." She gestured with a long, languid arm at the pair standing behind her. "Councilor Jarel and Councilor Quadesh will oversee your visit."

Daniel stepped forward and cleared his throat. "Councilor Damaris, thank you for your welcome. Allow me to introduce

Ambassador Bill Crawford, the representative of our government who will speak for the Tauri."

Anxious, Crawford pushed past the colonel with a deliberate aggression that wasn't lost on Sam. O'Neill bridled but said nothing, his hard eyes following the clearly nauseated Ambassador as he took center stage and began his rehearsed speech. It was a look cold enough to freeze rock, and Sam felt a beat of pity for the man. Only a beat; he was Kinsey's creature after all, and as dangerous as a snake. Of any variety.

As Crawford's polished words began to flow, Sam's attention wandered back to the face of the amber-eyed Kinahhi. Quadesh, Councilor Damaris had called him. He appeared to be much the same age as herself, olive-skinned and dark haired, and his eyes were now fixed politely on Crawford. Yet she couldn't shake the feeling that the man carried secrets, nor silence the cautionary alarms that were chiming in her head.

At last the speeches drew to a close, and the colonel muttered an irritable, "About goddam time," as he stepped forward. "Okay, now we've all said hello, how about we get this show on the road? We're busy people – places to go, people to see, bad guys to–"

Crawford turned, a smile on his lips and daggers in his eyes. "Thank you Colonel, that's enough."

That's enough? Sam winced. At her side Daniel murmured something that sounded like, "Oh boy." She doubted anyone had spoken to O'Neill like that in years.

Head cocked to one side, the colonel's voice was deceptively calm. "Excuse me?"

A whole head shorter than O'Neill, the ambassador bristled with the belligerence of a terrier yapping at a Rottweiler. When he spoke his voice was pitched low, for their ears only. "Let's get this straight from the outset. You may be the muscle, but I'm the brains. This mission is mine, and I won't let you screw it up. Got that?"

The colonel's fingers tightened their hold on his weapon, outrage evident in the tense, controlled movement. His voice was an angry rasp. "This is my command and you'll do whatever the hell I say."

"I don't think so."

Glancing up, the colonel offered the Kinahhi a tight, synthetic smile. "One more word," he hissed around the grimace, "and I'll pitch you back through the 'gate right now."

The ambassador's answering smirk spread like an oil-slick. "Why don't you do that? Senator Kinsey's just looking for a reason to re-ass you to latrine duty at McMurdo. Disrupting top-level negotiations – negotiations, I might add, that are of vital importance to our national security – would be just the excuse he's looking for." He stepped back, folding his arms smugly across his chest. "Go right ahead, do your worst. *Jack.*"

Daniel sucked in a breath through his teeth, and Sam took an involuntary step forward. She had no doubt that Crawford's threat was real; Kinsey had been trying to shut them down for years. "Sir?" Her voice sounded brittle in the angry silence.

O'Neill's attention darted to her and she held it with a look. *Don't do it, sir.*

His jaw clenched. She could see the anger coiled behind his eyes, like a living thing fighting to get out.

"Is there a problem?" The cool voice, dusted with disdain, belonged to Councilor Damaris.

It broke the moment, allowing Crawford to turn away and say, "None whatsoever, Councilor. Colonel O'Neill and the rest of our military escort will be pleased to see your city while we begin the negotiations."

Military escort? The colonel growled, but the looming tirade was halted by a firm hand on his shoulder.

"O'Neill." Teal'c's voice was so soft that Sam could barely hear him. "It is wise council to keep your enemies within your grasp, not beyond your reach."

"He's right, sir," Sam added quietly. "You'd just be playing into Kinsey's hands."

O'Neill pulled the cap from his head and stuffed it angrily into a pocket. "This is bullshit."

"Yes, sir."

He gave her an angry look. "Yes sir?"

She shrugged. "It's bullshit, sir. But what choice do we have?"

"Ah, look," Daniel interrupted quietly, clearing his throat. "I think I might…" He nodded over the top of his glasses toward where Crawford was now schmoozing with the councilors, "you know, join in."

The anger in O'Neill's face began to relax. "Join in?"

Tugging off his glasses Daniel started polishing them with a studied innocence. "Well, I do have experience in first-contact negotiations. Crawford can't deny that. "

"No," the colonel agreed. "No he can't." And then he smiled, a short, feral smile. "Go, Daniel. Snoop. Spy. Report."

Daniel gave a quick grin. "I'll catch up with you guys later." Casting Sam a 'here-we-go' look, he returned his glasses to his face and headed determinedly toward Crawford and the Kinahhi representatives.

O'Neill watched him go and sighed irritably, "So I guess we get to take the ten cent tour."

"I am Councilor Quadesh," the Kinahhi man said, bowing slightly in a formal greeting. "You are welcome in peace and freedom to the City of Hagarsa."

They stood in a bright, white plaza outside the Kinahhi Stargate complex, surrounded by squat buildings with flat roofs and shuttered windows that butted together like teeth in an overcrowded mouth. There was no grace or elegance here, just a determined pragmatism that would have made the Kremlin proud. At the center of the plaza was a structure that could once have been a fountain, or the plinth for a statue. Whatever it had once been, it was defunct. There was no water and no civic art. Instead, a tall metal archway stood incongruously at its side, glinting in the sunlight. And, oddly, there were no people. Not a soul. Not a sound. The silence was oppressive, and as Jack turned to take in the whole plaza his boots scraped loudly over stone. He almost winced, the noise sounded so intrusive. Instead he turned his eyes on their tour guide. "Nice to be here," he attempted to enthuse. After all, it wasn't this guy's fault that Crawfish had royally pissed him off.

At his side, Carter shivered and he realized that he too was cold. Although the sun shone, it was bigger and paler than the one he was used to and gave off far less heat. An old star, he thought. But there were no clouds and the aging sun was bright enough to give Jack good reason to slip his sunglasses over his eyes. He liked the protection they afforded, less from the UV light than from the penetrating stares of strangers. He was here to learn about these people and the less he gave away the better. "So," he said, waving a hand toward the tightly packed buildings, "where do we start?" He couldn't even see an alleyway between them and it made him claustrophobic.

"I understand that this is a coastal city," Carter chipped in. "In their report, SG-2 mentioned that you've actually built a city on the ocean. So I thought…" She glanced at Jack for a moment, seeking his approval. He gave a shrug, willing to go along with whatever she had in mind, "I thought perhaps we could see the city from here?"

Quadesh smiled. "We can indeed see Tsapan from the Hagarsan coast. What is your interest in it, Major Carter?"

Looking surprised at the question, she shrugged. "Well, it's quite a technological feat. It's something that's been mooted from time to time on our planet, as a way of dealing with over-population. So to see it in practice would be of great interest to us." She glanced over at Jack once more, a glint of resignation in her eyes. "Well, of interest to me, anyway."

"The technology interests you?" Quadesh pressed, his strange amber eyes sliding over Carter in a way Jack tried to ignore. Carter, he knew, could take care of herself. Still…

"Let's face it, Councilor – a floating city? It's cool." He scanned the plaza for an exit. "Which way?" He saw none, instead finding himself pinned by Quadesh's eyes. For a moment it felt as though the councilor could penetrate the dark shields of his sunglasses and see right into his heart.

Then Quadesh smiled and pulled what looked like a cell phone from his pocket. Genially he said, "It is not possible to walk to the coast, Colonel O'Neill. There are safer ways of traversing the city in these times."

Okay, so *that* set off all the alarms. Carter instantly flung him a concerned look and Teal'c shifted imperceptibly, his hand sliding up his staff weapon and its butt coming to rest solidly on the ground.

O'Neill cleared his throat. "These times being?"

Looking up from the device in his hands, Quadesh gave them an ambiguous look. "Times of trouble, Colonel. Times of trouble."

Crawford walked with a stiff back, as if his ego had taken up residence along his spine like some sort of personal Goa'uld striving for that extra inch in height. Daniel was reminded of his Greek mythology professor at the University of Chicago – small in stature, big in ego. He had no doubt that Crawford was intimidated by his presence, not to mention aggravated. But Daniel hadn't taken no for an answer – six years of working with the military had taught him the value of obstinacy – and even Crawford couldn't deny his experience in the field of alien diplomacy. "Just don't get in the way," the ambassador had warned before he'd turned his silken smile back to Damaris, leaving Daniel to trail along as they headed out of the 'gate room. Being at the back suited him, though, dividing his attention between Crawford's unbending gait and the councilor's elegant stride. You could learn a lot just watching.

Take Damaris, for example. She was an enigma. She wore her pride like a cloak, letting it catch up in her wake anyone who had failed to notice her power. Yet despite this pride, Daniel sensed an edge of unease in the woman – in all the Kinahhi – an unease that bordered on fear. In all his travels and encounters with new civilizations, Daniel had rarely come across an advanced, democratic society in which the head of state felt the need to be personally armed. His eyes fixed on the very serviceable weapon strapped to the woman's leg. What did she fear?

The white corridor down which they walked turned a graceful corner and abruptly came to a halt. At the end of the truncated hallway squatted a low desk, manned by a young soldier who jumped up as they approached. Next to the desk stood a metal arch that guarded the entrance to a lofty hall beyond. Through the arch Daniel could see a wide table, with ornate baskets of fruit dotting its length. It had been a long time since breakfast and his stomach growled hungrily, causing Crawford to fling him an exasperated glare. Daniel shrugged an apology and turned his attention to the soldier.

Young and eager, the soldier saluted, hand on heart, as Councilor Damaris approached the desk. She just nodded to the kid and drifted past, into the room beyond, setting little green lights flitting across the gray arch. She was followed by Councilor Jarel and three other Kinahhi bearing the cautious faces of bureaucrats everywhere. The green arch lights flickered again, as each of them passed through. Crawford was about to follow when the soldier on duty stepped forward and stopped him.

"One moment," he said, adjusting something on a view-screen in the side of the arch. Daniel peered around to get a better look and the soldier's eyes shot up and narrowed. "Please step back, sir."

Crawford glared at Daniel. "Get your nose out of there, Jackson." He offered the soldier an apologetic smile. "Is there a problem?"

Whatever had been bothering the Kinahhi seemed to have been resolved, and he stepped away from the screen. "No, sir. Please proceed."

With a warning glance at Daniel, Crawford stepped through the arch. Daniel watched the green flickering lights curiously. "Is it some kind of metal detector?" he asked. "Although that wouldn't make much sense, since Councilor Damaris just walked through it with–"

"Proceed through the *sheh'fet*," the soldier snapped, and when Daniel turned to look at him he saw a genuine agitation on the young man's face.

Sheh'fet? Judgment, in Hebrew. Or very like it. "Sorry," he said, "I didn't meant to interf–"

"Proceed through the *sheh'fe*t!" the soldier insisted, his hand jerking down to where, Daniel had no doubt, his weapon was lurking.

Holding his hands up carefully he started walking. "Okay, okay. No problem. I'm going."

He looked up as he walked underneath the arch, but couldn't see any lights. As he entered the vast, white space beyond the checkpoint he glanced once over his shoulder to see the young soldier staring intently at the screen on the low desk.

He had the sinking feeling that the lights hadn't flashed green for him. Which probably meant trouble.

Gaping in astonishment, Sam stared in the direction Quadesh was pointing, up into the skies above her head. "Wow." A ship the size of a school bus hovered silently overhead.

At her side, Teal'c raised an arm to shield his eyes from the sunlight as he too stared at the alien craft. "Its engines make no noise," he observed. "And they emit no jet wash."

Even the colonel seemed impressed. "Now *that's* what I call stealth mode."

"Yes, sir," Sam breathed. An engine that was utterly silent and that didn't even disturb the air as it landed? It brought a whole new meaning to the idea of a stealth fighter, not to mention the potential civilian applications. Of course there was the eternal question of a power source, but if the Kinahhi were willing to share this kind of technology… "Sir," she began excitedly, "if we–"

"I know, Carter," he said with a quick smile. "Check it out."

While they were speaking, the craft settled to land on the other side of the plaza and a mechanical ramp was gently extended. "Come," said Quadesh. "I will answer what questions I can on our way to Tsapan."

Excited by the prospect of getting up close and personal with this new technology, Sam was on Quadesh's heels, following him across the plaza. The ship, like the buildings, was white and blocky. It didn't seem built for either speed or beauty. And it had no windows other than those at the front. Not exactly passenger friendly, but–

"Major Carter?" A hand touched her wrist. It was Quadesh. He had stopped next to the metal archway she'd noticed earlier, and was watching her with an intense scrutiny that was unsettling. "Please, you must pass through the *sheh'fet* before we embark."

She glanced at the archway. "The *sheh'fet*?"

"And what would that be? Exactly." The colonel inserted himself between them, imbuing his light tone with just enough threat to cause Quadesh to drop her wrist and back off.

"It is nothing to fear," the councilor assured them. "We must all pass through. It simply provides a record of our passing."

O'Neill cast her a glance. "Passport control?"

"Maybe." She looked up at the metal arch. "More like a security check-point, perhaps?" It wouldn't look out of place at JFK.

He nodded, eyes moving to Teal'c. "T?"

"I have encountered no such device before, O'Neill." Which was a guarded way of saying it didn't look like something the Goa'uld had cooked up. Sam agreed. Whatever it did, this technology was native to the Kinahhi.

The colonel squared his shoulders and stepped forward. He would go through first, of course. She wondered if he was even conscious of these subtle acts of bravery, or if they were so ingrained into who he was that they were as natural to him as breathing. Either way, she noticed. Always had. "Do I have to switch off my cell phone and take off my shoes?"

Sam hid her smile as Quadesh stared at him, glanced down at the big, heavy boots, and said, "That is not required, Colonel O'Neill."

"Lucky for us all," he beamed, overflowing with false jollity. "After you, Councilor."

With a compliant nod of the head, Quadesh moved to the far side of the arch. There must have been a control panel there, because Sam could hear the soft beeps and burbles of technology before he stepped back out into view. "Please," he invited. "Follow me."

In two steps he was through. The colonel nudged her arm and nodded toward the top of the arch. Green lights were running across, like tracer fire. After a moment they disappeared. His eyebrows rose. *What do you make of that?*

"Green for go?" she guessed aloud.

As she was talking, she watched Quadesh move once more to the side of the arch – *sheh'fet*, he had called it – and touch the controls. The colonel shifted and didn't seem convinced by her guess. In fact, he looked downright uneasy. "Stay sharp," he muttered under his breath.

His tension was contagious, and she found herself lifting her weapon into her hands. She kept it neutral, but the familiar weight was comforting.

Then, with a final glance up at the arch, O'Neill took two steps through it.

There were no sirens. No alarms. Nothing happened. However, this time the running lights glowed blue. Blue for what? Through the arch the colonel was watching her carefully. All she could do was shrug. If the color was significant, she didn't know why.

Without further hesitation, she and Teal'c stepped through the arch to join him. Again, nothing happened but a swift display of blue lights.

After a moment, Quadesh appeared from the side of the *sheh'fet*.

Beneath his dusky skin, Sam thought she could detect a hint of pallor. And there was a definite sheen of sweat on his forehead that belied the cool air in the plaza. The tension ratcheted up a notch. "Everything okay?" she asked.

"Of course," came the reply. It was altogether too fast and too pat. "Let us proceed."

She cast a quick glance at the colonel to see if he'd caught the lie. His slight nod, telling her to keep digging, was all the answer she needed. "How does it work?" she asked mildly. "You said it records our passing. Is it a scanner? Is it connected to a central database or–"

"Please!" Quadesh held up a hand. It was trembling slightly beneath his long robes. "I cannot answer your questions. It is forbidden."

"I'm sorry," Sam said, immediately backtracking. The old adage about flies, honey and vinegar invariably paid off. It wouldn't pay to anger these people. "I didn't mean to embarrass you." She paused for a moment and saw a little of the tension ease from the councilor's face. Just a little. He still looked spooked.

"Come," he said, obviously making an effort to collect himself. "Let us embark." With a gracious gesture, he waved them up the ramp and into the Kinahhi aircraft.

Sam moved off silently, catching O'Neill's eye as she did so. "Curiouser and curiouser," he muttered quietly. She had to agree.

The inside of the ship was a surprise. No hard military benches or cramped airline seats here. Instead, deep, cushioned chairs in the Kinahhi's preferred color of white were grouped together, positioned next to floor to ceiling windows. Very urban chic.

O'Neill sat, settled his weapon more comfortably and glanced around. "Someone's been to Ikea."

She smiled at that, and at Teal'c's bemused expression as he came to look out of the picture window. "I did not see any windows on the outside of the ship."

"Must be some kind of one-way glass," Sam guessed.

Teal'c nodded and tapped it lightly with his finger. "It appears to be strong."

"It is an alloy," Quadesh informed them as the ramp hissed back inside the ship and the doors quietly closed. "Very strong. It can withstand the blast of a ground-launched projectile."

O'Neill's eyebrows rose. "And that's a common problem on your airlines?"

Not quite understanding the idiom, Quadesh simply said, "There are those who would do our people harm. It is against them that we struggle."

"Yeah." The colonel glanced away and out over the shining white city. "We kinda have a similar problem."

The Kinahhi smiled, his momentary discomfort either gone or effectively hidden. "Then perhaps our peoples will indeed become allies? We have much in common."

Sam returned his smile, although it felt forced. His amber eyes were like mirrors, reflecting herself back and giving away nothing. Uncomfortable, she looked away and out of the window. To her astonishment, the plaza was slowly receding beneath her; she hadn't even known they were moving. It really was quite a remarkable technology, and her excitement returned in force. "So tell me," she asked Quadesh, "how is this thing powered? How does it fly without aerodynamic lift?"

"Aerodynamic lift." Quadesh repeated the words with a nostalgic laugh and smiled again, that same mirror-like smile. "That then is how your own transports fly?"

"Yeah," she agreed, shifting awkwardly under his lightly patronizing gaze. "I guess that seems a little old-fashioned to you."

"A little. It is a very power-intensive method of transport, is it not?" Sam nodded her agreement, but held her tongue as Quadesh continued. "Here on Kinahhi we use a quite different technology, one that allows us to negate the force of gravity within a defined area. Thus our transports 'fly,' although not in the manner of a bird. It would be more accurate to say that they float."

Sam felt her eyes widen as she processed the information. "Anti-gravity technology? Wow, that's– That's way ahead of us. I'd love to see–"

"It negates the force of gravity?" The interruption had come from the unlikely source of the colonel. "As in… makes it go away? Nullifies it?"

"Within the defined area, yes," Quadesh replied. "We are, in effect, sitting atop a bubble of negative gravity."

Sam was about to speak again, but the colonel beat her to it. "How big?" he asked abruptly. "How big can the bubble get?"

Quadesh smiled, his eyes darkening. "I have told you more than, perhaps, is wise. The negotiations between our leaders will cover such issues of technology. I cannot give away our secrets, Colonel."

It was only because Sam was watching him that she noticed the frown of irritation flicker across O'Neill's face as he nodded brusquely and said, "Right." His eyes met hers for an instant, something surreptitious hiding in their depths. Without doubt there was a purpose to the colonel's interest. But what that might be, she had absolutely no idea.

CHAPTER THREE

"**O**kay, let me get this straight." Daniel spread his hands wide on the smooth, translucent surface of the table. "The *sheh'fet* reads minds?"

His words echoed around the white room before fleeing through the long, slit windows that sliced through the far wall, striping the floor with golden fingers of pale sunlight. Opposite him the Security Council sucked in a collective breath; seven straight-laced Kinahhi staring at him through suspicious eyes. Either his question or his tone had caused offense, it seemed. Their leader, the inscrutable Councilor Damaris, fixed him with a steady gaze. A hard woman, Daniel thought, as she blinked colorless eyes at him and her lips tipped up toward a thin smile. A hard, determined woman. She would give no ground. "That is too simplistic an interpretation, Doctor Jackson. The *sheh'fet* cannot 'read minds'. It simply measures physiological responses and determines the likely threat level posed by the individual being scanned."

The hairs crept up on the back of his neck, like moral fibers in revolt. "So even if they haven't done anything wrong, they're defined as a threat?"

Damaris nodded slightly, her smile fading. "A potential threat."

She didn't seem to appreciate the questions, and at his side he sensed Crawford shift uncomfortably. *He* probably didn't appreciate the questions either. Too bad. "And if someone is identified as a 'potential' threat? What happens then?"

Her lips pressed into a tight line, shoulders stiffening. "They are removed, Doctor Jackson. Surely the Tauri also remove those inimical to your society?"

"Well yes, but not before they're proven to have committed a cri–"

"We do indeed, Councilor Damaris," Crawford smoothly interjected, casting Daniel a flat stare that spoke silent volumes of outrage. "However, less efficiently than the Kinahhi."

"Efficiently?" Daniel glanced between Crawford and the Kinahhi woman, alarm rising. "How? Exactly."

The councilor's demeanor chilled. "Our methods," she told him, "are not part of these negotiations. You have asked for access to the *sheh'fet* technology, which we are willing to share in exchange for access to a number of resources on your planet."

Stunned, Daniel turned to Crawford. "So this is what Kinsey wants? This is why you're here? For their Big Brother equipment? This isn't going to protect Earth against Anubis or–"

"The security of the *United States* is of paramount concern to the Senator," Crawford snapped, jutting out his chin and endeavoring to look down his nose at Daniel. Not an easy task, given his height.

"What? He's going to install checkpoints on our street corners?" He couldn't believe what he was hearing. "This is… this is insane!"

"The Senator believes that this technology will protect us from those unfriendly to our country and–"

"–get him into the White House?"

"The Senator's concern is for the security of the–"

"Don't you get it?" Hands slicing the air with frustration, Daniel tried to make him understand. "We can't waste time with this stuff! There are more important things at stake. We shouldn't be wasting our resources–"

"That's rich coming from you, Doctor Jackson," Crawford snapped. "SG-1 has turned its back on countless military technologies – mostly, I might add, at your urging – on spurious moral grounds. This technology will guarantee the security of our nation."

"Arresting people *before* they commit a crime? Have you actually *read* the Constitution, Crawford? We can't–"

The subtle noise of chairs scraping over the opalescent floor drew his attention back to the Kinahhi representatives. All were now on their feet and as he and Crawford fell quiet the room descended into a disapproving silence. At last Damaris spoke, her voice heavy with disdain. "If the Tauri no longer wish to trade technology we must ask that you leave our world and–"

"No!" Crawford shot to his feet like a child threatened with curfew. "No. My apologies, Councilors. Doctor Jackson has no authority to speak on this matter." He turned, face taut with anger, to where Daniel sat, arms folded stubbornly across his chest. "In fact, he was just leaving."

"I don't think–"

Crawford was abruptly in his face. "Leave now, or you'll be lucky to get a job teaching first grade in Alaska."

Jaw set, Daniel glared back. "Are you threatening me?"

"No," Crawford replied with a small shake of the head, "I'm telling you, Jackson. For the record."

Daniel held his gaze for a long moment, weighing his decision. Crawford didn't give an inch and Daniel had no doubt he'd make good on his threat. Somewhere in the back of his mind he could hear Jack's warning voice, *Not now, Daniel.* For once, he listened to it. Slowly standing up, he got a marginally gratifying satisfaction from being able to look down on his rival. "This is a mistake," he warned. "For the record."

With that he nodded to the Security Council and strode toward the exit, wincing as Crawford's obsequious words trailed after him. "My apologies Councilors – there are some among our people who do not fully appreciate what you are offering."

Damaris replied, sharp as cut glass. "As there were among the Kinahhi. At first."

At first? Daniel felt his skin crawl. What the hell did that mean?

The ocean was blue and beautiful under huge skies striated with clouds cast in purples and pinks. From where Jack stood atop a barren cliff he could hear the crash and roar of the waves below and thought, for a moment, that there was almost enough beauty in the galaxy to compensate for all the ugliness it threw at you. Almost.

But it wasn't just the natural wonder of the ocean that caught his eye, and gradually he found himself gazing at the gem-like glitter of Tsapan – the ocean city. Even to his jaded eyes it was breathtaking. Floating above the waves the vast citadel shone and sparkled in the sunlight, its smooth surface punctuated by pinnacles and turrets, its walls a shimmering rainbow of colors.

"Wow," Carter breathed, always the mistress of understatement. "It's beautiful."

"Indeed it is," Quadesh replied. "Beauty bought at a price, so legend has us believe."

"What do you mean?"

Before Quadesh could reply, Teal'c spoke. "The design is Goa'uld."

Surprised, Jack turned back to the shining city. "Really? Where's all the Las Vegas chic?"

Carter smiled, but Quadesh was as sober as ever. "The legend tells us that Kinahhi was once ruled by the good and wise King Yahm," he told them. "He was beloved of the gods until his disdain for them grew so great that they sent Re'ammin the Thunderer to punish him. Yahm was cast into the ocean and Tsapan was built on the site of his defeat by the Kinahhi people he enslaved."

Jack flicked a curious glance at Carter. She just shrugged – *we need Daniel.*

"What became of Re'ammin?" Teal'c asked, his eyes fixed on the glittering city. "The name is familiar to me."

"He fled when the Kinahhi people rose up and used his magic against him," Quadesh replied with an indulgent smile. "The magic, of course, is the technology of Tsapan."

Jack's gaze returned to the city, which floated elegantly above the gentle waves. "It uses the same anti-gravity technology as your ships?"

"Ships?"

"Airplanes," Jack explained, waving at the sky.

Quadesh frowned. "I do not–"

"The colonel's referring to the transport we traveled in," Carter explained. "Is that how the city floats? Using anti-gravity technology?"

"Ah yes. You are correct, Major Carter. It has taken many generations for our people to understand the technology, but Tsapan is the source of all that we have learned. What once enslaved us has now set us free."

Jack smiled at that. "Nice irony." But his mind was already racing ahead, turning over the possibilities and speculating on the opportunities such technology might deliver…

"I'm sorry, Heather, I wish there was more I could do."

"Do you?"

"And yet," Teal'c said, scattering Jack's thoughts, "despite your freedom, you fear to walk the streets of your city and your leaders bear arms."

Turning away from the city, Jack fixed his gaze on the Kinahhi man. Teal'c made a good point and one that Quadesh seemed reluctant to address. When he spoke it was tight-lipped and defensive. "We do what we must to protect our society. Threats no longer come from mythical gods, Teal'c – they come from people who would destroy the freedom for which we have long fought."

Teal'c said no more, but Jack could sense the unease in his friend and knew better than to dismiss it. "Tell me," he said to Quadesh as they turned away from the ocean, "who are these people you're fighting?"

As soon as Daniel stepped through the gray arch the young soldier was on his feet and standing in front of him. "Let me guess," Daniel snapped, "that thing just told you I want to scoop out Bill Crawford's brains with a spoon and now you're going to arrest me?"

The young man blinked in surprise and said, "No. I've been asked to escort you to the Tauri quarters, sir. This way, please."

Blindsided, Daniel muttered an embarrassed, "Oh. Right. Uh, thanks." He'd definitely been spending too much time with Jack. He was beginning to channel the man. Falling in at the soldier's side he followed him through the white corridors of the Kinahhi government building and, clearing his throat, tried for a friendlier tone. "So… I'm Daniel."

The soldier cast him a sideways look and said, "Chief Officer Abdar."

He smiled and searched for something else to say. "I, uh, guess you've seen quite a few arrests, huh?"

The kid kept his eyes front and center. "Some."

"You must have a lot of prisons." No response. "You ever seen one? Been inside one?"

"I'm sorry, I'm not familiar with the term."

"Prisons? You know, places where you keep people who–"

He was stopped by a hand on his arm. "We must be careful here, Doctor Jackson." Abdar indicated a turn in the corridor. "The building was damaged two days ago and it is still being made safe." Daniel didn't have time to comment before they rounded the corner and he found himself staring through a crumbling wall and out into a street lined by square buildings. People hurried past, heads bowed, while men worked to repair the damage. Rubble still covered the floor and there was a crack along the ceiling that gave Daniel an ominous sense of claustrophobia.

"What happened?"

Abdar shrugged. "The Mahr'bal. Dissidents. The government is always a target."

"They attacked you?"

He nodded. "We've been at war with them since Libnah." When Daniel didn't reply, he added, "One of our colonial outposts. It was wiped out fifty years ago by a biological attack. Ever since, we've been at war."

"The Mahr'bal are an enemy state?" Daniel asked, raking a hand through his hair and getting that horrible feeling they'd bitten off far more than they could chew. It wouldn't be the first time the SGC had put itself in the middle of someone else's war. In his experience, it never ended well.

"No. They are of Kinahhi," Abdar told him. "They just don't believe in the same things we do. Freedom, technology, progress."

"So, what do they believe in?"

Abdar shrugged as they put the damage behind them. "The old ways. The old gods…"

"Old gods?" Instantly on alert, Daniel found himself glancing about as if expecting a contingent of Jaffa to come marching around the next corner.

Abdar smiled, shaking his head. "Every fool knows there are no gods. They were simply legends and myths to explain the inexplicable when our people were primitive and ignorant. But the Mahr'bal don't know reason. They're fanatics. They would have us all believe as they do, or die for our heresy. Here," he said, stopping before a narrow door. "We can leave here."

Pushing open the door, Abdar led Daniel into a sparse, white square. Windows and doors surrounded the empty courtyard and all was still and quiet. "This is where your people are to stay," he told them. "You will be safe here. It is within the security perimeter. For your own protection, however, you must not leave the quadrangle."

Blinking in the bright sunshine, Daniel squinted at the young man and nodded his thanks. "Are my friends here?"

Abdar shook his head. "They will return soon." He gave a curt smile. "Once your friends arrive, food will be provided. There are facilities in the rooms."

Daniel managed a weak smile. "Thanks." But the *sheh'fet's* flickering lights flashed disturbingly into his mind and he wished the accommodation didn't look quite so much like a prison.

Sam gazed out of the window of the transport as it flew them back across the city, trying to make out the features of the alien world. Ahead of them, she could see a vast complex which she guessed must house the Kinahhi Stargate. Ringed by a wide building, the inside of the complex was a maze of walkways and courtyards similar to the one from which they'd embarked on their excursion. It was almost a small city in itself.

"Looks like the Pentagon," the colonel muttered quietly.

She smiled. "Yes, sir."

Her thoughts soon drifted away from the Kinahhi city and back toward Tsapan. Its beauty was striking, especially in comparison with the utilitarian style of the Kinahhi. It wasn't only the city's beauty that fascinated her though, it was the technology. What kind of technology could float an entire city above the ocean? How did you even begin to create an anti-gravitational 'bubble'? It was no science she'd ever come across, and the prospect of challenging yet more of what she thought she knew about how the universe worked was intoxicating. Turning away from the window she smiled at Quadesh. "Would it be possible to visit Tsapan? I'd love to take a closer look at the technology it uses."

The councilor shook his head, a slight disapproving gesture. "I am afraid that's not permissible, Major Carter."

At her side she felt O'Neill shift. "Why not?"

Quadesh turned his amber eyes on him. "The city is a site of great importance to the Kinahhi," he said carefully. "As well as the root of our technology, for some it is also a site of religious importance. We cannot admit outsiders, on grounds of both security and cultural sensitivity."

"Some of the Kinahhi still worship the false gods?" Teal'c asked abruptly, and Sam winced at the irritation she heard in his voice. Not easily riled, this was the one subject on which Teal'c could rarely stay silent. And, for him, that was saying something.

Quadesh seemed surprised by the question, and for a moment Sam didn't think he was going to answer. He gazed at Teal'c, a calculation racing beneath the mirror-like surface of his eyes. "Access to the city of Tsapan is one of the major conflicts between the government and the Mahr'bal."

"Marbles?" Sam hid a smile at the colonel's quiet interruption, but Quadesh seemed oblivious.

"They do not approve of our use of the technology we have 'scavenged' – in their view – from the holy site."

Anger touched Teal'c's face. "There is nothing holy about the Goa'uld."

Quadesh simply inclined his head but his lack of an answer made Teal'c frown, and Sam still couldn't shake the feeling that the Kinahhi man was keeping something from them. She shifted in her seat, tense now, finding it difficult to sit still. It drew O'Neill's attention.

"What?" he asked.

"Nothing, sir."

"Yeah," he said quietly. "I know what you mean."

Still uneasy, Sam returned to her study of the city. They were barely skimming over the tops of the buildings, obviously coming in to land. But to her eye it was simply a blur of disappointment. If only she could spend half an hour in the floating city, just get one look at the technology... Next to her the colonel sighed heavily, pulled his cap out of a pocket and jammed it onto his head. When she looked over at him he gave her a frustrated frown. "Maybe we can trade for it?"

His mind had obviously been following hers, as it so often did. She nodded thoughtfully. "I suppose it's possible that's why Crawford's here."

"Oh, somehow I doubt that. Kinsey won't be after anything useful."

She was about to reply when white walls suddenly shot up either side of the transport and, with barely a bump, they came in to land. The doors hissed open and Quadesh rose to his feet. "I will take you to your accommodation now," he told them politely. "Your friend, Daniel Jackson, is awaiting you."

Sam flashed a wary glance at the colonel. "Short negotiations."

"Very."

They followed Quadesh out of the transport and found themselves standing in a narrow street, cast in alternating shadow and light. Their transport was parked – if that was the right word – in a row of similar ships.

"Taxis?" O'Neill suggested quietly.

She shrugged. *Maybe.*

"This way," Quadesh told them, already moving, eyes darting nervously at the dark, silent buildings. "We must hurry."

Daniel lay staring at the ceiling in one of the white, clean and boring rooms they'd been given. There was nothing there to spark his interest, no architectural curiosities, no inscriptions to translate. Simply a bed, a side table and a chair. Oh, and through the narrow door at the far end, a bathroom. En suite. Jack would be impressed.

His stomach grumbled and he wondered if the Kinahhi would be offended if he broke out his MRE's instead of waiting for the food they were providing. Then again, he doubted he could piss them off any more than he already had, so why worry? He sat up and reached for his pack, trying to decide between Country Captain Chicken or Jamaican Pork Chop. Not that it really mattered anyway; they all tasted the same – synthetic and slightly toxic. Meals-Ready-to-Eat were never exactly–

"Nice."

The word drifted through the door he'd left ajar and had the unique mix of sarcasm, humor and pertinence that could only be Jack O'Neill. Abandoning his pack, Daniel headed for the door and saw Jack, Sam and Teal'c following a tall Kinahhi man into the plaza. Jack was glancing around doing his lost tourist impersonation while, no doubt, actually taking in every strategic detail. Sam and Teal'c were a few steps behind, and neither looked entirely happy. Which just about mirrored his own feelings on the situation.

Stepping out of the room he raised his hand. "Hey."

Jack's attention snapped to him. "Daniel. Having fun?"

"Oh yeah," he replied sourly. "Oodles."

"Oodles?"

He shrugged, unwilling to say more in the presence of the Kinahhi man. Seeing him closer, he recognized him as Councilor Quadesh. Now *that* was an interesting choice of tour guide.

Quadesh drew to a halt, inclining his head politely to Daniel. Giving nothing away. "If you are ready to eat," he said, "I shall ensure a meal is brought to you."

"Steak?" Jack suggested. "With fries. And ice-cream – vanilla."

The Kinahhi merely blinked in response and Daniel felt obliged to intercede. "Thank you for your hospitality, Councilor. A meal would be welcome."

Quadesh smiled, barely. "For your own safety, please do not leave the quadrangle."

"Our own safety, huh?" Jack echoed, but it elicited no response as Quadesh turned to leave. Under his breath Jack muttered, "Our own safety, my ass."

Daniel had to agree.

Bill Crawford was an ambitious man. He'd learned early in life that success was less about what you knew than who you knew, and he'd spent the years since then trying to get to know the right people. His introduction to Senator Kinsey, at his former girlfriend's father's inauguration party, had been a godsend. Kinsey was a man whose ego required the sort of constant validation that Bill Crawford found so easy to provide, and in return he intended to ride on Kinsey's coat-tails all the way to Washington.

He just hoped Jackson and his gung-ho team wouldn't screw it up for him. Kinsey had warned him all about SG-1 and so far they were living right up to their reputation. On the plus side, if they really did screw up and he could prove it, getting the infamous SG-1 out of the Senator's side would earn him enough brownie points to retire on. So he had to take a risk, give them enough rope to hang themselves and hope they didn't throttle his negotiations in the process. It was a tight game, but Crawford had always enjoyed playing close to the wire. He liked the sense of power it gave him, he liked the notion that he was playing these suckers off against each other.

"Mr. Crawford?" The voice, smooth and bell-like, came from Councilor Damaris, bringing him back to himself. He moved away from the window, where he'd been staring out over the ugly Kinahhi city, and turned on the charm.

"You have a beautiful city, Councilor. We have no such beauties at home."

A delicate eyebrow rose. "Our city is designed to be strong, not beautiful, Ambassador."

He froze. The Kinahhi were an observant people. He needed to practice more caution, more subtlety. "Strength," he said, "has its own beauty and it is something that our government – especially Senator Kinsey – appreciates. Strength and security."

"On that we can agree." Amused, she motioned toward the door. "Your quarters are ready, Ambassador. And your military escort awaits you there."

Typical. The last thing he wanted to do was spend the evening butting heads with O'Neill and Jackson! Clearing his throat, he straightened his shoulders and offered an ingratiating smile. "It certainly isn't necessary to accommodate me with my escort, Councilor. I trust the Kinahhi implicitly."

"Of course," she agreed, pale eyes fixing him with a look he couldn't fathom. She turned away, resting an elegant hand on the windowsill. An evening breeze fluttered her robes and stirred her silver hair. But her face was rigid, a study in control. "Am I right in sensing some antipathy between yourself and your escort?"

He detected a tension in her, as if his answer was more significant than mere political maneuvering. She wanted it to be true, for reasons of her own. That made him curious. And it gave him an advantage. Carefully he said, "They are sometimes precipitous in their actions."

"Impulsive. Aggressive. Headstrong." Her voice was like gossamer on the breeze. "The *sheh'fet* identified them as such. They are not traits with which we are at ease, Ambassador."

Crawford moved to stand closer, lowering his voice and turning his eyes toward the silent city. The sun was setting now, its flabby yellow bulk painting the featureless skyline in shades of burned orange and rust. In a different place, it might have been beautiful. "I can assure you, Councilor, that the impulsiveness of Colonel O'Neill and his team has not gone unnoticed by our government. Senator Kinsey, in particular, has been-" he chose the words carefully – "inconvenienced by them on several occasions. You might say, they are a thorn in his side."

Damaris turned to him, her eyes bright against the sunset blush that glimmered on her olive skin. "Thorns can be removed," she said mildly.

Crawford's heart beat a little faster, but he kept his head. His father would have been proud. "Sometimes trying to remove the thorn only drives it deeper."

The councilor nodded. "It is important," she said, "to use the correct instrument."

Trying to swallow, he found his throat knotted tight. He had the distinct feeling he'd wandered out onto thin ice, suspended above water deep enough to close over his head before he had time to scream.

His silence drove the brightness from Damaris's eyes and she turned away. "It is late, Ambassador, and I am keeping you from your rest." He made a demurring noise in his throat, but she brushed it lightly away. "It is the wish of the Council that you remain with your people. The accommodation is quite comfortable, I assure you."

There was no choice but to acquiesce gracefully. "Thank you," he smiled. And then, more cautiously, "I look forward to resuming our conversation tomorrow."

Her careful eyes met his. "As do I, Ambassador. Come, I will walk with you to your quarters."

By the time Crawford arrived in the small quadrangle, SG-1 had made themselves at home. Jackson sat leaning against a white wall, legs crossed in front of him with his nose buried in a large book. O'Neill was close by, talking to the woman – Carter – while eating something from a metallic pouch and apparently ignoring the spread of food laid out on a low table on the other side of the courtyard. And the alien, Teal'c, appeared to be doing some kind of weird Tai-chi with the stick he always carried. Crawford clenched his jaw. He really didn't want to spend the evening with these people.

No sooner had he stepped into the square than O'Neill broke off his conversation and looked up. His eyes were unforgiving and Crawford met the stare head-on; no one bullied Bill Crawford. Slowly, O'Neill rose to his feet and wiped a hand across his mouth. "So, did you get Kinsey's little mind reading device?"

Scowling, Crawford glanced over at Jackson who met his look with a shrug. Returning his attention to O'Neill, he trod carefully. "The negotiations are still on-going, Colonel."

"I bet they are." Then, to Crawford's surprise, the man stepped closer and thrust his hands into his pockets. "You know," he said, forcing a conciliatory tone, "these people have other technologies. Better ones."

"I think it's for the Senate Committee to–"

"Ah!" O'Neill cut him off with a swift hand gesture. "Just listen, will you?"

Lips pursed, he listened.

"They have this anti-gravity device. It's impressive. The military and civilian applications would be huge."

Despite himself, his interest was piqued. Not only would this be another juicy bone to set at the Senator's feet, but it was clear that O'Neill was interested. And that was something he could use, that was leverage. "What kind of applications?" At his side he felt, rather than saw, Damaris stiffen.

"Think stealth aircraft. Think–"

"I am sorry, but that is not possible." The councilor stepped carefully between them. "Only the *sheh'fet* technology is under negotiation."

"I'm not interested in that," O'Neill said with a wave of his hand. "But this, though, this we could use. This we could–"

"It is out of the question."

"We could use it to help people, to–"

"It is nonnegotiable."

O'Neill glared off into the middle distance, teeth clenched. He was trying to hide it, but his disappointment was obvious. "And why is that?"

Damaris's expression was all ice, dripping hauteur. "I have no need to explain myself, Colonel O'Neill."

"Don't you?" he snapped. "I think it's kinda strange that you people are willing to trade us some useless piece of spying–"

"Enough!" The last thing Crawford needed was O'Neill screwing up a whole day's worth of trust-building. "Back off, Colonel."

"Don't you tell me–"

"O'Neill!" Teal'c appeared, one hand resting on the colonel's shoulder, his eyes fixed with a baleful look on Crawford. He had to struggle to hold that dangerous glare, but hold it he did. Never back down, his father had wisely advised. He never had. Angrily, O'Neill shook his arm free and spun away.

"This is bull," he growled as he stalked across the courtyard and into one of the rooms that lined the plaza, slamming the door and sending echoes ricocheting off every wall. Teal'c exchanged a wary glance with Carter, who was on her feet now, her gaze flitting between her friends and the slammed door. She shrugged nervously as Jackson closed his book with a dull thud and pressed his lips together into a worried line. Obviously O'Neill's behavior was unusual, even by his maverick standards – he wanted that technology, badly. The question was, why? Crawford stored the information away for later dissection and returned his attention to Damaris.

"My apologies," he murmured. "I shall contact my superiors about this incident as soon as possible."

The councilor's eyes were still fixed on O'Neill's closed door, a speculative look fluttering across her face before she turned her careful gaze back to Crawford. "There is much dissent among your people," she observed. "It is fortunate that you have come to Kinahhi."

CHAPTER FOUR

Daniel watched as Bill Crawford walked across the courtyard and disappeared into his own little bedroom – or was it a cell? In the Kinahhi security state there seemed to be little difference.

A soft sigh escaped Sam's lips.

"Well, that was interesting," Daniel observed to no one in particular. "What did I miss?"

She shook her head. "I don't know."

"O'Neill has demonstrated an unusual interest in the Kinahhi technology since our viewing of the floating city," Teal'c observed.

Floating city? Daniel's eyebrows climbed as his mind sketched an image of drunken buildings sloshing backward and forward at the mercy of the ocean waves. He felt queasy just thinking about it. "What is it? Like a giant ship?"

Teal'c shook his head. "Floating above the waves, Daniel Jackson. The Kinahhi gravitational technology is undoubtedly impressive."

Daniel was vividly reminded of the Nox – he'd have given almost anything to be able to take a look around their floating city.

"Actually, it's Goa'uld technology," Sam said, easing herself back to the ground and sliding O'Neill's half-eaten meal to one side. "At least, according to Quadesh."

Instantly interested, Daniel folded his legs under himself and sat down next to her. "That fits," he said, reaching out to snag the M&Ms from the MRE pouch. He doubted Jack would miss them. "I was talking to a soldier earlier. He mentioned a group of dissidents who worship 'old gods.'"

Sam looked startled. "A Goa'uld? I haven't sensed anything. Teal'c, have you?"

"I have not."

"I'm pretty sure it's just a myth at this point." Daniel dug out a red M&M and popped it into his mouth. "The kid was quite atheistic. In fact, the whole Kinahhi society seems entirely secular.

Which might explain why a disaffected minority would choose a defunct belief system as a rallying point. In a secular state, religion is radicalized."

Sam gazed at him, face blank.

"In other words, it's a handy tag. A way of defining your opposition to the establishment. It doesn't mean we've got a Goa'uld on our hands." He shrugged and rummaged around for another red M&M. "Besides, if we did, I doubt he'd be running the resistance."

"Daniel Jackson is correct," Teal'c agreed. "Were a Goa'uld present on Kinahhi, he would seek domination through overt means. And did not Councilor Quadesh tell us that the Goa'uld city had been long abandoned?"

"Yeah," Sam nodded. "From the technological progress the Kinahhi have made since then, it must have been several generations ago."

Daniel grinned. "Exactly!" It was fascinating how societies separated by distances too vast to comprehend could react so universally to the same problems. Humanity, it seemed, was one of the galaxy's constants. "Rapid technological advancement is a classic cause of religious revivals. I mean, you only have to think of the industrial revolution, which provoked a revivalist movement across the entire globe, to understand that–" Sam shifted and glanced at Teal'c. His eyes were glazed, as if he was about to retreat to a different place. Daniel reined in his excitement, cleared his throat, and made a mental note to jot down a few points in his journal that evening. "So," he asked, changing the subject, "who built the floating city?"

"I'm not sure," said Sam, brightening. "Actually, you probably know. Quadesh said the city was called Tsapan and it was built by someone called Re'ammin the Thunderer." She glanced over at Teal'c. "Right?"

"You are correct," Teal'c agreed. "That name is familiar to me."

It was familiar to Daniel too. He froze, red M&M halfway to his mouth, as a fist of fear curled around his lungs and squeezed. Tsapan. Re'ammin. Kinahhi. *Oh crap, I should have seen this coming.*

"Daniel?" Sam was instantly wary. "What is it? Do you recognize the name?"

He nodded and set the candies down. He had to swallow the suddenly cloying sweetness in his throat before he could say, "Re'ammin the Thunder is an epithet of–" He felt sick.

"Daniel!"

"Of Baal," he finished hurriedly. "It's a Canaanite epithet of Baal. Damn it, I should have known. Kinahhi literally means Canaan – it's an old Hebrew name. And Baal was the Canaanites' chief deity."

Sam's eyes went as wide as saucers and even Teal'c's usually impassive face fractured into a momentary picture of alarm. "We must tell O'Neill," he said immediately and took half a step toward Jack's quarters.

"No, wait." Sam was on her feet, a hand on his arm. She glanced down at Daniel and back at Teal'c. "There's no sign that he's here, right? No sign any Goa'uld has been here in generations."

Teal'c inclined his head in agreement, but his eyes were unconvinced.

"We all know what he–" Her fingers tightened on Teal'c's arm, knuckles turning white. "We can only imagine what Baal did to Colonel O'Neill. Janet said he must have died. Several times. He'd been in the Sarcophagus so often…"

Daniel looked away, unable to meet her gaze. He didn't have to imagine how Jack had suffered at the hands of that monster – he could remember every moment, in vivid Technicolor detail. The stubborn grunts of pain, his refusal to scream – at first. The cursing and obscene animal howls ripped from a man on the edge of sanity. But holding on, always holding on and never, ever giving up. Not even at the end when the wheezing breaths of escaping life faded into deathly silence. Until it started again. And again. And again… And Jack wouldn't let go. He wouldn't damn well let go!

His stomach rolled. "Sam's right," he said huskily. "He doesn't have to know."

Teal'c turned and crouched next to Daniel, laying his staff weapon carefully on the ground. "I do not believe O'Neill would appreciate this attempt to spare his feelings."

"I know," Daniel agreed. "He doesn't always know what's good for him."

Also sitting again, Sam nodded. "I don't buy all that way of the warrior crap, Teal'c. I don't care what he says, you can't go through that much trauma without being effected. Who knows how he'd react if we told him?"

Teal'c raised a curious eyebrow. "Perhaps you do not understand O'Neill as well as you suppose."

"And you do?"

"In many ways O'Neill and I are as brothers," Teal'c replied. "Keeping this information from him undermines his position as our commanding officer."

Daniel grimaced and saw Sam's jaw tighten; that was a difficult blow for the major to parry. "I don't know," he said. "Maybe Teal'c's right. If Jack found out we didn't tell him–"

"No." Sam was adamant. "You didn't see him when he came through the 'gate. His eyes, Daniel. He looked–"

Like a man barely aware of his own humanity? Broken? Tortured? Shattered? He'd been there, seen him break, seen him shatter. Not that she needed to know that. He stared down at the discarded packet of M&Ms. They looked too bright against the white floor. Of all his missing memories, why the hell couldn't this one have remained lost? "I can imagine," he mumbled eventually.

"If there was even a hint of a threat I'd agree with you, Teal'c," Sam pressed. "But there isn't. It's just an accident of history."

"Perhaps," Teal'c conceded. "What of the dissidents and their worship of 'old gods'?"

"You said it yourself, Teal'c. If Baal was here, he wouldn't be skulking around with fanatics. He's powerful – he wouldn't need to. This is just a coincidence."

Teal'c considered the point, head cocked to one side. "I have found that in life there are few true coincidences, Major Carter." Picking up his staff weapon he rose to his feet. "For now, I will do as you ask."

Daniel nodded his gratitude, although his feelings were still mixed. "If the situation changes..."

"We had better hope that is does not."

As Teal'c strode to the other end of the courtyard, Daniel heard Sam sigh. A taut expression touched her face, half-uncertainty and half-relief. Keeping secrets from her commanding officer wasn't something Sam Carter did lightly. "He'd do the same for us," he reminded her softly.

She nodded, but her disquiet didn't abate. "It's his command, he's allowed to."

"You could still tell him."

"No. It's better this way." She cast him a quick, regretful smile. "It's a moot point, anyway. The Kinahhi won't let us set foot on Tsapan."

The obvious frustration in her voice provoked a smile of his own, rising like hope through his bitter memories. "I'd pay top dollar for half an hour there. Tsapan! The site of the defeat of Yahm. It's a myth. It's like… it would be like finding the lost Ark!" He stretched out a hand. "It's right there, if only I could just reach it."

Sam laughed softly. "Bad luck this time, Indiana."

"Yeah," he smiled. "Isn't it always?"

His grin slowly faded as the moment between them lengthened into a companionable silence. Reaching down he picked up the packet of M&Ms and offered one to Sam, who refused, before tucking them back into Jack's MRE pouch. As his thoughts returned to Jack, Daniel's eyes rose to the door his friend had slammed on Crawford half an hour ago. Someone should probably go interrupt his brooding.

"So," said Sam, her gaze following his, "wanna draw straws?"

Jack paced the cell-like room, forcing himself not to kick out against the few pieces of metal furniture as he tried to figure out why he was so mad. Yes, Crawfish was a slimy toad with an agenda he'd pulled from Kinsey's ass, but he'd dealt with these people before. Hell, he'd been dealing with them for years! So why was the little worm pissing him off so much?

"What happened to 'nobody gets left behind'?"

Cromwell glanced over his shoulder at the frozen image of Henry Boyd's terror. "Well, what about him?"

"That's an entirely different scenario."

"That is the exact same damn thing, Jack."

The image pummeled into his mind and he cursed. "Let it go," he muttered to himself, slowing to a halt in front of the white wall.

"Move on." He pressed his hands against the cold stone, smooth beneath his fingers, and let his forehead rest there too. But Heather Boyd's face, sorrowful and accusing, still haunted him.

"I'm sorry, Heather, I wish there was more I could do."

"Do you?"

He let his head and hands take his weight, pushing against the unrelenting stone. Did he? Wasn't there more he could have done in the five years since it had happened? Couldn't he have done *something*? He remembered, vaguely, a late night conversation with Carter about black holes and the irrevocable laws of physics. He'd sensed her guilt too – she was the brains, after all. But even Carter hadn't been able to figure this one out, and if she couldn't–

There was a knock at the door. He sighed. "I'm busy."

After a short pause the door opened and he groaned softly to himself. This could only be one person. "Daniel, you speak twenty-three languages. What part of 'I'm busy' don't you understand?"

"Oh, I don't know," Daniel replied mildly, his footsteps moving from the door to the bed where he sat down. "The bit where you're so busy bawling out Crawford that you forget we're off world and the guests of–"

"Daniel…" He turned around, resting his back against the wall. "I didn't forget we're off-world."

Nodding slowly, Daniel said, "So… what happened?"

"Nothing happened."

Daniel's eyebrows rose in that I-don't-believe-a-word-of-it way he had. "Nothing?"

"Look, he pisses me off. Okay?"

Daniel shrugged. "He pisses me off, too. But you can't just go around yelling at heads of state and–"

"I didn't!"

Daniel cleared his throat and shifted on the bed, changing the subject but not admitting defeat. "What's so important about the anti-gravity technology anyway?"

Jack met his friend's shrewd gaze for a moment before looking away. "Nothing."

"Jack…"

"It's nothing!" The moment hung there until Daniel's silence eventually forced him to say more. "Okay, okay. I was just thinking about the memorial."

The surprise that crossed Daniel's face was swiftly followed by understanding. "Henry Boyd."

Jack nodded. "I thought maybe there was a way that Carter could MacGyver something to, you know, bring him home."

He smiled at that. "Have you asked her?"

"Not much point, is there? All Kinsey wants are his fancy mind readers."

Daniel sighed, his face darkening. He pulled his glasses off and pinched the bridge of his nose. "Thought police. Literally. Arresting people for potentially committing a crime."

"Didn't I see a movie about that?" Jack frowned. "I seem to remember little wooden balls…"

"Ask Teal'c. He's the sci-fi fan." Daniel sighed, rubbing at the back of his neck. "Point is, aside from the fact that it's utterly useless in protecting us from the Goa'uld, think about how Kinsey's going to use it."

"I know." It had nightmare written all over it. "They have some kind of terrorist situation here. Quadesh was pretty vague, but I get the impression all in the Kinahhi garden isn't rosy."

"Yeah," Daniel agreed. "Dissidents. Apparently they wiped out one of the Kinahhi's off-world colonies with a biological attack fifty years ago."

"Nice people."

Daniel grunted. "Nothing like a little internal dissent to breed paranoia and pump up the security state, huh?"

Biting his tongue – it was too late for one of *those* discussions – Jack nudged the conversation in a more useful direction. "You know what they're fighting over?"

Daniel sighed and glanced up with a decidedly troubled look. "Religion."

"Religion?"

He grimaced, as if he were to blame for the news. "Apparently the dissidents still worship the old god."

"Daniel? Are we talking about a Goa'uld?"

He looked away, squinting uncomfortably out of the small window into the plaza beyond. "Yes, but long gone." Eyebrows bunching in the middle of his forehead, he cleared his throat.

"There's absolutely no sign that he's still here."

Jack shook his head and resumed his pacing. Kinsey, the thought-police and now religious fanatics worshiping long gone, false gods? "Is it just me?" he asked. "Or does this whole situation reek?"

"Oh, it's not just you," Daniel assured him bitterly. Then he paused, face grim. "This technology is dangerous, Jack, especially in the hands of someone like Kinsey. We can't let him get hold of it."

"We won't."

But even as the words left his lips, Henry Boyd's face rose like a ghost in the back of his mind, abandoned and terrified, staring death in the face. *Don't leave me behind, sir. Don't leave me behind...*

It was late, quiet and tranquil. Nothing disturbed the midnight silence, but still Sam couldn't sleep. Usually it wasn't a problem offworld; the rhythms and noises of their usual camp life easily lulled her into the light, restful sleep of the soldier. But here in her lone cell, with the alien moonlight streaming brightly through the small window, sleep eluded her.

So her mind started chewing on the meatiest morsel it could find – the Kinahhi anti-gravity technology. If she could just get a look at it, just spend half an hour on that incredible floating city... The colonel had been right; the military and civilian applications of that kind of technology were amazing. Soundless aircraft, cities drifting over Earth's oceans to cater for the world's growing population, fighter planes that could–

A door closed softly and booted footsteps walked slowly out into the plaza. Instantly, she was alert and listening. However comfortable the room, Sam knew even the most innocuous of missions could turn dangerous on a dime. Sliding silently off the bed, she reached for her Beretta and stole to the window. Moonlight flooded half the courtyard, the line between silver and black absolute. Strolling across the open space toward the far wall, head bowed in thought, was a familiar figure not unknown for his nocturnal rambles. Sam watched as he sat down, his face lost in shadow and only his long legs emerging into the moonlight, and considered her options. Probably the wisest choice was to go back to bed and leave him to his brooding. But, despite her rational reputation, Sam Carter didn't always make the wisest choices. Holstering her weapon, she pulled on her boots and slipped out of the room.

The Kinahhi city was still – oddly silent compared with the usual honks, sirens and ant-like nightlife of any Earth city – and her footfalls sounded loud in the moonlight. O'Neill sat with his back against the farthest wall of the quadrangle, not far from the narrow ally through which Quadesh had led them that evening. Although he must have seen her approach, he didn't move or speak. Neither did she, simply sliding down the wall to sit at a respectable distance from him. She noted with approval that he'd chosen the most strategic vantage point, covering both their occupied rooms and the only apparent entrance to their accommodation.

When the silence stretched too long, he glanced over at her, dark eyes hidden beneath the bill of his cap. "Trouble sleeping, Carter?"

She nodded. "Something about this place. I don't know, it feels–"

"Creepy? Wrong? Like these guys are out-Kinseying Kinsey?"

Amused, she nodded. "Yes, sir."

He was silent again, gaze fixed on the far side of the courtyard. "Daniel's worried."

"About the *sheh'fet* technology?" That much she knew already, and as always he had a very good point. "It does sound very *1984*."

The colonel nodded. "I told him we'd stop Kinsey from getting it."

"Can we do that, sir? I mean, our orders–"

"I understand our orders, Major." After a moment he relented, and with a grim smile added, "You know me, Carter. I can make trouble as easily as Daniel can make peace. Screwing up inter-planetary negotiations is what I do best."

Even though she smiled, Sam felt a beat of disquiet pulse low in her guts. "Kinsey would wipe the floor with us."

"With me," he corrected quickly, casting her a warning look. "One man op, Carter."

She was about to object when his head cocked sharply to one side, listening. Words hung unspoken as she strained her ears to hear, but all was silence. Frowning, she shrugged a negative and he relaxed slightly. "This place is too damn quiet," he grumbled.

Too quiet, too creepy. Baal's shadow looming around every corner. She shivered and pushed the thought away. "Are you really considering it, sir? Wrecking the negotiations?" Her thoughts returned to the glittering city floating above the waves. Any chance of visiting would be over if the colonel provoked the Kinahhi too far. "I'd love to get a closer look at their anti-grav technology."

Subtly he froze, as if every muscle tensed at once. "Yeah," came the short reply. "Me too."

That much had been obvious in his confrontation with the Kinahhi woman. But the colonel's interest in new technology usually ended at the 'is it a weapon and can you make it work?' stage of the investigation. This interest in unproven, unmilitary technology was unusual to say the least.

He frowned at her. "What?"

She shook her head, trying to defray his irritation. "I'm just a little surprised that you're so interested, sir." Seeing his eyes narrow she hurriedly added, "Not that you're not always interested in–" She stopped digging, cleared her throat and began again. "Technology isn't usually something that excites you, sir."

Eyebrows rising ever so slightly he said, "Lots of things excite me, Carter. I just don't babble about them."

Oh!

Before she could find an answer his humor faded and he looked away, back out over the moonlit courtyard. "You ever think about Boyd and his team?"

The abrupt change in subject threw her, and like a speeding train it took a moment for her to switch tracks. "Uh, yeah," she said at last, not comfortable with the memory. SG-10 had died – were dying – a unique and horrifying death that she'd been powerless to prevent. Despite everything she knew about astrophysics, she hadn't known enough to save Henry Boyd and his team. She scowled at the memory. "I, um, often think that if we could have found a way to negate the gravity, just for a few seconds–" Suddenly his point hit home like a well-driven nail. "Oh my God, that's why you're interested in the anti-gravity technology, isn't it?"

O'Neill shrugged his half-hearted agreement. "Probably wouldn't work, right? I mean, we're not talking about floating an airplane here – we're talking about a black hole." He looked at her again, a mute appeal in his eyes. "Right?"

He wanted her to disagree with him; she could hear it in the unspoken plea in his voice. But reluctantly she had to nod. She wouldn't
lie or give false hope. "The technology might be usable. But you're
right, sir, we're talking about a whole different league in terms of
power. Nothing I've seen here could have any impact on the gravitational force of a black hole. I mean, we're talking about the implosion
of a *sun*."

"Yeah," he sighed. "That's what I thought."

Of course, no sooner had she convinced him it was impossible,
than her mind started running with the problem. Could there be a
way? Could it be possible? Five years on, could she bring these people home to their families? A frustrated sigh slipped past her lips, "If
I could just *see* the technology, or even some schematics. Anything!
I mean, maybe it's possible. Maybe there's a way to create a bubble
– like they use to float the city – that would give them enough time to
get through the 'gate."

"Really?" He shifted until he was facing her. "I mean, it's possible?"

"Maybe. I don't know. I don't even know how this technology
works!" She sighed. "And it's not like I'm going to find out any time
soon."

His mouth compressed into a thin line. "No, not if I wreck the
negotiations."

"And if you don't wreck them, Kinsey gets his security technology."

He snorted grimly. "Caught between a rock and Kinsey's ass."

Sam didn't answer, watching the conflict play over his face for
a moment before she looked away. In the colonel's universe no one
ever got left behind, but that black-and-white ethos sat uncomfortably
amid the gray-streaked world of politics. There were bigger issues at
stake than the lives of Henry Boyd and his team, and they both knew
it. But Sam also knew that nothing, no amount of logic or realpolitik,
could assuage O'Neill's guilt at leaving anyone behind.

Nothing.

Bill Crawford was watching the morning through the stinging
eyes of sleeplessness, his head muzzy with a vague, insomnia-

driven headache. A yawn threatened, but he buried it as he followed his young Kinahhi escort through the sterile white corridors of their Stargate complex. He hadn't slept well in the alien bed, his stomach was objecting to their strange food, and he felt stretched taut with irritation and impatience. A mood that hadn't been helped by spending breakfast in the unpleasant company of a silent, brooding Jack O'Neill and his equally uncommunicative cohorts.

The night hadn't been entirely fruitless, however, and that thought eased his frustration. In fact, his inability to sleep had proven extremely useful. Lying in bed, staring at the moonlight streaming through the window, he'd heard footfalls outside. First one set, then another. Then a quiet conversation, spoken in whispers, had echoed off the plaza's smooth walls and come to him like a gift.

"I, um, often think that if we could have found a way to negate the gravity just for a few seconds–" Major Carter had whispered. *"Oh my God, that's why you're interested in the anti-grav technology, isn't it?"*

Black holes, lost teams. It was all new to him. But Crawford was a quick study, and everything he really needed to know had been right there. Not so much the words themselves, it had been the emotion simmering underneath that had delivered the prize. Need. Crawford knew a thing or two about need. It was what drove men, what allowed him to manipulate them into satisfying his own desires. O'Neill needed that technology to silence some personal demon of his own. It was a powerful piece of knowledge. Valuable.

Tradable.

He hadn't forgotten his conversation with Damaris the previous evening. If she was looking for the right instrument with which to control SG-1 then he might just have it. For a price. After all, O'Neill had all but said he wouldn't interfere with the negotiations if it jeopardized the chance of gaining access to the gravity technology. All he needed to do was persuade Damaris to dangle a carrot, and O'Neill would follow it like a mule. And with him, his team. Jackson had a big mouth, but he'd never cross the colonel. That much Crawford knew. Loyalty was all-important to these people, suckers that they were.

His escort slowed and Crawford realized they were already at the entrance to the lofty white hall where he'd spent most of the previous day. They had arrived a little early, however, and as he stepped through the doorway he glimpsed Councilor Damaris in close confab with a Kinahhi man. The whispered conversation was urgent and serious, brows creasing and hands moving in swift anxious gestures. Before his ears could pick up their words his escort announced his arrival and the councilor's head snapped around in uncharacteristic irritation. She muttered something inaudible to the man she'd been talking to, who turned his familiar amber eyes on Crawford before nodding briskly to Damaris and sliding noiselessly from the room.

"Trouble?" Crawford asked mildly.

Her irritation was gone, replaced by an affected smile. She waved a dismissive hand. "Another security alert. Please don't concern yourself, they are quite common." And then, after a short pause she politely asked, "I hope you slept well?"

"Very well," he lied, "thank you."

And so the negotiations resumed. Smoke and mirrors – always made him feel at home.

"What do you mean, 'no'?" Daniel hissed urgently, matching Jack stride for stride as they followed Quadesh through the long, white corridors toward the Stargate. He couldn't believe what he was hearing!

"No." Jack repeated, staring straight ahead. "As in negative. Nadda. Not gonna happen."

"Why not?" This made no sense. "You agreed we'd tell Hammond to scrap the negotiations for the *sheh'fet*. You said we'd stop Kinsey from getting his hands on it."

Jack cast a glance at Quadesh, two paces ahead, and deliberately shortened his stride. He lowered his voice when he spoke, "There are other issues, Daniel."

"What other issues?" Jack's face remained impassive, but Daniel had known him too long to be fooled. "You talked to Sam?" he guessed. "About the gravity technology?"

A slight tightening around the eyes was all the 'yes' he needed.

"You know the Kinahhi won't trade it."

Jack tugged at the bill of his cap, pulling it lower and hiding his eyes. "They won't if we slam the door on them."

Struggling for patience, Daniel glanced at his watch – half an hour before they were due to check in with the SGC. Still time. "Look, Jack, if Kinsey gets that technology–"

"He'll have to explain where it came from, right? Or reverse-engineer it." Eyes front, his face was shadowed and Daniel had the distinct impression he was trying to convince himself of his own words. "Then he'll have to get Congress to approve it," Jack carried on determinedly. "And they never would, right? The wishy-washy liberals would get involved…" He slowed, reached out and grasped Daniel's arm to slow him too. His eyes shone intently from the shadows, his voice low and earnest. "His daughter's nine years old, Daniel. She can't even remember her father. If there's a *chance*…"

It was a low but effective blow. "I just think there's a bigger picture. We have to put–"

A hammer-blow to the gut. Flying, weightless and breathless, ears exploding in pain and thunder. Smashing against unforgiving stone, head cracking in gashes of white light and scarlet. Crumpling to the ground under a hot, hard rain. Struggling for air in the liquid, choking dust. Ebbing into a numb, ringing silence.

Pain everywhere and nowhere, Daniel dimly began to hear voices through the white-noise in his ears. Screaming. Panic. Chaos. And then an urgent yell. "Daniel!"

He moved, lifted his head and groaned as something behind his eyes exploded with a new flash of pain.

"Daniel?" Again, the voice. Closer. Louder.

Opening his eyes, he peered blearily through a new world of gray while his sluggish mind fought to understand where he was. He could hear more shouting now, shrieking and wailing. Someone rushed past him as he pushed himself onto his knees. At least everything seemed to be working, although his breaths came in short, choking gasps. But the outside world had somehow intruded into the corridor because the sky was above him and–

"Daniel!" A pair of strong hands grabbed his shoulders and yanked him upright. "You okay?"

Trying to answer was a mistake, and the lungful of dust he'd inhaled threatened to rip him inside out as he coughed it up. "Easy," the voice said, a firm hand patting his back. It was Jack, he realized. "Come on, we need to get you out of here before the rest of the building comes down."

Head spinning, he struggled to his feet and looped an arm around Jack's shoulders. Half-dragged and half-blind, he staggered through the mayhem. "I got him!" Jack was shouting, the noise pounding Daniel's head against a vicious white-hot anvil.

Stumbling over rubble, they were assaulted on all sides by the wail of sirens and terror. But at last the air began to clear. He could breathe more easily and the fog inside his mind lifted. Although his glasses were long gone, he began to make sense of the world. They were outside, the air was full of smoke, and ahead of him he could see Sam crouched next to the prone form of Teal'c. The sight slammed into him hard. "Teal'c?" he croaked.

Sam looked up, rising to her feet. Her face was pasty beneath a layer of dirt, her uniform bloody. "He's hurt, but it doesn't look bad." She stepped closer and winced, her eyes fixed on the side of his head. "How about you?"

Gingerly he reached up and touched his temple; his fingers came away scarlet. "Oh, you know. I've been worse."

"You've been dead," Jack pointed out, easing him toward the ground. "Now sit." The world was still woozy and he wasn't going to argue. As he sat he saw, for the first time, the chaos behind him. Half the side of the building was missing and what remained hung in ragged strips, like torn flesh.

"What happened?"

"Bomb blast," Jack said shortly, glancing up and over his head toward Sam for confirmation. She nodded her agreement.

Daniel's mind flew back to the previous day and his conversation with the young soldier. "The Mahr'bal," he said, coughing again. "The dissidents."

"Dissidents, my ass," Jack spat. "They're terrorists."

He didn't reply, his eyes suddenly caught by a woman kneeling in the dust not ten feet away. In her arms lay the still form of a small child whom she rocked silently, over and over and over while around them the air filled with the sounds of grief and horror. His stomach roiled and he had to grit his teeth hard against a sudden rage that filled his eyes with tears; for all his talk of compromise and mutual understanding, in that moment he knew what it was to hate.

Suddenly, Sam made a small, distressed noise, low in her throat. Jack was picking his way across the wreckage of the building, toward the woman and her dead child. He hesitated at the last moment, face grim and God only knew what memories passing through his mind, before resolutely crouching at the her side and talking quietly. Daniel buried his face in his hands, feeling the blood seep through his fingers from the wound on his head.

Nothing was worth this sort of pain – no cause, no ideology, no historical grievance.

It was evil, pure and simple. And the Goa'uld certainly didn't have a monopoly on that.

CHAPTER FIVE

Teal'c opened his eyes to a white, sterile ceiling and a moment of confusion. Instinctively his mind reached for the symbiote and the queasy reassurance he received from its presence, but he felt only absence. A flutter of panic brought him fully awake, trailing his memory along behind. The prim'tah was gone – dead – and he was free. But his freedom had come at the price of his strength, a trade that was inevitable and yet still disconcerting even after so many months.

"Teal'c?" The face that loomed into view above him belonged to Major Carter. Pale and dirt-streaked, she smiled with relief. "How are you feeling?"

He considered the question carefully before he answered. His head throbbed and a piercing, red-hot pain cut through his shoulder. "I will endure."

She smiled, her fingers reaching out to touch his forehead. "Yeah, well, you've got quite a bruise. And they removed about six inches of glass from your shoulder."

Insignificant wounds – his prim'tah could have treated them in under an hour. Swallowing his frustration, Teal'c made himself sit up. The world spun, but when Major Carter attempted to steady him he fended her off with a warning look; she knew him better than to ignore it. Once the room had stopped tilting he glanced around and discovered that he was lying amid a long row of beds, all occupied. Beyond the ward, through a narrow set of doors at the far end, he could hear the muted sounds of disorder and grief. It reminded him of the aftermath of battle, of the desperate minutes and hours in which you scoured the dead for familiar faces. The memory stung and he spoke the first thought that entered his mind, "Where are O'Neill and Daniel Jackson?"

Major Carter nodded toward the bed behind her. "Daniel's okay – nasty concussion, but otherwise fine. And the colonel's trying to find someone who'll open the 'gate for us." A cloud shadowed her eyes as her gaze drifted down the ward. "I guess we were lucky."

He followed her gaze, the wounded stretching the length of the room in a row of white-shrouded victims, all engaged in their own personal battles to survive. "It seems that the Kinahhi are justified in their security measures."

"Yeah. Lot of good it did them."

"Indeed." Desperation, he knew, was a merciless master who felt no compassion. "There is little that can deter the determined, as our dealings with the Tok'ra have demonstrated."

She shifted uneasily onto the balls of her feet and plunged her hands into her pockets. "I don't know that you can compare–"

"Unpack your suitcases kids, looks like we're staying." Major Carter started at the sound of the loud, familiar voice; Teal'c merely inclined his head as he watched O'Neill approach.

Despite his ebullient tone, Teal'c could sense a genuine anxiety radiating from his friend. It curled tightly in his own gut, occupying the space once reserved for the prim'tah.

Major Carter's eyes darkened. "They won't let us leave?"

"No one in or out – 'security measures'."

"The first cry of every tyrant." The voice was slightly slurred, but unmistakably Daniel Jackson.

O'Neill turned, barely concealing his obvious relief. "You're awake!"

"Uh – I think so." Daniel Jackson winced, a hand drifting to the dressing on the side of his head.

"Headache?"

"More like agony, actually," he grimaced. "Thanks for asking."

A slight smile touched O'Neill's lips, but he said no more. And into the moment's silence Major Carter intruded, her anxiety obvious. "Sir, I don't like this."

O'Neill's attention snapped back into focus. "Me neither. But short of actually storming their 'gate room – and don't think I didn't consider it! – we're not going anywhere."

"What does Crawford say?" Carter pressed. "Surely he's not happy that they've–"

"Perhaps," Teal'c suggested, "you can ask him yourself?" Bill Crawford was pushing through the narrow doors at the end of the ward. Next to Councilor Damaris, who accompanied him, the ambassador appeared especially stunted and graceless. The image was most amusing.

Teal'c felt the end of his bed dip as O'Neill perched on it, legs stretched out and arms folded across his chest in a gesture of belligerence that Teal'c doubted was accidental. In battle, appearance was sometimes more important than strength – a phenomena the Jaffa knew all too well. The ability to engender fear in your enemy was a warrior's greatest weapon. Sitting there with his legs barring access to their small corner of the ward, and a scowl hovering like stormclouds on his brow, O'Neill presented a forbidding figure. Crawford attempted to conceal his discomfort as he approached, but the fact that he stopped several feet from O'Neill spoke of the colonel's victory.

The ambassador cleared his throat. "I'm glad to see you're okay," he said, with all the sincerity of a Goa'uld.

"No flowers?" O'Neill pinned Crawford with a look. Apprehension rippled across the man's features, but he didn't flinch from the silent confrontation. In the end it was O'Neill who spoke again. "Something else you wanted?"

Stepping forward, the Kinahhi woman endeavored to relieve the tension. "Please allow me to offer the sincere apologies of the Security Council, Colonel O'Neill. We are most distressed that you have been involved in this unfortunate business."

"Distressed enough to open the 'gate and let me get my people to a doctor?"

Her brow furrowed. "Let me assure you, Colonel, our medics will take excellent care of your people. No offense to your own medical personnel, but I assure you that they will receive more effective care here on Kinahhi."

"Yeah well, *no offense*, but I don't trust your medics."

Crawford took a warning step forward. "Colonel…"

"Oh *what*?" O'Neill erupted. "Grow a spine, Crawford! Don't you see what's happening? They're holding us here!"

"For what purpose?" Damaris shot back, fire blazing in her eyes. It was incongruous in her otherwise impassive face.

"Why don't you tell me, Councilor?"

"Believe me, Colonel O'Neill," Damaris said, in a voice just colder than ice, "if we meant your people harm you would already be harmed."

"Is that a threat?"

"Simply an observation."

Nothing else was said, and the silence grew long and tense. At last Damaris addressed Crawford, her tone imperious. "The Stargate will be reopened in the morning, once the security sweep is complete. You may contact your people then."

And with that she turned on her heel and strode away. Crawford didn't follow immediately, fixing O'Neill with a deadly glare. "You're walking a fine line, O'Neill. McMurdo's only a phone call away."

O'Neill remained as inscrutable as any Jaffa. But as Crawford hurried after Damaris, Teal'c saw a twitch in the colonel's jaw and knew that he sensed the menace. Danger was all around them, hidden behind polite smiles and veiled threats. He had made an enemy in Councilor Damaris – an enemy who, Teal'c instinctively felt, was more dangerous than she appeared.

The fat Kinahhi sun was slouching toward the horizon by the time SG-1 were 'escorted' back to their quarters. The evening shadows were long and scruffy, and the fading sunlight did little to warm the stone quadrangle. Somehow the chill seemed appropriate, Jack thought, as he listened to a kindergarten-soldier ordering them to stay put. He wasn't blind to the not-so-subtle shift in their treatment by the Kinahhi, and he bore the change with as much civility as he could muster. Under the circumstances, it wasn't much.

"Yeah, yeah," he called after the backs of their departing escort, "for our own protection. I get it!" Protection, his ass! He'd been in enough prisons to recognize the shape of their walls, whatever the décor. Bottling up his frustration, he turned back to the rest of his team with a flat smile. "Well this sucks."

Daniel, chalky behind his spare glasses, nodded a faint agreement and eased himself onto the cold tiles. "They're afraid, Jack," he said, leaning his head against the stone wall and closing his eyes.

He was right, of course. Even Jack could see fear and distrust creeping through these people like a disease. Given what he'd witnessed this morning, could he really blame them? The woman and her dead child had been an incarnation of grief so intense he'd barely been able to move toward them, shackled as he was by his own memories of a small, broken body...

"Sir?" Carter's voice startled him out of the quicksand memories.

She met his gaze with a silent question. *Everything okay, sir?*

Avoiding her eyes, and the question, he moved to sit next to Daniel. "Like I said, this sucks."

Carter nodded dutifully, but he wasn't entirely convinced she shared his sentiment. Her attention drifted and she absently gazed up at the tops of the buildings that surrounded them. A speculative light danced through the shifting greens and blues of her eyes, lending them a luster that was– Not something he should be noticing. He cleared his throat. "Carter?"

She blinked, startled. "Sir?"

"You're thinking."

Eyebrows rose in surprise. "Well, I– I was just– "

"Thinking. About what?"

She shook her head, an instinctive gesture of denial, and then abruptly changed her mind and squatted in front of him. In a low voice she said, "I've been thinking some more about the anti-gravity technology." Her gaze darted to Daniel and back again. "And about the Goa'uld city."

Oh, he *so* knew where this was going. "What about it?"

She grinned her contagious grin. "I was thinking, we really should check it out. I mean, if we're going to be stuck here anyway…"

"Stuck *here*," he pointed out, thudding his boot against the flagstones for good measure. "I doubt day-trips are on the itinerary, Carter."

Next to him, Daniel shifted and raised his head. He still looked sick, but his eyes had lost none of their astuteness. Despite the appearance of dozing, he'd obviously been listening to every word. "On the other hand," he said, "this is probably going to be our last chance to take a look at the city."

"If the deal with the Kinahhi goes ahead," Carter agreed, "Crawford won't let us anywhere near this place again."

"And if it doesn't go ahead no one will be back."

Damn it, he hated it when they played this kind of tag-team logic. Especially when they had a point. If they never returned to Kinahhi…

"What happened to 'nobody gets left behind'?"

"That's an entirely different scenario."

"That is the exact same damn thing, Jack."

Gritting his teeth, he forced himself to be objective. He hadn't missed the anger in the councilor's face back at the hospital and knew that, whatever happened, this was his last chance to get a look at the anti-gravity technology. But at what cost? Daniel was doing a passing impersonation of Casper the Friendly Ghost, and for all Teal'c's Jaffa stoicism Jack knew exactly what a six-inch wound to the shoulder felt like. *Exactly.*

And the wisest thing to do with two injured team-members was to play it safe. Dig in until he'd located an exit route, then evacuate the injured and get the hell out of Dodge. Racing across the city on a covert mission to visit a floating city – however cool that sounded – had 'disaster' written all over it. He glanced at Teal'c for support; Teal'c understood command, he'd carried the burden longer than Jack. But the Jaffa simply raised his uninjured shoulder in half a shrug. "It will not be an easy task to evade the Kinahhi surveillance equipment."

Even as Teal'c spoke, Jack knew what was coming next. "Leave that to me, sir." Carter exchanged an excited smile with Daniel. "We'll only be gone a couple of hours, max."

A couple of hours? Yeah, and then– Hang on. "*We'll* only be gone a couple of hours?" He glanced suspiciously between the two. "*We?*"

At least they had the good grace to seem awkward, although there was something else in the looks shooting between them. It planted a grave seed of suspicion. If he didn't know better, he'd have thought they were deliberately hiding something. But they wouldn't do that, would they? Not his team. "It makes sense for Daniel and me to go," Carter explained, with a conviction disproportionate to the situation. "I mean, I need to see the technology. And Daniel–"

"Has a severe head injury." Was he the only one conscious of the fact?

Daniel fingered the dressing on the side of his head. "It's nothing. I'm fine. And anyway, I have to go–"

"No. You don't." This was just not going to happen. "You and Teal'c stay here, while Carter and I–"

"Tsapan." Daniel said the word softly, as if it had some weighty significance.

It certainly seemed to hold some for Carter, who stopped dead and stared. "Daniel!"

"He has a right to know, Sam, before he decides whether or not to go."

She shook her head, jaw clenched. There was a reason Carter never won at poker; her eyes gave away far too much. And right now they were brimming with apprehension as she frowned down at her fingers, tapping an anxious rhythm on the stone floor.

"What's going on?" Jack asked quietly, fixing Daniel with a steady look. There was a compassion in his friend's face that made his hackles rise.

"Tsapan," Daniel repeated. "The floating-city. There's something you need to know."

Inside, Jack felt his mental defenses rally. After all these years it was an instinctive response to the imminence of something – anything – that might upset his carefully constructed, rigidly controlled inner landscape. "What about it?"

Daniel's eyes flicked to Carter and back again, and Jack matched the movement. The same sympathy shone in her face, laced with something else. Fear? Guilt? "Tsapan was the name of a mountain on Earth," Daniel explained quietly, "Mountain Divine Tsapan."

Still not having a clue, Jack's patience was running thin. Carter chewed at her lower lip, a frown tugging at her brow, as Daniel very carefully said, "It was the legendary home of Baal."

Breath hitched in his lungs. *Acid. Daggers. Black, agonizing death. Then white light, again and again and again–* Damn it. Jaw clenched he found himself staring at his fists, white-knuckled as the rage boiled up in the pit of his belly. *Acid. Daggers.* Don't think about it, don't think. "So it's what?" he asked stiffly, focusing on his hands. "A second home for his playboy lifestyle?"

"There's no evidence he's been here for centuries, sir." Carter was trying to reassure him, as if he were some hopeless PTSD vet who could blow any minute. Hell, maybe she was right. His fists grew tighter, and he refused to listen to the rage pulsing in his ears. How dare she imagine she knew how he felt? How dare she pity him?

"It's possible we'll learn something," Daniel added in the same treading-on-egg-shells tone. "Something we can use against him, or against the other System Lords."

Hard intel – that had been the mission the first time too, hadn't it?

Get the intel then get the hell out. Only that time he'd ended up rotting in an Iraqi jail for four months, and the time after that? He balked at the memories of that hell-hole and blew out a short breath, looking up and right into Carter's eyes. Open and honest, but not intruding. "Sir," she said earnestly, "Daniel and I discussed it yesterday – we can handle this alone. And if I could just get a look at the technology then–"

"*Yesterday?*" His anger, like magma under pressure, found the vent it needed and erupted. Its force shot him to his feet. *Acid, daggers, death. You bastard!* Sucking in a deep breath he fought to keep himself together. When he spoke, his voice was deadly quiet. "You knew about this *yesterday*?"

Carter's face froze, chin jutting out. Oh, she knew what she'd done all right. "Daniel and I talked about it last night, sir."

He nodded, his rage making the gesture short and jerky. "And why the hell didn't you tell me?"

"I didn't think–"

I didn't think you could handle it, sir. "Damn it!" he snarled, and Carter blanched visibly. "Baal could be hiding around the goddam corner, Major, and you *didn't think* I should be aware of that?"

"He's not around the corner," Daniel interceded, also standing, and turning a whiter shade of pale in the process. "He's not here, Jack. That's why we didn't tell you. You didn't need to know."

A short gasp hissed through Carter's teeth.

"You didn't think *I* needed to know?" Jack repeated icily.

"Major Carter and Daniel Jackson sought to spare you from revisiting unpleasant memories, O'Neill," said Teal'c. His steady voice cut through Jack's blinding anger, although it was tinged with disquiet. "I warned them that you would not see the matter in such a light."

Damn straight! He whirled on Carter. "Daniel, I can understand. But you, Major, you I should damn well report!"

Carter nodded slightly. "Yes sir. I'm sorry, sir. I just didn't want you to–"

"I don't care what you want, Carter," he barked savagely. "Just do your job."

Mortified, she dropped her gaze to the ground. "Yes, sir."

And then he turned on Daniel, skewering him with a look that would have sent a parade ground of recruits running for cover. "Tell me everything."

"There's nothing more to tell," Daniel replied, although unlike Carter he wasn't cowed. Instead, there was unabashed and honest sympathy in his face, because he'd been there, he'd seen it all. Jack shrank from his gaze, trying to preserve whatever shreds of privacy and dignity remained. Daniel shrugged. "It's no big deal."

Furious, Jack backed up a step. "Oh no. It's a big deal. And if either of you *ever* pull a stunt like this again, and I swear to God I'll…I'll–"

Unable to look at them, afraid of what he might do – or reveal – Jack turned and stalked away. There was nowhere to go but his cramped little cell of a room, and he couldn't face that, not now. He cursed under his breath; he wanted to hit something. Or someone. Crawford, perhaps? Or Kinsey? Or Baal. *Acid. Daggers.* Sonofabitch. *Black, agonizing death. White, terrifying dawn–*

"Sir?" Carter's voice rang loud in the silent courtyard, but he didn't stop walking. "Sir, if I can see the technology I might be able to figure out a way to save Henry Boyd and his team."

His footsteps faltered. Boyd, someone else falling into an agonizing death, trapped in that infinite moment of terror.

"And let's not forget the *immense* personal satisfaction, not to mention archaeological significance, of locating the site of Yahm's defeat," Daniel added brightly. "Which, I appreciate, isn't exactly your priority right now, but nonetheless…"

Daniel was trying to lighten the tone, trying to give him a way back from the fury that was driving a wedge through the team. Typical Daniel. For a long time Jack stared down at the dull leather of his boots, dark against the white stone floor. His team was like a lifeline. They'd dragged him back from the brink every time – they never left him behind, not ever. Not even when he was chewing off their ears for trying to help him, for trying to protect him. "Yam?" he said eventually, his voice rattling with an emotion he'd rather hide. "Baal defeated a vegetable? I'm impressed."

He heard a soft snort of laughter from Daniel and it released something inside him. The knot in his chest began to loosen as the fury settled back down into the dark places where it habitually lurked. Grudgingly, he turned. Daniel, still white as a ghost in blood-streaked clothes, was watching him with a carefully neutral expression. He was hiding what he knew, and for that Jack was profoundly grateful. Teal'c stood at his side like a sentinel, staff weapon braced against the ground, watching and understanding. And Carter… She was on her feet now, but her head was slightly dipped, and she stared contritely at the floor a few feet ahead of him. He knew his words had hit her hard, and he was still too angry to regret them. She should have known better. She *did* know better, which was at least half the problem.

"So…?" Daniel asked, speaking for them all as they awaited his decision.

So… Take a day-trip to Baal's pleasure dome, breach his orders and cause all kinds of merry-hell? Or play by the book and get his injured team home safe and sound?

It would have been an easy choice if Henry Boyd hadn't drifted into view – still alive, still dying, still missed every day by his wife and a daughter who'd forgotten her father's face. And so, in the end, it wasn't a choice at all. Despite Baal, despite Kinsey's threats, and despite his injured teammates, there was only one decision to make.

"We'll need a ride."

CHAPTER SIX

The city was dark and silent, spread out below them in shifting shades of gray. There was no movement in the streets, few lights, and above them the glitter of alien stars shed a delicate sheen over the faces of Sam's teammates as they crouched on the roof of their accommodation.

Below them lay a security checkpoint, the gray arch of the *sheh'fet* glowing with a soft green light and guarded by three well-armed men. In other circumstances they might have taken them out with zats. But not here. If the alarm were raised, Sam doubted they'd make it off the roof.

"Now what?" Daniel whispered.

"We'll have to jump," she whispered back, nodding toward the neighboring building. It was close, butted up toward theirs, but still a good two meters away.

Daniel's eyes widened. "Jump?"

"You'll be fine."

"You remember I don't like heights, right? I mean, I have mentioned that before – several times, I think."

"Not too late to change your mind." The voice was the colonel's. He came up behind them and crouched next to Daniel. "You still look like Casper."

"Casper can fly."

Sam smiled weakly. The anger radiating from the colonel was palpable, and most of it seemed to be directed at her; the fact that he refused to look at her was a dead give-away. Daniel was forgiven though, or so it seemed. Obviously it was only her motives he doubted. Fine, whatever.

With a quick glance at the checkpoint below, O'Neill moved to the edge of the building. "I'll go first," he whispered. "Then Daniel, Carter and Teal'c. Okay?"

Sam nodded along with the rest of them, but the colonel ignored her as he turned and rose to his feet. He took a few steps backward, eyed the jump and then ran and launched himself across the chasm. Landing smoothly on the other side, he disappeared into the shadows. Sam held her breath, watching the men below. One of them glanced up toward the skyline for a moment, then turned back to his conversation.

"Your turn," she whispered to Daniel.

He blew out a short, nervous breath and nodded. "Did I mention I hate this?"

"Fear will make you strong," Teal'c reminded him quietly, and with a hint of amusement Sam didn't miss.

Daniel twitched an eyebrow. "See you on the other side – I hope."

As he approached the edge of the building, O'Neill's face emerged from the shadows. The colonel made a hurried beckoning gesture, so Daniel nodded and ran full-tilt toward the gap, flung himself into the air, arms windmilling, and hit the other rooftop. For a moment Sam thought he was going to topple backwards, but then O'Neill had a fist in the front of his vest and yanked him close. He took a good look at Daniel's face before depositing him carefully on the ground. Daniel had lost some blood, and despite the Kinahhi pain-killers, his head must have been hammering even before the acrobatics. Not that he'd ever complain. There were Marines who could learn a lesson or two about stoicism from Dr. Daniel Jackson.

Her turn now. Carter took a couple of deep breaths and prepared for the jump. She was somewhat surprised to see O'Neill waiting on the other side; she'd assumed he'd leave her to her own devices in his current mood. Not giving herself time to consider the drop, Sam ran and threw herself into the air. There was a moment of total exposure, nothing above or below, and then her boots jarred against the stone roof and she stumbled forward under the force of her own momentum. A hand grabbed her arm, steadying her, and she looked up at the colonel. He held her gaze for an instant, nothing but cold starlight reflecting in his dark eyes. "Go make sure Daniel's okay," he said. "I think his head's started bleeding again."

With a nod she pulled her arm from his grip and turned toward her friend, who lay propped up against a low stone wall around the flat roof. His face was pale as moonlight and a dark streak of blood dribbled from beneath the bandage. Sam grimaced and crouched in front of him. "Maybe this wasn't such a good idea."

He shrugged. "Probably not. But it'll be worth it. Another book I can write and never publish."

She smiled and reached for her med-kit, looking for a fresh dressing. "Stranger things have happened." She considered the point. "Actually, pretty much every day around here."

Daniel gave an amused snort of agreement as behind her she heard the soft thud of booted feet hitting the roof; Teal'c had landed.

"Let's hurry it up," ordered the colonel. "Daniel, you sure you're okay?"

"I'm fine."

"Carter?" The colonel didn't trust Daniel's self-assessment any more than she did.

She pressed a new dressing over the cut on Daniel's head and began to fasten it in place. "He's not bleeding heavily, sir. I think he'll be okay."

"I'm fine!" Daniel protested. "I said I'm fine."

"Yeah," O'Neill replied. "You always say that." Then he turned to Teal'c. "Belay the rope."

While Sam helped Daniel to his feet, and he tried to pretend he wasn't even slightly woozy, Teal'c tied the rope and after a moment they were ready to descend. "Same as before," O'Neill ordered. "Daniel, make sure your harness is secure. If you pass out I don't want you ending up as pizza on the sidewalk."

Daniel winced. "Nice image."

The colonel didn't answer, dropping over the edge of the building and disappearing. It didn't take long for the rest of them to follow and hide in the shadows of the silent street below. "The taxi stand was back that way," O'Neill whispered. "Keep your eyes open."

Carefully they moved out. Sam was glad of the gun in her hands; dark windows stared down at them, like the blank eyes of the dead. The unnatural silence spooked her, amplifying even the smallest sound until she found she was jumping at shadows. Although what she had to fear, she didn't know. Kinahhi soldiers, perhaps? Or the dissidents? Or Baal.

That thought drew her eyes back to O'Neill, leading them resolutely through the streets. She could see the tension in the square set of his shoulders and knew he had his own fears. Sometimes she thought she'd like to know the details, to have facts to counter the horrors of her imagination. Other times she thought it was best she didn't know. She wasn't sure she could live with that much anger. And yet he did. Every day. Somehow he had retained his humanity and his perspective despite, or perhaps because of, the inhumanity he'd suffered. It was one of his most admirable—

A soft sound hissed from behind her and Sam whirled around, weapon raised. "Sir," she called, quiet and urgent.

"Carter?"

"I heard something." Scanning the street she strained her ears to listen. "A scraping sound."

He was beside and past her in two steps, fingers tight on the trigger of his P90 as he poked into the shadows.

"I hear nothing, O'Neill," Teal'c reported after a moment.

"Me neither," Daniel agreed.

The colonel nodded and lowered his weapon slightly. But he didn't loosen his grip. "Let's keep moving."

Rattled, Sam followed. She couldn't shake the feeling that all those dark windows hid eyes that were watching them and waiting for just the right moment to strike. She shivered and closed the gap between herself and the rest of the team.

As they approached the street corner, O'Neill slowed and waved them all toward the walls of a shadowy building. "Down there," he whispered, peering around the corner. With the tip of his gun preceding him, he turned into the new street. "It's clear."

The road stretched darkly ahead, and to one side was the rank of Kinahhi transport ships. So far, so good.

"I hope you know how to hot-wire one of these things, Carter."

"Piece of cake, sir." She hoped.

Drawing nearer to the first transport, Sam was surprised to see the doors open and a faint light glowing within. She approached carefully, weapon raised, and stopped at the doorway. Daniel was behind her and quietly whispered, "This is convenient."

"Yeah," she agreed. "Very."

Standing flat against the ship, to one side of the door, she looked over at the colonel on the opposite side and waited for his signal.

He gave a slight nod and counted down on his fingers. Three, two, one…

They burst into the small ship with silent efficiency, weapons trained in all directions. It was empty. O'Neill nodded to Teal'c. "Cockpit."

As they disappeared, Sam searched the wall for the controls and sent the door sliding firmly shut. It made her feel marginally safer.

Daniel was still looking around, weapon at the ready. In this light she could see a glassiness to his eyes that she'd previously missed and it worried her. "Why don't you sit down?"

He didn't need a lot of persuading, and sank carefully down onto a long cushioned bench and closed his eyes. She'd taken half a step toward him when O'Neill emerged from the cockpit with Teal'c in tow. "It's clear," he reported, glancing around the cabin. "Well, this is handy."

Sam nodded. "You think it's a trap?"

"That would imply they knew we were coming."

"In which case why let us get this far?"

No one had an answer to that, and they stood silently for a moment. "So?" Daniel murmured drowsily. "What do we do?"

O'Neill shrugged. "Never look a gift-horse in the mouth, right?"

"Unless it comes from Troy." The colonel graced him with a long, blank stare until Daniel peeled open his eyelids. "The Trojan horse?" He gave up. "Never mind."

Sam caught the flicker of amusement on the colonel's face; she knew he loved to bait Daniel. "You look like crap, Daniel," was all he said. "Get some rest."

Turning to her, his face hardened as he nodded brusquely toward the cockpit. "Carter, get this thing in the air." At least he looked her in the eye when he spoke, though there wasn't much forgiveness there.

With a sigh she said, "Yes, sir."

"And keep me posted. We wouldn't want you to forget to tell me something important, would we?"

Jaw tight, she bit back her irritation and just nodded. "Yes, sir." And pardon me for giving a damn!

Teal'c stood by the window, the dim inner light allowing him at least some view of the street beyond. It remained quiet, but he felt more comfortable standing watch. He sensed a threat in the dark, silent city.

Behind him, Daniel Jackson was sleeping. He was unwell, and Teal'c grew concerned for his welfare. However, there was little that could be done until they returned through the Stargate, and meanwhile Daniel Jackson was a strong man. He would endure, as Teal'c did himself. His wounded shoulder burned, and he once more regretted the loss of his symbiote. The feeling was immediately followed by the sour taste of shame; he refused to mourn the means of his people's enslavement – of his own enslavement – whatever the cost.

"What's taking her so damn long?"

The question came from O'Neill, who was pacing the small cabin like a caged tiger, more troubled than Teal'c had ever seen him. No doubt the imminent prospect of encountering Baal's palace was weighing on his mind. Among other things. "I am sure Major Carter is working as fast as she is able," Teal'c said, still keeping a wary eye on the street outside.

O'Neill grunted, unconvinced. "We're like sitting ducks here."

There was no denying the point. But he doubted their current situation was the cause of the colonel's restlessness, merely a convenient expression of deeper anxieties. Teal'c knew the man well. And he understood O'Neill's anger at the actions of Daniel Jackson and Major Carter, however well intentioned. In that, he had also played a part. "I should have informed you of Baal's connection with this planet, O'Neill," he confessed. "I did not do so at the insistence of Major Carter and Daniel Jackson. I believe I was mistaken."

"Yeah," was the clipped response. The pacing continued, forcing Teal'c to elaborate further.

"Major Carter and Daniel Jackson did not mean to undermine your authority," he said, lowering his voice so that it did not travel beyond O'Neill's ears. "They do not always think as we do."

He was answered by a long silence, punctuated only by the soft thud, thud, thud of O'Neill's boot kicking against the side of the cabin. "Daniel's not a soldier," he said at last. "I expect that kind of thing from him. But Carter, she should know better."

"Major Carter made a mistake." Teal'c turned slightly and saw O'Neill standing with his back to him, still kicking irritably at the wall. "Mistakes can be forgiven."

O'Neill turned, eyeing him warily. "You think I'm being too hard on her?"

Choosing not to answer directly, he decided on a more oblique response. "I believe you suspect that Major Carter's decision was not entirely objective. Perhaps you should examine your response in a similar light?"

The shutters closed. "Right."

Too close, Teal'c reprimanded himself. There were certain things O'Neill refused to admit, even to himself. Saying no more, Teal'c let silence fill the space between them. Unlike the Tauri, he understood that the meaning of silence was all too often drowned by the words employed to hide it. And so he left O'Neill to his thoughts and returned his gaze to the streets outside, still dark and filled with a different and more menacing silence of their own.

"Sir?" Major Carter's triumphant face appeared from the cockpit. She was not smiling, but he could see subtle defiance in her eyes. "We're in business."

He was floating, everywhere and nowhere. He could see everything, feel everything, but touch nothing. He could hear screaming – enraged, hopeless, defiant screaming. He knew the voice, he knew it too well. And he felt the pain as if it were his own.

Their concerns are not ours, the voices whispered. Intercession is not permitted.

But he's dying! He could feel the life seeping out of him, see his soul falling into shadow.

Death is the fate of the unenlightened.

And he could see it now, the darkness. Like a maw of some hideous evil, ravenous for new blood. And his screams were fading, his hope was fading, and he could see him falling. Falling, falling, falling into darkness...

"NO!"

The sound of his own cry jolted him out of sleep, his harsh breathing the only sound in the gloom.

It was dark.

Why was it dark?

Disoriented, head imploding with pain, he felt soft fabric beneath his hand as the tried to sit up. The screams, the darkness, the crushing pain in his head... "Jack?"

Strong fingers reached out and seized his arm. "I am here, Daniel Jackson." Teal'c? "We are aboard the Kinahhi transport ship, and approaching the city of Tsapan."

Tsapan? Yes. Yes, the Kinahhi. Tsapan. Baal. He remembered and pressed a hand against his throbbing head. "Why's it so dark?"

"Colonel O'Neill did not think it advisable to advertise our arrival."

Tactics, right. That made sense. He opened his eyes cautiously, afraid it might intensify the nauseating pain inside his head. It didn't, and through the gloom he could just pick out the figure of Teal'c crouching before him. "I think I was dreaming."

The Jaffa's eyes blinked, a glint of light in the dark. "I believe you were."

Those screams, the memory was like a foul slime coating his mind. He covered his eyes and tried to will the image away – no one should scream like that. No one should survive that. No one should have to live with those memories.

"Daniel Jackson, are you well?"

He nodded between his hands and sucked in a deep breath. "Bad dreams, Teal'c."

There was a long, pregnant pause. "Do you wish to speak of them?"

Daniel shook his head. Maybe it would help, but they weren't his dreams to share. There was only one person who had a right to hear them, but Daniel doubted that conversation would ever happen.

Bury it deep, he told himself. And leave it there.

The silence in the cockpit was unnatural and excruciating.

Jack sat staring out the window, feeling the tension twist in his chest as the glittering rainbow city drew closer and closer. Baal's palace – just the thought was enough to send little darts of fear shooting through his chest. Even his restless fingers were idle, scrunched into tight fists on his legs as he watched the city grow larger and larger through the wide window. *There's no one there, O'Neill,* he reminded himself. *Been a long time since you were afraid of the dark.*

No, not afraid of the dark. Afraid of the light. The white light that heralded another desperate dawn–

"NO!"

The muffled yell came from behind them, back in the cabin. Daniel. Carter flung him a concerned look – the first time she'd looked at him since she'd eased the Kinahhi ship into the air – and he half rose to his feet. Then he heard the muted rumble of Teal'c's voice and Daniel answering quietly. A dream, probably. Wouldn't have been the first time Daniel had startled himself awake, all cold-sweat and disorientation, especially since the whole 'higher being' incident.

Satisfied that Teal'c was handling it, Jack eased himself back into the seat and cast half a glance at Carter. Teal'c's words still lingered in his mind, illuminating his own actions with a clarity that made him wince. She'd only wanted to protect him and he'd bitten her head off like he was dealing with a raw recruit on the parade ground.

Just do your job.

Except, he knew he'd have done the same thing for her. For any of them. And so would she. Which was exactly the problem. What was okay for Daniel or Teal'c didn't wash for *Colonel* O'Neill or *Major* Carter. There had to be a distance between them, they had to be careful. They had always been so careful, especially Carter. But this…? He'd had no choice but to yank her back into line, however hypocritical he felt.

He sighed. She must have heard it, because she cast him a sidelong glance. What was she thinking, he wondered. Was she as pissed with him as he'd been with her?

Probably. And he probably deserved her anger, just like she deserved the apology he could never offer. But he still wanted to make things right. He hated this tension, especially now, when they were about to face who-knew-what, and Baal's phantom was lurking around every corner. He needed his team in one piece. He just didn't know how to begin with Carter – he never had.

Clearing his throat he leaned forward in his seat, elbows on knees, and looked out at the city. Up close, its beauty was flawed. Generous curves in peeling gold swelled out in an ample under-belly as Carter skimmed the ship around its base, looking for somewhere to land. Nothing. Pulling back, she took them up in a steep climb past plump towers, stretching toward the true beauty of the stars. Jack wondered how he'd ever considered the city beauti-ful; it looked like a fat, painted whore, corrupt and rotting beneath cheap perfume and tacky lingerie. A parody of beauty, just what you'd expect from a snake-head.

"Any ideas, sir?" Carter's voice radiated cool restraint.

"I'm looking." He moved closer to the window. Somewhere dark – but not too deep. Always think about your exit. Especially here. "What about there?" A flat rectangular space drifted beneath them. An abandoned roof garden perhaps? It was barren now, half shaded and half bathed in starlight.

Following his line of sight, Carter dipped the ship. Towers soared above them as she hovered above the empty roof. "There's no way to tell if it's structurally sound," she warned. Which meant they might end up in the basement with half the city crumbling in on top of them.

"Better idea?" It was a genuine question, not sarcasm.

She gave a little shake of her head. "No sir, and we don't have a lot of time."

True enough. The last thing he wanted when they got back was a welcoming party. "Okay, take us down," he decided. "But keep your foot on the gas, just in case."

"Yes, sir."

It was elegantly done, a gentle landing that he barely felt. For a moment after the ship came to rest they both sat still, holding their breaths. But there was no cracking of stone, no screeching of metal under torque, just silence.

Slowly he breathed out. "Thank you for flying Kinahhi Air-ways."

Carter almost smiled, but at the last moment the corners of her mouth flattened into a resigned line. Bowing her head she pushed herself out of the pilot's chair and headed for the door. "I'll go get Daniel and–"

"Carter?"

She turned, her usually expressive eyes guarded. "Sir?"

He nodded out the window. "Good job." It was less of an apology than a peace offering.

Lips pressed tight, she nodded. "Thanks."

Then she was gone and he could hear her quiet voice talking to Daniel, and Teal'c's baritone rumbling soothingly beneath. It did little to ease the knot in his belly; they were here, Baal's palace. Deserted or not, he was taking no chances.

Fingers clenching, he rose and went in search of his weapon. If the bastard was here, he wouldn't be taking him alive. No damned way.

"Stay close," the colonel barked from up front. He didn't need to repeat the order. Dark and damp, the only sound on Tsapan was the constant howl of the sea wind through derelict towers and empty streets. It tugged at clothing and surprised them with sudden gusts whenever they turned a corner. Lights hung like phantoms above them, and Sam guessed that the power required to drive the anti-gravity device unintentionally illuminated the abandoned city.

She kept her hands on her weapon as they moved cautiously through the streets, heading down as she'd suggested. The power plant had to be at the bottom of the city. But there was no sign of life, no sign of life recently passing.

Caaaaaaaaw!

Almost jumping out of her skin, Sam jerked her gaze and weapon up toward the sky – the wide wings of a sea-bird wheeled away. Feeling foolish, she lowered her gun only to catch O'Neill doing the exact same thing. "What kind of bird flies around at night anyway?" he grumbled, tugging his cap lower and resuming his wary exploration of the city.

'A nocturnal one' was the obvious answer, but she refrained from pointing it out. They were all jittery, the colonel especially, and even Teal'c held his weapon ready for use. Only Daniel seemed oblivious to the danger, pausing periodically to peer at something in the gloom, holding up his flashlight and muttering quietly to himself until O'Neill chivvied him onwards.

Eventually he refused to be herded, waving off the colonel's abrupt order. "Wait. Just wait a minute." Impatiently, O'Neill returned to where Daniel stood staring at a wall. No, Sam realized, not a wall. A door. "I think I've found something." There was writing on it, an alien script that Sam couldn't recognize. Carefully, Daniel brushed his fingers across the words and said, "This isn't Goa'uld."

Teal'c took a step closer, peering over Daniel's shoulders. "It is not."

"It's Kinahhi."

O'Neill frowned, dark eyes shadowed. "Meaning?"

"Meaning that the Kinahhi use this door." He pushed at it, but it wouldn't budge. "Might be a way down to the power plant."

With a nod, O'Neill pushed at the door too, then shouldered it hard. Still nothing. "Teal'c, see if you–"

A shadow passed overhead.

Heart leaping into her throat, Sam flattened herself against the wall. Above them, high amid the turrets, loomed the silent, blocky shape of a Kinahhi transport.

"I hope that's not our ride home," Daniel murmured quietly.

It stopped, hovering. Then slowly it began to descend.

"We've been made!" Sam hissed.

O'Neill whipped his head back and forth, assessing their options, then made a decision. "Teal'c," he barked, "the door. On three."

One, two– Thud! The door splintered under their combined weight, as Teal'c and the colonel stumbled through and bright yellow light spilled out into the street. Grabbing Daniel's sleeve, Sam tugged him in after her.

"Sir, the light!"

"I know, I know!" O'Neill was scanning the room for the source. There! She saw it too, a large amber globe fixed to the brightly colored wall. In two strides he was across the room and brought down the butt of his P90 hard, smashing the globe and plunging them all into safe, protective shadows.

Until a flashlight darted around the room.

"Turn it off!" O'Neill snapped.

It remained on. "Look," Daniel said, the light fixing on a narrow opening and a flight of stairs leading downward. "A way out."

"Or a dead end."

"We're not getting out the other way," Sam pointed out, backing up toward the staircase. Outside the Kinahhi ship must be landing; she hated that she couldn't hear it. She wondered how many soldiers they'd brought. SG-1 wouldn't stand a chance in a firefight, especially with Daniel and Teal'c already wounded. "Sir, the only other option is to hand ourselves over."

His snort of disdain was inevitable. "Teal'c, get Daniel down there. Carter and I'll cover your six."

Weapon raised, Sam moved to the stairs as Daniel and Teal'c headed down into the unknown. She risked a quick glance at O'Neill, standing so close his elbow bumped hers as they began their slow retreat. His face was determined and some of the tension she'd seen before was gone. He probably found the adrenaline rush relaxing.

"Heads up, Carter," he murmured. Beyond the shattered door the bulking shape of the Kinahhi transport crept into view. Slowly they retreated down the stairs, cramped and claustrophobic, barely daring to breathe and waiting for the first shot with every step.

CHAPTER SEVEN

A brooding General Hammond sat at his desk, ostensibly reviewing the base's Standard Operating Procedures before the morning's SOP meeting with his team leaders. But no sooner had he scanned a sentence – always the same sentence, it seemed – than his eyes found themselves drifting up to the clock ticking quietly on the wall. It read 18:59, which gave SG-1 just one more minute to report before they were officially considered out of contact.

He watched the red second hand tick relentlessly onwards. Tick, tick, tick, tick. The minute hand moved, landed on the twelve, and right on the button the phone rang.

"Hammond."

"Sergeant Davis, sir. SG-1 are six hours past their deadline."

"I'm on my way." Closing the SOP manual with guilty relief, he pushed himself to his feet and headed toward the control room. It was not unusual for SG-1 to miss their scheduled report times – he sometimes thought they actually courted disaster – but on this mission it was a surprise. The only danger he'd anticipated them having to face were the Earth-bound machinations of Kinsey. Or, at most, being irritated to death by the smarmy little diplomat they'd been forced to baby-sit. So what the hell could have gone wrong?

Davis was studying the silent 'gate and turned when Hammond stepped into the control room. "No contact at all, sir."

"And there's no problem with the 'gate at our end?"

"No, sir. SG-13 came back without incident just an hour ago."

"Very well," Hammond decided, "dial up Kinahhi. Let's find out what the hell's happened to our people."

The stairs seemed endless. Above him the faint glow from the surface had faded and only the dancing beams from Teal'c's and Daniel's flashlights cast any light below.

Carter fell back at his side, their footfalls and her steady breathing loud in the cramped space. "I don't think they're following us, sir."

"Doesn't make any sense. They must have seen us."

"Perhaps we're not the reason they're here?" she whispered. "Whoever they are."

"So why the hell were they trying to land on our heads, Carter?"

"Coincidence?"

She didn't sound convinced, and neither was he. But perhaps she was right, unless… He stopped, Carter automatically stopping with him. Ahead, the booted steps of Daniel and Teal'c slowly faded along with their dancing flashlights, leaving them alone. He said nothing, listening, silencing his breathing as he'd long ago learned. Waiting for the other side to give away their position.

Time drifted, lengthened and contracted, measured only by the slow count down from one-hundred to six, five, four, three, two, one…

Nothing.

He moved, the rustle of his jacket sounding loud and out of place. "I think we're alone."

"Yes, sir. We should– Argh!"

Brutal, narrow hands slid around his neck, throwing him flat against the wall. Cutting off his air. There was a strange, hungry snuffling and a wave of foul breath washed over his face as he blindly hit out. His fist connected with flesh and bone, hard and leathery. Its fingers briefly lost their grip on his throat, and Jack managed to gulp some air as he slid his hand over the strange, angular features and found its chin. He pushed up, hard, snapping its head back as he slammed his knee up, crunching painfully against solid bone. But it was the other guy who let out the thin shriek, his sinewy fingers slipping loose as he fell back and disappeared into blackness.

"Carter?" Jack barked. "Carter!"

The solid thwap of flesh hitting stone, laced with another groan of pain, was his only answer, followed by a hissing, scrabbling sound fading into silence. And then a breathless, "I'm okay, sir."

Thank God! He found his flashlight. The crisp, white beam sliced the darkness and half-blinded Carter. She flung a hand over her eyes and yelped.

"Crap, sorry."

Swinging the light away, he just caught sight of a pallid, emaciated figure scampering up the stairs until it literally disappeared into the wall. Heart racing, he'd taken half a step to follow when Carter grabbed his arm, "Sir, wait. There could be more."

"More *what*?"

In the scant glow of his flashlight, Carter's face was pale. "Kinahhi?"

Perhaps. He rubbed at his bruised throat. Whatever had attacked them, they were strong. Half of him wondered if Baal had left something nasty behind, some shadow of his evil to plague the city. The idea made him shiver. "Come on," he told Carter. "Let's get out of here."

She nodded, clearly spooked as hell. He didn't blame her. The hair on the back of his neck was still on end, as if a thousand pairs of unfriendly eyes were watching his back.

Waiting.

The thin shriek echoing down the staircase froze Daniel midstep. "What was that?"

At his side, Teal'c slowly turned to look up into the blackness above. "I do not know, Daniel Jackson."

"We should go back. Jack might need–"

Teal'c's hand landed firmly on his arm. "We must not. The stairs are too narrow for us to be of any assistance should O'Neill and Major Carter be under attack. If they are not, we would only hinder their escape from the Kinahhi. We must do as O'Neill ordered and proceed."

Daniel said nothing, letting the growing silence on the stairs enfold him. Teal'c was right – cold military logic – but that didn't make it any easier. For a moment he closed his eyes and allowed the headache to overwhelm him. Damn it hurt, like a hand contracting into a fist behind his eye. Ruthlessly he pushed it aside, squinting determinedly into the darkness through a nausea he kept at bay with nothing but willpower. He refused to become a liability.

There were no more screams, only relentless silence. Reluctantly he turned back to the steep stairs below. As he stood staring, he thought he saw something in the dark. "Teal'c, turn off your flashlight."

Wordlessly, the Jaffa obeyed and they were plunged into total darkness. Gradually, Daniel began to see a soft amber light far below, reflecting dimly on the wall where the stairs turned an abrupt corner.

"It appears we are almost at the bottom."

"Yeah," Daniel agreed. "Question is, what's waiting for us down there?"

The smiling face of Bill Crawford filled the monitor, flickering with hazy static as he did his best to reassure a deeply skeptical George Hammond. "They're being well cared for by the Kinahhi medics, General. And they're getting some well deserved rest."

The general was glad the video link only went in one direction; it allowed him to scowl to his heart's content. "Nonetheless," he insisted, "I'd like to speak to Colonel O'Neill." With his team out of contact, he certainly wasn't going to take the word of Kinsey's puppet as evidence of their safety. He wanted to hear it from the horse's mouth, and frankly he just didn't buy the story that SG-1 were "resting". Resting? When the hell did they ever rest?

Crawford glanced off to one side, obviously being prompted, before he returned his attention to the camera. "I'm sorry, General, but the Kinahhi insist that the 'gate be deactivated immediately. It's a breach of protocol for it to have been opened at all during this security lock-down."

Angry, Hammond took a step forward and wagged a finger at the blind image of Crawford's face. "Now you listen to me, Ambassador. Unless I see evidence that my team are alive and well within the next ten minutes I'll–"

"Is there a problem, General?"

The good-ole-boy tone grated in Hammond's ears like nails on a chalkboard. "Senator Kinsey," he said stiffly, turning around. "I thought you were on your way back to Washington."

The Senator didn't crack a smile. "I came to say goodbye, General." He glanced over at Crawford. "I repeat, is there a problem?"

Schooling his features to an impassivity he found difficult, Hammond switched off the mike and considered his next move. To admit that SG-1 were, to all intents and purposes, missing was to give Kinsey too much information. He wanted to neither confirm any suspicions the Senator might be harboring, nor offer a weapon with which Kinsey could intensify his attack on the SGC. On the other hand, to allow Kinsey to effectively bully him into backing down was tantamount to abandoning his people. And he'd walk barefoot over hot coals before that ever happened.

In the end he chose what he hoped was a middle path. Turning his back on the Senator, he spoke quietly into the mike, weighting every word with a promise of dire consequences. "I expect to speak with Colonel O'Neill first thing in the morning," he told Crawford. "And I will hold you personally responsible for ensuring that I do so."

Without letting Crawford reply, he severed the video link and squared up to Kinsey. The Senator's blue eyes, narrow and calculating, moved from Hammond's face to the monitor and back. "SG-1 letting you down again, General? I told you you'd regret sending such a troublesome–"

"The only thing I regret," Hammond snapped, "was having to send that imbecile Crawford with them. They deserve better." Straightening his shoulders and brushing off the sudden outburst, Hammond lifted his chin and added, "Now, if you'll excuse me Senator, I have work to do."

He hadn't even reached the door before Kinsey spoke again, menace apparent in his quiet lilt. "You should know this, General. If SG-1 in anyway jeopardize our negotiations with the Kinahhi, they'll be out of the SGC so fast they won't even have time to kiss their own asses goodbye."

Hammond didn't dignify the threat with an acknowledgement, pulled open the door and left without pause. But he couldn't stop Kinsey's words from trailing him down the corridor like the stench of stale cigarette smoke.

Something was going on. And, as always, he was on the wrong side of the Stargate to be able to do anything but wait, and pray that his faith in SG-1 would be rewarded yet again.

The corridor at the foot of the stairs opened out widely into an ornate circular chamber filled with concentric rings of elegant pillars, at the center of which flickered and hummed an incongruous column of lights and glowing crystals. An add-on, if ever he'd seen one. But what caught Daniel's eye wasn't the technology, it was the mosaic ceiling above. Glittering like a rainbow sky it bathed the room in a multihued light, lending it a silent, breathtaking quality that was enough to render him speechless. This was what it was all about, touching a myth. Touching something that no one on Earth had seen for thousands of years – if at all.

Despite the throbbing in his head, he craned his neck, "Wow." Then he reached for his camera. The ceiling needed study, and far more time than Jack would be likely to give him. Snapshots would have to do. But it was priceless, utterly priceless. Yahm, depicted as a sea-serpent – how apt – was writhing on the end of a lightning bolt wielded by a god whose fist was a swirling black mass of thunder; no doubt Re'ammin the Thunderer. Otherwise known as Baal. Baal the bloody, Daniel's mind silently reminded him. Baal the merciless. Baal the sadistic son-of-a–

"Daniel Jackson, I believe I've found what we seek," Teal'c's quiet voice was loud in the still room and Daniel snapped his head down suddenly. Too suddenly! The rush of blood exploded in a flash of pain behind his left eye and the next thing he knew…

"Daniel Jackson?" Teal'c's face loomed over him. Oddly, Daniel realized he was now staring up at the ceiling from the floor. A new lump forming on the back of his head testified as to how he'd gotten down there. "I believe you lost consciousness."

Daniel grimaced – he'd fainted? "I, uh, like the view better from down here." Which wasn't entirely a lie. The fist of thunder looked different from this perspective, and he snapped a picture of it for good measure.

A single raised eyebrow remained Teal'c's only response, for at that moment footsteps echoed through the chamber. Teal'c rose, whirling his staff weapon into a defensive stance as Daniel tried to scramble upright. But his woozy head just sent the room spinning in anarchic circles and he had to close his eyes before his last meal returned for an encore.

Through the revolving darkness he heard Teal'c rumble. "O'Neill. Major Carter."

Thank God!

"Teal'c, we– What happened to Daniel?"

Opening his eyes again, he valiantly squinted up at the rest of his team. "I'm fine," he assured them, although the mantra was wearing a little thin. "Spent too long looking up."

"Up?" Jack replied, glancing briefly at the ceiling. "Why?"

"It's interesting."

O'Neill gave him a long look but didn't bother to argue. Next to him, Sam stood gazing curiously around the chamber. But she seemed unsettled, and something about the way she clutched her weapon reminded Daniel of the shriek they'd heard in the darkness. "We thought we heard something," he said, glancing between them. "A scream. Was it you?"

O'Neill raised an eyebrow. "I don't scream." But as he said it a shadow passed over his face, and he abruptly glared down at the toes of his boots. They both knew it wasn't true.

Ignoring the moment, or perhaps trying to ease it, Sam added, "We were attacked by some kind of creatures."

"Creatures?" Daniel waved away Teal'c's offered assistance as he pushed himself to his feet. "What kind of creatures?"

"Strong, skinny ones," Jack replied, recovering. He pulled at the collar of his jacket, and through the soft light Daniel could see vicious red welts forming on his neck. "Kind of human."

"Kinahhi?"

"Maybe. Either way, we need to make tracks and–"

He stopped mid-thought as Sam unexpectedly wandered away from them, heading toward the wide column in the center of the room. "Sir," she called quietly, "I think this may be it."

"I believe Major Carter is right," Teal'c agreed. "This appears to be the central core of the anti-gravitational matrix."

Jack flung a wary look at the shadowy staircase. "You've got ten minutes, Carter."

She turned. "But Colonel, I'll need–"

"Nine and fifty-five seconds. Teal'c, Daniel, stay with her. I'm going to scout the room, see if I can find another way out."

Sam bit back any further protests, slung her weapon out of the way and all but rolled up her sleeves as she got to work, muttering quietly to herself. Teal'c stationed himself between them and the staircase, staff weapon at the ready. And Daniel...? Folding his legs beneath him, he sank back to the floor and lay down, camera in his hands. He actually did get a better perspective from down here, and if it also eased his hammering headache then who was he to complain?

The whispered conversation of his friends was the only noise in the vast chamber as Jack stalked through the forest of pillars, searching for a way out that didn't involve a return trip through the Kinahhi Halloween special. *Clutching white fingers in the dark, coming out of nowhere...* How the hell had they managed to creep up on him like that? No sound. Not a single sound.

He shivered; the place gave him the creeps. The whole damn city stank of decay and something worse. There was evil here. Not just the ancient evil of the palace's creator, but something else. A sense of dread that was all too alive.

Keeping his P90 raised, he turned a slow three-sixty as he walked. Shadows streamed out from the pillars, wide and slovenly in the diffuse light cast by the gaudy ceiling. But there was nothing there, no monsters hiding in the darkness. No ghosts.

He glanced up at the mosaic that was so enthralling Daniel. The face of the god wasn't familiar; it didn't wear the neat, trimmed beard of an urban sophisticate or possess the flat, dead eyes of a psychopath. Jack looked away and banished the thought – memory was a distraction. The danger was here, not in the past. His throat still burned from the fingers of the man – creature – who'd attacked him on the stairs. He had no desire to run into Skinny Legs and his creeping compadres again.

He checked his watch – six minutes left. It wasn't nearly long enough for Carter to get what she needed, but he was too antsy to lurk in this maze of shadows longer than absolutely–

A scuffing sound behind him yanked his heart up into his throat. Spinning around, finger on trigger, he scanned the shadows and pillars. He didn't breathe, straining to hear over the hammering in his chest.

Nothing.

Damn it. The shadows were deep here, back toward the wall of the chamber, dark and deep. Tension ran across his skin, crawling up onto his scalp as he backed slowly away from the ghost of a sound. Head toward the light, toward the guys, toward–

Fingers brushed his shoulder. He jerked around so hard he almost lost his balance. Only twenty years in the field kept him from firing. A figure, half lost in darkness, stood before him. *Baal! Shit.*

Fear clouded his eyes, suffocated him.

Baal!

His hands shook, his voice was dry and useless. But he stood his ground and faced the nightmare that had haunted him ever since he'd–

Wait…

Sluggishly, reason clawed through the panic. Baal hiding alone in shadows? No Jaffa? Baal dressed in Kinahhi robes? Like lightening in slow-motion, realization struck. *It's not him.*

"Get out where I can see you," Jack rasped, "or I'll put a bullet in your head."

The figure moved, tall and slender, but not him. Not *him*. And not white like the creatures who'd attacked them on the stairs. It was a man, and as he emerged from the shadows Jack's breath caught in surprise. "Quadesh? What the hell–"

The Kinahhi councilor raised a narrow finger to his lips and whispered. "No one can know I am here, Colonel O'Neill. My life depends upon it."

Still sick with receding panic Jack lowered his voice, but not his weapon, and said, "You've got thirty seconds before I start yelling. You've been following us. Why?"

A hint of a smile wavered across the man's face. "You did not really think you could evade our security so easily, Colonel?" When Jack didn't respond, Quadesh simply shrugged and added, "I hid your escape from my superiors. Had I not done so, you would all now be in custody. Or worse."

"And you did that because…?"

"Because I believe I can trust you, Colonel. And I think you may already suspect that all is not well here on Kinahhi."

"We got an inkling," Jack admitted, still staring at the man over the barrel of his gun. He didn't feel like lowering it. "Why don't you keep talking?"

Quadesh paused, as if marshalling an inner strength. At length he appeared to make a decision, both hands twisting around a slim metal tube he clutched like a talisman. "Although the Security Council talks of dissenters, Colonel, there is no real dissent on Kinahhi. No freedom of thought or expression. The *sheh'fet* sees to that – anyone harboring seditious thoughts simply disappears."

A sickeningly familiar scenario. "Disappears where?"

Quadesh stilled, hands tightening around the slim tube. "Here, Colonel. They are brought here."

Holy crap. His mind raced back to the creatures, hungry and violent, on the stairs. "What happens to them?"

"I do not know. But none return. I suspect they are killed."

He was probably right, it was the MO of every tin-pot dictator he'd ever encountered. Tortured, dehumanized. Then murdered. Was that who they'd encountered on the stairs? Escapees? Inmates? He lowered his weapon, slightly. "Why are you telling me this?"

Stepping forward, Quadesh's voice dropped. "So that you can tell your people. Stop them from signing the treaty with Kinahhi and instead help us to gain our freedom!"

Us? An image flashed into Jack's mind; the woman cradling her lost child, drowning in grief. "Are you one of them?" he demanded coldly. "Do you plant bombs? Kill kids?"

Quadesh's face paled. "No! No, you misunderstand Colonel. I have never–" Closer still, his amber eyes were full of fear. "This is the first time I have dared to act against the Security Council. I am not a murderer, Colonel O'Neill. I swear to you." And then, hastily, he held out the narrow tube he'd been clutching. "Please, take this as a gesture of my goodwill."

Reluctant to let go of his weapon, Jack studied the tube suspiciously. "What is it?"

"What you need," Quadesh insisted, a hint of a smile returning. "It is why you have come here, Colonel."

Jack raised his eyes. "And why have we come here?"

"You wish to rescue your friends from a planet trapped within the event horizon of a black hole." The hand proffering the metal cylinder began to tremble. "You wish to understand our gravitational technology."

And how the hell did he know all that? "Says who?"

Quadesh bit lightly on his lower lip, eyes shifting as if considering his options. And then his narrow shoulders lifted in an apologetic shrug. "Your Ambassador."

"Crawford?"

The councilor nodded. "I overheard him talking to Councilor Damaris. He had heard you discussing the possibility with Major Carter."

That night when he couldn't sleep, out in the courtyard. "The rat-bastard!"

"It is all here," Quadesh promised. "All the schematics held in the Kinahhi database – a copy, of course. They will not know it is missing and it is more than your Major Carter will glean here." He glanced over his shoulder, pushing the tube toward him. "I must go before I am missed. Please, Colonel, consider my plea."

His lips suddenly dry, Jack stared at the tube. Dare he take it? Could he live with himself if he did? The Security Council had already refused to trade the technology, so taking the schematics was tantamount to stealing from a would-be ally. It went against everything he stood for, everything he'd fought for when he'd brought down Maybourne's rogue NID agents who'd been doing the exact same thing.

And Kinsey! If he got wind of this it would be the end of Colonel Jack O'Neill. And if Jack went down, he had no illusions about the rest of SG-1. Kinsey was after their blood.

But none of that changed the fact that Henry Boyd and his team were still out there, still lingering in terror on the point of death. Or that this was probably their best chance of getting home… *And nobody gets left behind.*

Letting go of his gun, he reached out and let his fingers close slowly over the cool metal tube. A glimmer of satisfaction passed through Quadesh's eyes as he stepped backward.

"Thank you, Colonel." He bowed, hands pressed over his heart. "The people of Kinahhi thank you."

Jack said nothing; he hadn't done it for the people of Kinahhi and he didn't deserve their thanks. "I need a way out," he said by way of a reply. "Not the stairs."

Quadesh nodded and pointed a slender finger toward a thick pillar standing at the far end of the chamber. "In there is a conveyor.

It will take you to the surface."

Jack gave a curt nod. "I take it we won't be discussing this again?"

"We will not," Quadesh agreed. "I just pray that I was not seen leaving the city." Then, with a short, nervous nod he turned and hurried into the shadows. Jack watched as he touched something on the mosaic surface of a pillar and a door slid silently open. Quadesh looked back once and gave a half-hearted gesture of farewell before he stepped inside and disappeared.

In the silence that followed, Jack hefted the slim tube in his hand. It was light, weighed almost nothing. And yet it was heavy with danger, possibility and risk.

CHAPTER EIGHT

Daniel sat with his eyes at half-mast, his interest divided between the man opposite him and the sparse lights of the Kinahhi city below as they skimmed silently back toward their lodgings. He tried not to think about the climb up the side of the building that awaited them, concentrating instead on keeping the pain in his head at bay. What he wouldn't give for the sight of Janet Fraiser right now, morphine in hand and a lecture on her lips.

To distract himself, he returned his attention to Jack, who gazed unseeing out the window. Even by Jack's standards he'd been taciturn since dragging them – over Sam's muted frustration – to the elevator in the depths of Baal's palace. Daniel wondered if he'd seen something down there that had spooked him. Something that had reminded him of Baal's other fortress…

He was about to speak, although he wasn't entirely sure what he would say, when Jack moved. He reached into his pocket and pulled out a Mainstay energy bar, carefully opened it and started chewing. In Daniel's current state, the aroma of faux-lemon and vanilla made him nauseous, so he closed his eyes and deliberately sent his mind to the banks of the *Payom*, where the desert wind blew softly at sunset and the scent of frangipani filled the air. And Sha're's fingers found his, warm and strong. The pain and the nausea receded as the memory whispered gently through his mind. A lifetime ago. He'd been a different man back then. He'd–

The rustle of plastic intruded on his sweet melancholy and he lifted his heavy eyelids. Jack was wrapping the remainder of his Mainstay bar carefully and tucking it back into his vest. His face was still pinched with a hidden concern. But perhaps thoughts of Sha're had brought the right words to Daniel's mind, because he suddenly knew what he had to say. Sha're had always known what to say, even when they'd been divided by language. "I was wrong, Jack."

"About?"

"Trying to protect you from this."

A slight movement of his eyes served as both agreement and forgiveness. "I know what you were trying to do." He paused, turning back to the window. "And I appreciate it."

Daniel let the silence ride for a moment, then added, "I don't know if I could have done it. Gone there, after what you—"

"Yeah." The word, short and clipped, cut him off. "Well, they pay me to be a hard-ass." He sat forward, fidgeted and pulled his cap out of a pocket. "What about you? How's the head?"

A blunt change of subject, but that was Jack for you. At least he was talking. Going with the flow, Daniel reached up and touched the dressing on his temple. His fingers came away dry. "Feels like I drank too much moonshine."

A smile edged across Jack's face. "That stuff packed a punch."

"Yeah." He remembered the first time he'd spent the night drinking Skaara's concoction with Kasuf. Sha're had stood over him the next morning with such a look of amusement and irritation in her soft eyes that, despite the hangover, he'd been forced to smile. Sha're, Kasuf, Skaara… Abydos. All gone now, all its people gone. The loss hit him, as if often did, out of the blue.

Jack must have seen it in his face because he stood up and clasped a reassuring hand on his shoulder. "Get some rest," he said gruffly. "We'll be there soon."

Daniel nodded, swallowing the taste of grief as Jack headed up toward the cockpit. But he'd left something behind, a slender metallic tube was tucked between the seat and the wall. "Jack?"

He turned. "Yeah?"

"Is that yours?"

His friend looked, shrugged and shook his head. "Nope. Now rest, while you can."

Thinking no more of it, Daniel let his mind drift back to Abydos and the short days that had seemed destined to last forever…

Bill Crawford couldn't sleep, which wasn't unusual. Sleep was an elusive creature that rarely visited his restless mind. *Sleep is for wimps*, his father had liked to say. Although he suspected that sleep was really reserved for the dull, for those who had nothing more important to do with their pathetic lives than waste half of it between the sheets. He wasn't one of those people; his life had purpose and if the cost of success was a good night's sleep then it was a small price to pay.

On occasions, insomnia even proved invaluable. This morning

was a case in point. He was staring out from the window of his new quarters, housed high above the city and – at his request – far from O'Neill and his team. A reward, so to speak, for the little tidbit of overheard conversation he'd been able to pass on. A week's worth of trust earned in a moment, all thanks to his chronic lack of sleep.

And from his new vantage point he was able to watch the dawn maneuvers of a small phalanx of Kinahhi soldiers trotting through the streets below. They were the only people moving, men on a mission. Something was afoot. Another bomb, perhaps? Nervously he moved away from the window and was just resolving to ask Damaris what was going on when three swift raps on his door made him jump. Glad that he was already dressed, he moved quickly to answer. And for a moment he regretted the absence of SG-1. If the Kinahhi had double-crossed him…? Swallowing a fluttering fear, he opened the door, shoulders back and chin as high as he could thrust it. "Yes?"

A Kinahhi soldier stood before him. "Ambassador Crawford, Councilor Damaris requests that you join her immediately. A grave matter has arisen that cannot wait."

The fluttering fear didn't abate. "Regarding what?" His voice sounded higher and more snappish than he'd intended.

"Espionage," the soldier told him sternly. "Your military personnel have been arrested outside the perimeters of the security zone."

"They *what*…?" Crawford stormed from his quarters and along the corridor, leaving the soldier to catch up. Unsure whether to yell or laugh, he couldn't help the triumph that flared in his gut. SG-1 had been arrested? Arrested!

This is your last mistake, O'Neill! I'm going to serve your head to Kinsey on a goddam platter!

"We went for a walk!"

The colonel stood like a pillar of outrage in the center of the courtyard, arms folded across his chest. They'd been shepherded back to their quarters after their ignominious arrest, just moments from the rope that would have taken them onto the roof and to safety, and O'Neill was not taking it well.

Sam watched him from where she and Teal'c stood, arms and legs spread against the wall. The Kinahhi soldier patting her down was none too gentle as he rummaged in her pockets. "Hey!" she protested, as a hand strayed a little too close to forbidden territory. What the hell was he looking for anyway?

Her vest lay in a puddle of the team's belongings two feet away, everything tipped out and scattered across the previously pristine floor. Ammunition mingled with old Mainstay bar wrappers and the Naked Lady playing cards the colonel always carried and didn't think she knew about.

"Take off your boots," the soldier demanded.

She rolled her eyes and was about to protest when she caught the subtle nod from O'Neill, ordering her to co-operate. Fine! She bent to unlace them. If GI Joe wanted to hunt around in her boots – which she'd been wearing non-stop for the past thirty-six hours – it was his hard cheese. Literally. "Enjoy," she said, offering them to him with an unfriendly smile.

Sadly, his reaction was lost in a buzz of excitement that bustled into the far corner of the plaza. The infuriated tone of Bill Crawford preceded him like the whine of a mosquito. Just what they needed.

"Oh great!" O'Neill muttered.

The ambassador was accompanied by Councilor Damaris and a small entourage of soldiers, led by a grizzled man who looked like he meant business. The councilor seemed as frosty as she'd been during their previous encounter in the hospital. Her eyes found O'Neill, and she strode toward him with a ferocity at odds with the Kinahhi's usual languor. "Explain yourself, Colonel," she demanded.

"With pleasure," came the surly reply. "As I've said to your people here – a hundred times! – we *went for a walk*!"

Damaris folded her arms across her narrow chest. "I do not believe you."

"We were bored! We've been stuck in this place for days. Days! We were going stir crazy."

Crawford appeared at the Kinahhi woman's elbow. "You've crossed the line this time, O'Neill. Not even Hammond can protect you now."

Whatever his thoughts, the colonel gave nothing away. "We went for a walk. It's not a crime where I come from." He threw a glare at Crawford. "At least, not yet."

The councilor was unimpressed. "Perhaps I would believe you, Colonel, were it not for the fact that data of extreme sensitivity was downloaded from our central computer last night. A copy was made. What do you know of that?"

Interesting, Sam thought, but nothing to do with us. Except Crawford looked like he could barely restrain his triumph, all but hopping up and down at the councilor's side. What was he expecting?

"I can barely download my email," O'Neill said coldly. "I don't know anything about your central computer."

Crawford glanced up at Damaris with a sly smile. "The colonel is indeed technologically inept." His menacing gaze drifted, then came to land squarely on Sam. "Major Carter, however, is something of a genius."

What the hell was he trying to do? Frame them? "I'm flattered, Ambassador," she snapped, struggling for what dignity she could muster with half her kit on the floor and her boots missing. "But I don't know anything about it, either. I'm sorry, Councilor, you must have some kind of internal leak because it's nothing to do with us."

Leaving O'Neill, the councilor stepped over their scattered belongings toward Sam. She was trailed by the old soldier who walked with the swagger of command, a man used to his own power and not afraid to use it. He almost looked more dangerous than the councilor. Almost. Up close, her colorless eyes were forbidding and Sam had to repress a shudder. For a long time Damaris just stared at her, as if trying to dig out the truth from within. Then she turned and addressed the soldier at her side, "Search their quarters."

"Oh come on!" O'Neill protested.

Damaris whirled on him. "You will be silent! Thirty-eight Kinahhi citizens died in the blast yesterday. And if I find that you are in league with the dissidents who terrorize our city, then you will suffer the full weight of our law!"

The colonel's gaze didn't waiver. "I'd rather die than help the people who planted that bomb."

"For your sakes, I hope you speak the truth."

O'Neill looked over the councilor's shoulder, toward Crawford who had started poking around in their quarters as their packs were dragged out and emptied onto the stone floor. For a brief moment Sam had a feeling he knew more than he was letting on. Suddenly nervous, she watched the soldiers search their belongings with a keener interest. They seemed so certain that there was something to find. But she knew they had nothing, she hadn't even had time to make notes on Tsapan before–

"Oh, hey, careful with that!" Daniel's voice came from the other side of the courtyard, where he sat propped groggily against a wall. One of the soldiers, surly and bullish, held up a digital camera. Daniel's camera! Daniel had been taking photos of Tsapan's mosaic ceiling...

Forcing herself not to react, Sam stared in morbid fascination as the soldier studied the device. He clearly didn't know what it was, and she prayed Daniel wouldn't enlighten him. Or that Crawford wouldn't notice the exchange. Inevitably, the question came. "What is it?"

"Oh, it's ah...a barometer."

A barometer?

The soldier frowned. "Explain."

Clearing his throat, Daniel considered. "It– You press the button and it takes a snap-shot – so to speak – of the, uh, climate. Air quality. That kind of thing. You know?"

Still unconvinced, the soldier pressed a button and the camera bleeped obligingly. He probably got a good shot of the inside of his nose.

"We use it to determine if alien environments are safe for us," Sam added. "It's quite a useful device, actually."

Deliberately unimpressed, he made a show of dropping the camera carelessly amid the growing pile of belongings. Daniel winced as it clattered against the butt of his weapon, but there was relief buried in his eyes too. There was more at stake here than a few pictures of a mosaic.

Breathing more easily she turned away, hiding a smile as she watched Teal'c glaring silently at the unfortunate soldier ordered to search him. She almost felt sorry pity for the scrawny red-haired kid patting down the Jaffa's muscular arms and legs – had to make the guy feel inadequate, she figured.

Time moved on and the soldiers became increasingly disconsolate as they realized that no missing documents were to be found. The colonel, who hadn't moved from the center of the courtyard, eventually called out to the councilor. "You satisfied yet?"

Damaris was not. She stalked toward O'Neill, Crawford trailing along behind, unable to hide her disappointment. "There is still the matter of your unauthorized absence," she said coldly. "And for that reason I shall be requesting that General Hammond withdraw your team from our world, Colonel. If you cannot respect our law, you cannot remain."

The colonel was unfazed. "Fine by me. We wanted to leave yesterday, remember? Maybe if you had let us…"

He let the sentence hang, but the Kinahhi woman picked it up. "Yes, many things might be different." She addressed the soldier at her elbow. "Return your men to their duties, Commander Kenna, and prepare to open the Stargate." He nodded and smoothly withdrew as the councilor turned back to O'Neill, "Gather your belongings. You have one hour."

With that she spun on her heel, but Crawford couldn't resist a final dig before he was swept away in her wake. "I'm *so* looking forward to writing my report, Jack."

The colonel's flat smile was dangerous. "Yes. I bet you are."

If Crawford heard he didn't respond, scurrying after Damaris like a lapdog. The Kinahhi soldiers fell in efficiently and quickly behind them, apparently doing their best to trample as many of the team's belongings underfoot as they went. But at last they were gone, although Sam had the distinct feeling that cameras, if not eyes, were still watching them. Clearly the colonel had the same thought, because he cast her a warning look and simply said, "Get ready to move out, people."

She nodded, but her attention lingered on him as he bent to gather his scattered kit. He headed straight for his vest and slipped it on, methodically replacing items in the pockets almost without seeing them. His eyes were scanning the ground the whole time until a hand shot out and snatched what looked like an old Mainstay wrapper from beneath a pile of unopened MREs. Without missing a beat he stuffed it into the pocket of his BDU pants and went on picking up his things.

Mindful of Big Brother, Sam said nothing. But she made a mental note to ask him about it once they were safely back at the SGC. He was keeping secrets, she'd put money on it. And when the colonel kept secrets it was never, ever good news.

CHAPTER NINE

Things were starting to fade, graying out around the edges. Daniel had the distinct impression that he wasn't doing so well.

"Daniel?" The voice seemed to come from nowhere, which was when he realized his eyes had drifted shut. He levered them open and saw Sam's face hovering in front of him. "Hey," she said softly. "How you doing?"

The answer *I'm fine* flitted through his mind, but even he knew it sounded ridiculous. He opted for the truth instead. "Ah, not so good."

Sam nodded, her hand stretching out to touch his forehead. "You're a little warm," she decided. "Hang in there, we'll be home soon. Think you can stand?"

He risked a nod, but the subtle movement tightened the vise around his head. "Just give me a moment." She did. Several as it turned out, and when he opened his eyes again Teal'c was also crouching at his side.

"I will assist you, Daniel Jackson."

With Teal'c's help, he stood. The world was fading to gray, and he had to breathe short and sharp to keep his stomach from revolting entirely. God only knew how he was going to survive the roller coaster trip through the 'gate. He plastered what he hoped was a smile onto his face and willed himself not to succumb to the creeping grayness. "Let's go."

Kinahhi soldiers in drab uniforms fell in around them as they left the plaza. Time was measured in footsteps, one foot, then the next, one foot, then the next, as they walked interminable white corridors toward the Stargate. Had it really been this far? Perhaps they were being taken somewhere else entirely?

As if at the end of a long tunnel, he suddenly heard Jack's voice. "Quit stalling, I need to get him home. Now!"

Stalling? Daniel lifted his head, making his vision swim, and saw Jack and Sam standing before a tall narrow door. Jack looked about ready to C4 the thing out of his way, but one of the soldiers blocked his path. "You must await the arrival of the Security Council."

"Screw the Council! One of my people needs–"

The door hissed open behind him and the soldier stepped out of Jack's way with obvious relief. Jack nodded toward Daniel and Teal'c to follow as he and Sam pushed through the door and into the massive 'gate room where they'd arrived just a few days earlier. A flutter of white robes told Daniel that the Security Council was present, but his vision was too unfocused to pick out many faces. He recognized Damaris though, and Quadesh. The latter stood in close conversation with a man Daniel didn't know, but even through his muzzy head he could sense the tension in the room.

"Carter," Jack ordered, "dial it up."

"That will not be necessary." Councilor Damaris waved one of her soldiers toward the DHD that sat behind tall, clear panels.

Ever suspicious, Jack nodded Sam in the same direction. "Make sure he doesn't dial a wrong number."

The idiom probably went over the councilor's head, but Jack's distrust was hard to miss. "Your people," she observed dryly, "are truly in need of our assistance."

"Yeah," Jack agreed, "like a hole in the–"

He was cut off by the distinctive and vastly reassuring clank of the Stargate spinning into action. Daniel felt a burst of relief at the sight. Thoughts of Janet and morphine ran through his mind as fast as the chevrons engaged. Chevron six locked and he thought he was on the home straight when–

KABOOM!

The blast came from behind the DHD, knocked him flat, and sent him shooting across the smooth floor and into the opposite wall. He felt the impact, hard stone smashing against arms raised protectively over his head. Then, with a flash of brilliant light, everything went black.

Teal'c was on his feet instantly, choking in the dusty air. "O'Neill!" he yelled, coughing as the dirt caught in his throat. He could see and hear little. Sirens were wailing and the air was thick, glowing a strange, luminescent blue. It took a moment for Teal'c to realize that the Stargate had opened.

He took a step forward, his booted foot coming into contact with something soft on the floor. Squatting down, he rolled over an inert body and found himself staring into the dead eyes of a Kinahhi soldier. Alarmed, he rose to his feet. "O'Neill!"

Someone behind him groaned loudly. Turning toward the sound he saw Daniel Jackson through the murky air, curled in a miserable heap next to the wall. Afraid of what he might discover, Teal'c hurried to his friend's side and carefully rolled him onto his back. Well-practiced fingers checked the pulse of the carotid artery. It was strong; his friend was in no immediate danger. As if to prove the point Daniel Jackson's eyes fluttered open, bleary and disoriented. "What…?"

"I believe we have fallen victim to another dissident attack."

"Again?" He coughed, but the cough quickly turned into a retch and a pitiful groan.

Teal'c eyed the open Stargate. Certainly the Kinahhi had earned few favors from them, and for a moment he entertained the thought of simply carrying Daniel Jackson through the 'gate and abandoning the Kinahhi to their fate. However, he had other teammates to consider first. "Do not move," he instructed his friend. "I shall return."

The dust was falling like soft rain now, clearing his view. The sight it revealed was grisly. The Kinahhi Council lay stricken, white robes dirty and bloodied. Amid their ranks Teal'c saw two of his own; O'Neill was groggily pushing himself to his hands and knees, head swaying from side-to-side. Major Carter, who had been much closer to the blast, sprawled motionless some feet away.

He ran to her, stepping over the motionless soldier at her side, and dropped into a crouch. The blood trickling from her nose and left ear was disturbing. "Major Carter?" He shook her gently by the shoulder. "Major Carter, can you hear me?" There was no response.

Lowering his cheek to her lips he felt a faint puff of breath against his face. As he straightened he saw O'Neill, frozen halfway to his feet, staring at them with scarcely concealed panic. "She lives," Teal'c said.

O'Neill surged back into motion. "Where's Daniel?"

"In need of assistance." He gestured toward the wall.

"Get Carter home," was all the colonel said as he strode through the devastation toward his friend. While he was moving, soldiers swarmed through the door into the 'gate room, bringing help. The men tended to their own, the living and the dead. Teal'c scooped the limp form of Major Carter into his arms and rose to his feet. O'Neill joined him momentarily, holding Daniel Jackson upright with an arm firmly around the man's waist. "Go," O'Neill ordered.

Walking carefully up the steps with Major Carter in his arms, Teal'c was on the threshold of the event horizon when an exclamation stopped him.

"Colonel O'Neill!" It was a woman's voice, cold as crushed ice. "Stop, or I will order my men to open fire!"

Back stiffening, Teal'c slowly turned. Six soldiers had them in their sights. Behind them stood a bloody and disheveled Councilor Damaris. O'Neill and Daniel Jackson were still at the foot of the steps, and Teal'c could see the brief calculation in the colonel's eyes. But it was obvious that they would not be able to escape to safety. With a grimace, O'Neill carefully lowered Daniel Jackson to the ground and turned around, hands raised. "Let us go, Councilor. This had nothing to do with us."

The Kinahhi woman almost screeched her response. "And you expect me to believe that?"

"Why would we do this?" O'Neill persisted. "Our own people got hurt."

"And many of ours are dead!" Her hand lashed out toward the DHD where bloodied soldiers lay broken and still. "Even– Even members of the Council! Quadesh, our–"

"Quadesh?" Teal'c did not miss the beat of alarm in O'Neill's voice. "Quadesh is dead?"

The councilor, however, was oblivious. She stepped closer, voice harsh. "Do not attempt to feign sympathy, Colonel. It will not absolve you of this crime."

O'Neill said nothing. Following his line of sight, Teal'c saw the slender form of the Kinahhi man who had guided them through the city. He lay prone, a soldier respectfully straightening his legs and arms. In the process of so doing, the young man pulled something from Quadesh's hand. Turning the item over carefully, he glanced up with a look of confusion on his young face.

"Take them away!" Damaris ordered, reminding Teal'c of their current plight. "We will deal with their treachery once–"

"Not gonna happen." O'Neill's weapon was raised and leveled. "Teal'c, get Carter out of here. Daniel–"

"Jack, I don't think I'm going anywhere." Daniel Jackson looked like a man clinging to consciousness by his fingernails. "Sorry."

O'Neill settled his weapon more comfortably against his shoulder. "Teal'c, that was an order."

"If he moves," Damaris countered, "you will all die." Behind her, the weapon of every Kinahhi in the room was raised and pointing in their direction.

No one stirred and the moment stretched long and taut, as brittle as blown glass.

Suddenly a voice broke the silence. "Councilor!" Commander Kenna stepped in front of his own men, blocking their line of fire. "Councilor, there is something you must see."

"Not now! Take it to—"

"You must." He held out a small, blackened device. "We found this."

Cross, her attention rested only briefly on the object. "What is it?"

"It's a detonator." The answer had come from O'Neill, and when Kenna turned his eyes on him he added, "Right?"

The soldier nodded, tight-lipped. "Colonel O'Neill is correct."

"And so you incriminate yourself!" exclaimed Damaris. "I think—"

"It does not belong to O'Neill," Kenna interrupted, although he seemed reluctant to confess as much. "Councilor, we found the device in the hand of Councilor Quadesh."

Damaris froze. After a moment her mouth opened, then closed again and opened once more. She seemed deprived of all speech. O'Neill, however, was not.

"Quadesh?" He sounded as shocked as the councilor appeared. "Are you sure?"

"I am," Kenna told him. "And why should you care, Colonel? This discharges you of responsibility."

A glimmer of disquiet passed over O'Neill's face; it was the equivalent of an emotional storm in most other Tauri. "I'm just surprised. He, uh, seemed like a nice guy. You know, not that we saw a whole lot of him." Kenna's eyes narrowed suspiciously, and O'Neill cleared his throat. "Well, now that's cleared up, we'll be heading home. Okay?"

Still reeling, Damaris fumbled for an objection. In the end, all she could muster was, "Now do you understand what we face?"

"Understand what?" the colonel asked. "That you have enemies? We all have enemies, Councilor."

"And we all do what we must to protect our people from them, do we not?"

"Within reason."

"Reason?" The councilor's smile spoke of shock and desperation as she waved her hand around the devastated 'gate room. "Where is the reason in this?"

There was a long pause and Teal'c could sense a shift in O'Neill's demeanor. When the colonel spoke again his voice was kinder. "The trick is, Councilor, to defeat the enemy without getting down and wrestling in the mud with them."

Her lips pressed into a defiant line. "We do what we must."

"Yeah." Slowly he bent down and helped Daniel to his feet. "Hope that works out for you."

Then he turned and fixed Teal'c with a steady look. *Go!* Teal'c had no hesitation in following the silent order. The deadweight of Major Carter was beginning to tax even his strength, and the increasingly bluish tint to her lips was perturbing. With a slight bow to the Kinahhi Councilor, he turned and stepped into the fierce embrace of the wormhole, glad to shake the dust of Kinahhi from his feet. Forever, he hoped.

Lieutenant James glanced up briefly, hands poised over the 'gate controls. "Sir, it's SG-1's IDC."

At last! But Hammond's relief was tinged with apprehension. "Open the iris." Like a camera shutter, the titanium shield twirled back to reveal the iridescent glimmer of the event horizon, rippling gently and expectantly. The general held himself still, waiting. He'd ordered Crawford to ensure that SG-1 get in touch, and to his surprise it seemed that the man had followed his orders – although the delay between the 'gate opening and the transmission of SG-1's IDC remained unexplained. Bracing himself, Hammond lifted his gaze to the video screen, hoping to see O'Neill's face appear at any moment.

Instead, Lieutenant James sucked in a quiet breath. "Sir."

The wormhole shivered and Teal'c stepped out, Major Carter's limp form in his arms. Hammond grabbed the intercom, heart plummeting. "Medical teams to the 'gate room, now!" Then he turned and bolted down the stairs.

By the time he reached the foot of the Stargate, Teal'c had laid his unconscious friend on the ramp and O'Neill was lowering a woozy Dr Jackson down at her side. They all looked battle-damaged. "What the hell happened?"

O'Neill grunted. "Got caught up in some local politics, sir."

Behind him Hammond heard medical personnel pour into the room, clattering gurneys in their wake. The diminutive figure of Doctor Janet Fraiser pushed her way past him and onto the ramp. She crouched at Carter's side, checking her pulse, peering into her eyes. "Did she take a hit?"

"Bomb blast," O'Neill replied. "Close quarters."

She glanced over her shoulder and barked, "Get her down to the infirmary."

Stepping over the major, Fraiser knelt in front of Daniel. "Hey," she said, fishing a penlight out of her pocket and checking his pupil reflexes. "Do you know where you are?"

"About five minutes away from a morphine shot?"

She smiled and stood up. "Two, if you're good."

Gurneys trundled to the foot of the ramp and Carter and Jackson were whisked away, Fraiser trotting ahead and issuing orders until the closing blast doors cut off the sound of her voice. Behind Hammond the wormhole collapsed in on itself, and suddenly all in the 'gate room was silent.

Slowly O'Neill rose, and he and Teal'c trudged off the end of the ramp. The colonel looked troubled, and not just because his team had gotten hurt. Which provoked a question in Hammond's mind. "Where's Crawford?"

O'Neill shook his head and snatched off his cap, dislodging a small cloud of dust. "Still negotiating." He paused for a beat, dark eyes serious. "Sir, we need to talk."

Not liking the sound of that one bit, Hammond simply nodded. "Hit the showers, Colonel. Debrief in an hour."

As O'Neill and Teal'c trailed wearily out, Hammond glanced up at the control room. He thought he could feel the eyes of Senator Kinsey boring into him, but only Lieutenant James was up there quietly going about his business.

Shaking it off, the general followed his team from the room and tried to imagine what kind of trouble SG-1 had gotten themselves into this time.

The water was hot, blasting off the grime that caked his hair and skin, easing the stiffness in his neck. Jack figured he must have landed badly when the blast had thrown him back; it felt like a distinct case of whiplash. But the hot water helped. He stood for a good ten minutes, letting it pound his aching muscles, while he ferreted through his mind and tried to sort out the confusing events of the past twelve hours. Top of the urgent list was the matter of what, exactly, he was going to tell Hammond.

The documents – he'd had a brief look and they appeared to be blue-prints – were still concealed inside the Mainstay wrapper and secured in his locker. They sat there, evidence of his guilt, and he had half a mind to burn them.

Quadesh had detonated the bomb, despite swearing he wasn't involved with the terrorists. Jack had been suckered in like an old fish who should have known better. He'd taken the bait because he'd *wanted* to believe Quadesh. He'd *needed* to believe the councilor wasn't involved so he could let himself accept the stolen plans.

But if he kept them now, wouldn't it be tantamount to being in league with the terrorists? The woman and her child were vivid in his memory; he refused to be part of that. Ever. But if he destroyed them, he'd be abandoning Boyd. Again. And no one gets left behind. Ever.

He let his forehead come to rest against the cool, white shower tiles. *There's no such thing as a free lunch.* The cliché ran thinly through his mind and brought a grim smile. He should have known better. He should have damn-well known better! People don't just walk up to you and give you *exactly* what you're looking for out of the goodness of their hearts. There's always a price to pay. In this case, he was afraid it might just be his soul.

"O'Neill? General Hammond requires us at the briefing in less than twenty minutes."

Teal'c's call roused him from his contemplation. He grabbed his towel and started to dry off. By the time he emerged into the cool air of the locker-room, Teal'c was already dressed.

Jack reached for a clean T-shirt. "I'm gonna stop by the infirmary on my way."

Inclining his head, Teal'c sat back on the bench and waited. Obviously he intended to tag along. While Jack dressed he could feel his friend watching him. He ignored him for as long as he could, pulling on his pants and standing to reach into his locker and stuff the Mainstay wrapper into his pocket. But Teal'c's gaze didn't budge, and at last Jack was forced to turn and face him. "What?"

The eyebrow rose. "You appear distracted, O'Neill."

He sat and pulled on his boots. "I do?"

"Ever since our visit to Baal's palace." There was a pause, and Jack hoped his friend had gotten hold of the wrong end of the stick. "Something occurred there that disturbed you."

He concentrated on pulling his laces tight. "You mean other than the creepy guys that attacked Carter and me?"

"I do."

Damn him. Jack glanced up, toying with the truth. If he told Teal'c, he'd have to tell the rest of his team. And then they'd all be part of the lie, because he knew hell would freeze over before they ever breathed a word to Hammond, or anyone else, of what he'd done. When the proverbial hit the fan, they'd all be caught in the stink. However, if he kept the secret to himself he kept the blame to himself. And so with a small shrug he said, "I guess it creeped me out. You know...Baal."

Teal'c's cocked eyebrow screamed disbelief, but Jack refused to be drawn out. He'd made his decision. He was keeping the plans, and he was keeping them to himself. For now.

He stood and slung on a shirt. Blue today, just for a change. "I'm going to check on Carter and Daniel."

"I shall accompany you."

As they walked together along the corridor, Jack was struck by the obvious hole in his own logic. Protecting his team from the consequences of his decision was all well and good, but without Carter, who the hell was going to make sense of the plans?

By the time Daniel made it to the briefing, Hammond was on his feet and in full swing. Jack sat rigid, hands folded on the table, lips pressed into a tight line, while Teal'c watched them both with silent fascination. None of them heard Daniel's polite knock on the open door.

"Arrested?" the general exclaimed. "Colonel, are you telling me the Kinahhi ejected you from their planet?"

Jack grimaced. "Well, not exactly ejected so much as reluctantly allowed us to–" He stopped when his eyes landed on Daniel, eyebrows climbing. "Daniel? Does the word 'rest' mean nothing to you?"

Hammond's head snapped around, and even Teal'c turned so that he could stare at the newcomer. Daniel offered a weak smile. "I persuaded Janet to let me, uh, take a walk. General, I really need to discuss the Kinahhi technology with you because–"

"Already covered it, Daniel." Jack was tetchy, tapping his pen on the tabletop in a short, staccato pattern. "Now, go and lie down before you–"

"No." Daniel moved into the room and pulled out the chair next to Teal'c. He sank into it quickly, before his knees could give way. "Jack, I know you don't want to break off relations with the Kinahhi, but we can't let Kinsey–"

"Easy son." Hammond took his seat again with a quick, curious glance at Jack. "Colonel O'Neill's already told me about the technology under negotiation. And I agree with him that it–"

"No!" Daniel objected again. "I'm sorry, General, but if we let Kinsey get his hands on it he'll use it to…to…to destroy everything we stand for! Our rights to–"

"Doctor Jackson!" Hammond's voice cut right across him, as soft and strong as silk. "I agree with Colonel O'Neill's suggestion that we *break off* negotiations with the Kinahhi, but–"

"But you–" Wait. *Break off* negotiations? He glanced at Jack and received a 'now-do-you-believe-me?' smirk in return. "Oh."

Hammond smiled slightly, but there was little pleasure in it. "However, I have to tell you, I have no influence over Senator Kinsey. This is his project."

Looking between the two men, both grim and resigned, Daniel felt his heart sink. "We can't just let him get away with this. Jack, you know how important this is…"

Jack made a face, as if his conscience had been pricked, and turned to Hammond. "What if we designated their planet as hostile?

Seemed hostile to me."

The general shook his head. "With Crawford still there, Kinsey won't buy that. In fact, he's more likely to order an investigation into the reasons for your team's arrest, Colonel."

Clearing his throat, Jack cast half a glance at Teal'c, who remained pokerfaced. Daniel suspected that their attempt to bring home the anti-gravity technology hadn't been mentioned. He sighed and Jack slumped in his chair, the heels of his hands pressing into his eyes. They were both exhausted – neither had slept for a good twenty-four hours. And thanks to Janet's miracle drugs there was too much cotton wool in his brain for Daniel to think clearly. But he knew there had to be a way. There had to be something they could do to keep Kinsey's paws off the Kinahhi's *1984* technology. "What about the President?" he suggested at last.

O'Neill's hands dropped from his face, faintly hopeful. "Go over Kinsey's head, sir?"

"I can try," Hammond offered, although there was doubt in his voice. "But with the election coming up the President has more pressing concerns."

Snorting in disgust, Daniel ignored his headache and sat forward. "More pressing than the potential destruction of our civil liberties? If Kinsey gets this technology we–"

"Think about this, son," the general suggested. "If the President loses the election to Hayes, Kinsey will become Vice President. What'll that mean for our civil liberties?"

It didn't bear thinking about. Letting his aching head drop into his hands, Daniel felt the stirrings of despair in his chest. Kinsey as Vice President? Good God...

Across the table Jack's chair pushed back, the soft brush over carpet the only sound in the pensive room. "Yeah, well," he said defiantly, "that's never gonna happen."

Daniel closed his eyes and mentally crossed his fingers. Kinsey in the White House? He'd rather see Anubis in the Oval Office.

CHAPTER TEN

The next morning Sam awoke to the noisy clatter of the infirmary, at least three hours earlier than she would have if Janet had let her go home. But when she'd suggested the idea the night before, the doctor's eyes had narrowed and she'd rattled off a litany of injuries. The only one Sam could remember was 'possible concussion'. But long experience had taught her that arguing with Janet Fraiser was pointless, so she hadn't even tried.

Daniel, however, clearly possessed talents she lacked because he'd managed to sweet talk his way out long before lights-out, and he hadn't come back. Levering herself upright, Sam ignored the sudden sway of vertigo and put a hand to the bruise on the back of her head. It hurt! Her face felt tight too, and her roving fingers found a neat little row of stitches near the hairline close to her left ear. Other than that, she felt pretty good. Too good to waste time in bed. Pulling back the bedcovers she looked around to see if her uniform was anywhere in sight.

"Oh, no you don't." Dr Janet Fraiser strode into view, her shoes click-clicking on the vinyl floor.

Sam grimaced. "I feel fine."

"Uh-huh," Fraiser nodded. "Lie down."

Knowing resistance was pointless, Sam did as she was told. "Really, Janet," she protested, "I feel fine. Great!"

The doctor produced her ubiquitous penlight. "That's what you all say." The bright light flashed into Sam's eyes. "Any nausea? Headache?"

"No," Sam assured her. And when Janet fixed her with a searching look she added, "Really! Actually, I'm a little hungry."

Slipping the penlight back into her pocket, Janet stepped back and cocked an eyebrow. "Okay, Sam. Go get some breakfast. I want you back in two hours, though, for a follow-up CAT scan. There's no fracture, but you took a nasty blow yesterday. I just want to make sure it's not a concussion. Okay?"

Sam smiled, sat up and swung her legs over the side of the bed. "Okay. Thanks, Janet."

Her feet hadn't even touched the ground before the doctor added, "And you're officially off-duty. Make sure you tell Colonel O'Neill."

"The colonel? Why?"

"Make sure you tell him," Janet insisted, waving vaguely toward the door. "He's been… hovering." The doctor lifted an eyebrow and Sam found herself studying the weave of the hospital blanket. *Hovering?* "Didn't say why, exactly – but I don't want you working until I've had another look at your head. Okay?"

She nodded, although her mind was drifting back to the Kinahhi plaza. The colonel was hiding something, she remembered. Question was, would he tell her what? And if not, could she ask? Dared she?

By the time she'd showered and changed, her stomach was growling, and she decided to satisfy her hunger before her curiosity. She opted for pancakes in the commissary and all but swallowed them whole. Still hungry, she grabbed a Danish on the way out and headed back to her lab. There were one or two results she wanted to check on, and despite Janet's warning she doubted it would aggravate the goose-egg on the back of her head.

When she opened the door to her lab, she was greeted by the slightly stale air of a few days' disuse. It was the familiar, reassuring scent of homecoming and she relished it. Danish in one hand, she pulled out the relevant files and had just dropped them onto her workbench when a familiar voice spoke from the doorway, "I thought Fraiser said no working, Carter."

She glanced up with a smile as the colonel sauntered into her lab. Hands thrust into his pockets he looked pensive, and the half-smile he briefly offered was uncomfortable. Maybe he still hadn't forgiven her for hiding Baal's ancient link to the Kinahhi? Her own smile faded. "Something I can help you with, sir?"

At first he didn't say anything, just paced the short length of the room and back before quietly closing the door and turning to lean against it. "Best guess," he said after a long moment. "From what you saw in the floating city, what are the odds of you being able to come up with something to bring Boyd's team home?"

"From what I saw? Not good, sir. I really didn't have time to see much at all. I couldn't even begin to try and replicate it without more information or–"

"What if you had it?"

Her eyes widened. "What do you mean?"

"What if you had more information?" His face was set, deadpan. "What if you had blueprints?"

Holy crap! She vividly remembered him snatching up the old Mainstay wrapper from their jumbled kit after they'd been searched. "Sir, do you have them?"

"Answer the question, Carter. What are the odds?"

She shook her head. "Unless I saw the schematics I couldn't say. Maybe. But we'd have to generate a hell of a lot of power, sir."

"But is it *possible*?"

"I'm sorry, Colonel. I just don't know. It might be. It might not." He said nothing, his eyes fixed on her as if trying to see into her mind and read the answer there. Good luck to him. "Sir? Do you have the plans? The ones Councilor Damaris said had gone missing?" And how the hell had he gotten hold of them?

At last the colonel looked away, brow furrowing as he pushed away from the door. One hand withdrew from a pocket, long fingers clutching the Mainstay wrapper. So she'd been right!

He glanced up from under his eyebrows and dropped the wrapper onto the workbench. "No one knows about this," he said. "And neither would you, if I had a choice. But you're the only one who has a chance of making sense of it."

Sam reached across the bench, but as her fingers touched the foil his hand closed over hers. "If you open it, then you know. You don't have to, this isn't an order. It's not even official. It's your choice, Carter."

Her choice? Hardly. "If there's a chance I can save Henry Boyd and his team, sir, I'm not going to ignore it. There is no choice."

A flash of something lit up his eyes. Understanding, perhaps? Or regret. But he lifted his hand and nodded. Picking up the wrapper, Sam reached inside and pulled out the wadded documents. The paper – if that was the right word – was tissue-thin, but strong. Undamaged, the plans rolled open on her desk. The language and markings were obscure, but it was unmistakably a blueprint. She looked up. "I'll need Daniel to help translate the specs and–" The colonel was already shaking his head. "What?" she asked.

"Need to know, Carter. The fewer people who know, the better."

Sam nodded slowly, smoothing out the blueprints. "You don't want Daniel or Teal'c to know?"

"The plans are *stolen*, Carter."

He didn't need to say more. If the truth came out they'd both be facing a dishonorable discharge, perhaps worse. And if Daniel and Teal'c knew... "You want to protect them." She hadn't missed the irony.

But he obviously had. "I wouldn't have told you unless I had to."

She smiled and shook her head. "You don't think they'd want to help?"

"Oh, I know they would. Point is—"

"Point is, it's okay for you to protect us but not for us to protect you, right?" She couldn't help herself, and it was worth risking his anger to see those eyebrows climb in astonishment.

"Excuse me?"

"I said—"

"I heard what you said." The eyebrows contracted back into a frown. "And it's a completely different situation."

"Is it?"

"I'm in command." He fixed her with a weighty look. "That's the difference, Carter. It's my call. My responsibility. Always."

Lowering her eyes, she gazed at the spidery drawings in front of her. "Not this time, sir. My choice, remember? This isn't official." He said nothing and she looked back up. "We need Daniel's help."

Irritably, he shoved his hands back into his pockets. "And if I tell him, he'll have no choice either will he? He couldn't refuse, anymore than you could."

"Or you," she pointed out. And from his mild look of surprise she gathered that he hadn't considered that before. "It's a matter of honor, sir. For all of us."

There was a slight pause – she could see him weighing her words – before he grunted his reluctant agreement. "I'll go find Daniel." Turning, he opened the door. Then stopped, his fingers tapping an uncertain pattern against the handle. "Carter?"

"Sir?"

"I understand why you didn't tell me about Baal." She winced; the less said about that the better. But he wasn't finished. "I appreciate it, but it can't happen again."

"It won't," she promised. "I'm sorry, sir."

He nodded slightly. "Me too."

And then he was gone, leaving her alone with the strange Kinahhi plans and a whole new conundrum to drive away the more perplexing problems of her life.

"Okay," Daniel said, pacing across his office, "let me get this straight. Councilor Quadesh followed us to Tsapan, cornered you behind a pillar, and gave you the plans to the anti-gravity technology? Just like that?"

Jack sat sprawled in a low chair, flicking sightlessly through one of the many books cluttering Daniel's office. He glanced up, annoyed by the skeptical tone. "Something like that."

"And you didn't tell us?"

"I'm telling you now."

Daniel stopped, cocked an eyebrow, and added, "Don't you think that's a little… convenient?"

"He wanted a favor."

"A favor?" Carter lifted her nose from the blueprints she was studying, like a tiger scenting prey. "What favor?"

"He wanted me to raise the concerns of the dissidents with Hammond." Jack snapped shut the dull tome with a loud thud. "Obviously, it'll be a cold day in hell before that happens."

Eyes dancing between Carter and Jack, Daniel frowned. "Ah, why not?"

"Are you kidding?"

"No. Why not raise the concerns of the dissidents? Given what Quadesh told you–"

"Quadesh blew up the damn government, Daniel!" Good God, was there no cause the man wouldn't champion? "He was a terrorist. You saw what he did."

Daniel's face flattened and sobered. He nodded. "I saw, Jack. But if it's true that people disappear just for holding the wrong opinion…"

"*If* it's true."

There was never any black and white for Daniel; he always had to try and see everyone's point of view. It was something Jack had grudgingly learned to respect, even if it did make his life a hell of a lot more complicated. "Look," he began, in a more conciliatory tone, "I–"

"O'Neill." The interruption came from Teal'c, who stood, hands behind his back, watching the proceedings with his usual equanimity. "Do you not think it is curious that Quadesh went to such lengths to enlist your assistance, only to alienate you by detonating the bomb in the Kinahhi 'gate room?"

Jack turned and stared, as did Daniel. Teal'c wasn't exactly a chatter-box, so when he did open his mouth it was always worth listening. "You think he was set up?"

Teal'c raised an eyebrow. "The Kinahhi knew that the documents had been copied. If they suspected Quadesh's involvement, this would have served to both remove the enemy within while ensuring that his credibility with you was destroyed."

Flopping into the low chair next to Jack's, Daniel spoke quietly. "Teal'c, you're suggesting that the Kinahhi blew up their own government."

"I am."

"That's insane!" Jack objected.

"Yeah, but Teal'c's right," said Carter. "Why would Quadesh give us the plans and ask for our help, then risk injuring or even killing us in the explosion? That doesn't make sense either."

Frustrated, Jack ran a hand through his hair and leaned forward. "So where does this leave us?"

Daniel gave a dry laugh. "With no one to trust?"

That wasn't quite true. "There's one person," Jack said, glancing over. "Hammond."

"Something else to tell the President?" Possibilities flew across Daniel's face. "If the Kinahhi are willing to destroy their own government to prevent us from hearing the case from the dissidents, that might be enough to persuade the President to break off the negotiations."

Jack smiled. "It might."

"On the other hand," Carter added, "General Hammond might be forced to hand the blueprints back."

Stop Kinsey or save Boyd? Again, the same choice. Jack grimaced and pushed himself to his feet. "Get as much out of it as you can, Carter. Daniel, help her with the translation." He took a deep breath, gritting his teeth against the silent voice of Henry Boyd – *don't leave me behind, sir!* "I'm going to see Hammond."

General George Hammond sat at his desk, staring at the man in front of him. A cold, outraged anger bubbled in the pit of his stomach, but he refused to allow it to show in his voice or his face. "If what you're telling me is true, then SG-1 will be guilty of stealing alien technology. That's a very serious allegation."

Dark eyes narrowed and the man leaned forward, his hands spread widely on the edge of the general's desk. "I'm aware of that. But the evidence is overwhelming."

"I'd like to see that evidence, Mr. Crawford."

A feral smile split the man's narrow face. "Of course." From his jacket pocket he pulled a small device, not much bigger than the palm-pilot Hammond's daughter had bought him for Christmas. The one still sitting in his desk, unused. As Crawford touched a button on the top of the smooth, gray device the whole thing became a screen and the general could see tiny figures moving about in what looked like a dimly lit room. "This," said Crawford, "is Councilor Quadesh illegally accessing blueprints for sensitive Kinahhi technology."

Hammond looked. Truth be told, he could have been watching anything. "This is hardly convincing."

The ambassador didn't seem bothered. He pressed the button again. "And this," he said, "is SG-1 stealing a Kinahhi transport." Hammond recognized his team flattened against the side of a square, alien craft before executing a textbook search-and-secure maneuver. Very elegant. "Colonel O'Neill has already told me about their visit to the Kinahhi floating city. I agree it was reckless – perhaps a little imprudent – but no damage was done and no–"

"No damage? I assure you, General, a great deal of damage was done to our negotiations." Crawford paused and allowed himself a self-important smile. "Fortunately, I was able to smooth things over."

"Ambassador, unless you can show me hard evidence that my team has stolen schematics from–"

A cursory knock on the door interrupted them, and Hammond winced at the timing as Jack O'Neill poked his head into the office. "Sir, I need to–" Then the colonel saw Crawford and froze. "I'll come back."

"No!" Crawford exclaimed. "Come on in, Jack. We were just talking about you."

Jack? The disrespect was deliberate and did nothing to quell Hammond's irritation. But the ambassador did have a point. "Come in, Colonel. I'm sure you'll be able to clear up a few matters for us."

Cautiously, O'Neill stepped into the room. He eyed Crawford with a mixture of contempt and suspicion, leaning back against the far wall with his arms folded firmly over his chest. You didn't need to be a genius to read that body language. Hammond felt a moment of discomfort – was O'Neill hiding something? "So what's going on?"

A foot shorter than the colonel, Crawford strutted like a peacock. "As you know, Councilor Quadesh has now been revealed as a dissident. The Kinahhi have evidence that he stole technical designs from their central database – designs for the anti-gravity technology you were so keen on gaining, Colonel."

"Fascinating." O'Neill glanced down at his watch, adjusted it, and started playing with its buttons.

Crawford plowed on. "In addition, they have footage of your little adventure to the floating city of Tsapan. And of Quadesh, seen close to your guest quarters that very night!" He paused, triumphant. "What do you have to say to that, *Jack?*"

O'Neill looked up from his watch, bemused. "Sorry, I must have stopped listening when I realized you were talking."

Repressing a smile, Hammond decided it was time to step in. "Colonel, did Councilor Quadesh give you any stolen technical designs?"

There was a minute pause before O'Neill said, "No, sir."

"That's good enough for me, Colonel." He turned back to Crawford. "And it's good enough for you too."

"But the Kinahhi–"

"Searched us before we left the planet!" O'Neill snapped. "They found nothing, Crawford, and you know it."

Hammond rose. "I suggest, Mr. Crawford, that you tell the Kinahhi to investigate this among their own people. From what I've heard, they've got enough trouble there without importing more."

Crawford's face darkened, a mass of bruised dignity and outrage. "I can assure you that they will investigate. And I have no doubt that we'll find SG-1's fingerprints all over this mess!" Leaning forward, he hissed, "You won't be able to protect them for long, General."

"I think you've said enough, sir," Hammond growled. "I suggest you leave, before I have you removed."

Snatching up his little palm-pilot, Crawford fixed him with a killer look. "Make the most of your last days in that chair, General." Then he turned, flinging a parting barb at O'Neill. "You too, Jack. I hear McMurdo is great this time of year. I'm sure you'll have a ball."

He left the threats hanging in the air like a bad smell as he stalked out of the room. O'Neill said nothing, pushing his hands into his pockets and meeting Hammond's gaze with a wary look. The general sighed as he sat and leaned back in his chair, studying his second in command. He trusted him. He trusted him to do what was right for his people and his planet. But there was something in his eyes that spoke of concealment. "You've made an enemy there, Colonel."

O'Neill shrugged. "He's his master's servant."

"Yes, he is," Hammond agreed, trying to read the truth in the colonel's deadpan features. "Was there something else you wanted to see me about?"

"Oh, it was—" Blinking, as if he'd forgotten entirely, O'Neill hedged. "It was Daniel, sir. Actually, the whole team. They took a beating on that last one. I was gonna ask to be pulled from the mission list for a couple of weeks."

Hammond frowned. "Doctor Fraiser has already spoken to me, Colonel. SG-1 is on stand-down for fourteen days. There was a memo…"

"Ah. Well, that explains it then." O'Neill flashed him something between a smile and a grimace. "I'll go… read my memos. Sir."

Letting him leave with an amused shake of his head, Hammond felt his humor fade as the door swung shut and his office slid into silence. Colonel O'Neill was hiding something. But one thing he knew for sure – if O'Neill was keeping secrets then there was a damn good reason for it. For now, he'd let it ride and hold onto his faith in his people. SG-1 had never, ever let him down. And if it came to a choice between Jack O'Neill and Bill Crawford, then he knew damn well who he was going to trust.

There was no choice at all.

CHAPTER ELEVEN

The living room in Sam's house had become the temporary headquarters for SG-1. Books were piled in cockeyed heaps, empty coffee mugs decorated every free space, and a makeshift chalkboard half obscured the window, cutting the light and making the whole room dimly reminiscent of the SGC. Even in the middle of the day the lights were on.

Daniel sat slumped in a deep chair, one leg dangling over the arm, stomach rumbling. He glanced at his watch and hoped Jack would be back with the take-out soon. To distract himself from thoughts of hot and sour soup, he buried his nose in the stack of photos he'd taken of the mosaic ceiling on Tsapan. He'd finished his translation of the documents hours ago; the Kinahhi language, as it turned out, was closely based on Goa'uld and hadn't proved a challenge. At least for him. Sam, however, was having problems. She'd been staring at her computer screen all day, trying to make sense of the incomprehensible diagrams in front of her.

On cue, she sighed heavily. "Daniel?"

He glanced up. "Mmmm?"

"This figure," she tapped the screen, "you're sure it means two hundred?"

"I'm sure." His nose was already back in the photos; she'd asked the same question four times. "Just like I was last time."

"Sorry."

Teal'c shifted where he sat on the floor, stood and came to peer over her shoulder. "You do not believe that this technology will be able to aid Major Boyd?"

Sam looked defeated. It wasn't an expression Daniel had often seen on her face, and he found it oddly troubling. "Theoretically, this device could produce an anti-grav field of massive proportions. Far stronger than anything we saw on Kinahhi. I just don't know how we'd power it. A naquadah reactor – even a naquadria reactor – wouldn't be nearly enough." She landed a controlled fist with a little thump on the desk. "I shouldn't have told the colonel it was a possibility, Teal'c. I mean, a black hole! What was I thinking?"

Teal'c raised an eyebrow. "You were thinking of Major Boyd and SG-10."

With a rueful grimace she nodded. "Maybe if I had an unlimited budget and a team of researchers…"

The rest of her words faded as Daniel found himself staring in astonishment at the photograph in his hand. He hadn't noticed it when looking at the images on-screen, but as he studied the mosaic of the Thunder-god wielding a fist full of swirling black clouds, he was struck by a lightning bolt of his own. "Uh, Sam?" Slowly he undraped his leg from the arm of the chair and sat forward, still studying the picture.

"What is it?"

Glancing at her over the tops of his glasses, he said, "This is interesting." He handed her the photo. "It's the ceiling on Tsapan."

Pushing herself away from the computer, Sam took the picture. She stared at it for a moment, but its significance eluded her. "What about it?"

"Look." He pointed at the thunderhead. "See how it's swirling?"

She looked more closely at the dark mass, black in the center and fading to silver-streaked blue at the edges. Like a whirlpool or a– "Oh my God, it's a black hole."

"Yes!" Daniel exclaimed. "Exactly what I thought. Teal'c?"

The Jaffa took the photo from Sam and studied it carefully. "Re'ammin the Thunderer," he mused. "The name is–" His head jerked up. "I have been foolish, Daniel Jackson!"

"You have?"

He handed the photograph back with a clipped motion that spoke volumes about repressed irritation. "It is a tale told on Chulak to frighten children into devotion to the false gods."

Sam smiled slightly. "The Jaffa bogeyman?"

"Perhaps. It is said that Re'ammin the Thunderer sought to challenge the gods. His power was vast. He could darken the sun and cast *whole worlds* into oblivion."

"Whole worlds?" Her eyes widened.

"But the gods would not let his hubris go unpunished. His Divine Palace was destroyed, his spear shattered and his shield rent asunder. He was made mortal and fled the power of the gods, taking his broken shield and hiding his face in the mud of Asdad." A slight hint of a smile touched Teal'c's lips. "A fitting fate for any who would seek to challenge the power of the gods."

Daniel smiled at that, but Sam didn't seem convinced. "If this Re'ammin is really Baal," she said, "the myth is wrong. He's still alive."

Teal'c cocked an eyebrow. "It is possible that the myth refers only to his host."

"Maybe. But if–"

"Actually," Daniel interrupted, "Baal is a god of rebirth. Death and rebirth. As a Canaanite deity he was said to have defied Death, in the form of Mot, but was eventually taken down into the under-world only to be restored to life after Anat, his sister…" He stopped, glanced at their blank faces, and cleared his throat. "The point being, Teal'c's legend could well relate to Baal. And if it's right and if *this*", he waved the photo for emphasis, "is what it looks like, then–" He left the thought hanging.

Sam picked it up, her tone awed and wary. "Then, at some point, Baal possessed a technology powerful enough to manipulate massive gravitational forces. As a weapon."

"And cast whole worlds into oblivion."

A grim silence filled the room. The thought of Baal in possession of such technology… Daniel shuddered. He was all too aware of the man's – monster's – capabilities.

"The question is," said Sam, her voice hushed, "why hasn't he used it against the other System Lords?"

"I do not believe Baal still possesses the weapon," Teal'c said. "The tale tells that he was punished and his power destroyed. It is unlikely that the System Lords would have allowed him to remain in possession of such a technology."

Daniel wasn't so sure. Gazing out the window, he didn't see spring sunshine; he saw a claustrophobic torture chamber. He saw Jack dying, again and again, pinned to a metal grid until it fell away beneath his lifeless body. Daniel's mouth straightened into a thin line as he struggled to control the memories. Henry Boyd, he reminded himself. Focus on the present, focus on what's needed.

"Daniel?" It was Sam.

He glanced up, flinching at the concern in her eyes. "I was just wondering… Why do you think Baal abandoned Kinahhi?"

She dismissed it with a shrug. "Quadesh said the Kinahhi rose up against him."

"So why didn't he come back? With ships? Why didn't he crush them?"

She shook her head, but Teal'c had an answer. "Because the System Lords had forbidden it. To return would have meant his death."

Daniel nodded in agreement. "Baal–" He cleared his throat and scowled down at the floor; the name tasted foul. "Baal still uses gravitational technology."

Sam fixed him with an inquisitive look. "The Tok'ra intelligence report said he was researching gravitational fields, but we've never seen any details."

He shied away from her implicit questions. He couldn't tell her the truth. "It's nothing on the scale of Kinahhi. No floating cities or ships. It's much–" In his mind he was right back inside the gravity well, immersed in the creeping hopelessness and terror of his friend. "It's on a smaller scale," he finished, grating the words out between his teeth.

Sam glanced at Teal'c, but his face gave away nothing. Obviously realizing that she wouldn't get more of an answer, she simply accepted the fact and moved on. Trust. It was all about trust. "So what does it tell us?"

"That he still has the technology to manipulate gravity. But that he doesn't – or can't – use it as a weapon. Question is, why not?"

He could see the thoughts racing through Sam's eyes, making connections, taking quantum leaps. Slowly she started to nod, hovering on the verge of understanding. "If he had the power to create or manipulate a black hole, he'd need some way to withstand the gravitational field himself."

Enjoying the thrill of the intellectual chase, Daniel sat forward. "Without it, causing a black hole would be suicide, right?"

"Absolutely," Sam agreed. "Anything within the event horizon of a black hole – including light – is pulled into the singularity. He couldn't even escape through a Stargate. SG-10 proves that." Her excitement growing, she jumped to her feet. "He must have had something, some way to be able to create the black hole and then escape."

"A shield!" Daniel exclaimed.

Sam's face lit up. "Of course! An anti-gravity bubble that could surround a ship."

"His 'shield was rent asunder,'" Teal'c added, the warmth in his voice betraying his own eagerness. "And by so doing, the System Lords rendered his weapon useless."

Hope and doubt were at war in Sam's eyes. "Why not just put it back together?"

"Perhaps he couldn't?" Daniel suggested. "What if that's why he was forbidden from returning to Kinahhi? What if half the shield is there – the anti-gravitational technology – and half somewhere else? Rent asunder."

Thoughts racing, Sam began to pace. "Power. That's what's missing. A power source large enough to counter the gravitational pull of a sun." She stopped, skewered him with a look. "So where? Where would the power source be?"

A good question. Daniel mentally skimmed back over Teal'c's Jaffa legend and came up with an answer, of sorts. "My guess is Asdad."

"Where?"

"Asdad." He glanced over at Teal'c. "Re'ammin took his broken shield and hid his face in the mud of Asdad. Right?"

"He did."

Asdad... For some reason, the word tasted bitter. Shrugging it off, Daniel took a deep breath. "So, we just have to figure out where that is." He stood up. "I'll start looking for references." Over the years his journals had filled with obscure Jaffa mythology, transcripts of alien texts, legends and histories. Surely somewhere among all that he'd find–

"Daniel?"

Sam was watching him. "You know what this probably means, right?"

He did. "Wherever Asdad is, it's going to be right under Baal's nose." And Jack would have to face head-on what he'd spent the best part of a year repressing, ignoring, and denying. Daniel glanced at her worried face. "When we know something, I'll talk to him."

Worry turned into a wry smile. "Good luck."

Teal'c simply nodded his approval. Their previous, aborted attempt at protecting Jack had backfired spectacularly, and so this time there was no option but the unadorned truth.

Daniel hoped it would be easier for him. Although, in reality, he knew it could never, ever be easy. He could barely comprehend how Jack had stayed sane: *what I do know is that I'd have gone nuts without you. I'd have given up. You didn't let me.*

With a heavy sigh, Daniel turned to his books and started looking for answers.

It was late, night crawling into the gray hours of the early morning.

A jaw-cracking yawn, at least the third in as many minutes, finally prompted Sam to call it quits. Despite her weariness, the excitement made it difficult to break away from the project, even to grab a few hours sleep.

Ever since Daniel's breakthrough discovery, things had started to fall into place. Knowing now that she only had plans for half the device, she'd quit trying to make a square peg fit a round hole and simply focused on what was in front of her. And, power aside, the alien device was taking form in her basement with a technological elegance that was clearly not Goa'uld in origin. Which explained why Baal had never managed to build a new shield – this was evidently something he'd scavenged, not created.

But the deeper she delved into the blueprints, and the better she came to understand what she was seeking to build, the more questions rose to the surface. Because, contrary to her initial assumption, the blueprints were not of the Kinahhi powered anti-grav generator she'd briefly glimpsed on Tsapan. Instead, they had to be the designs for Baal's shield itself. Which was unexpected, and raised questions of its own.

Standing up, she stretched, yawned again and headed for the stairs. It was quiet in the house, and as she drifted into the living room she saw Daniel sprawled out on the sofa, snoring softly. Teal'c had disappeared into the spare room some time around midnight and only the colonel was still awake, slumped low in the armchair next to Daniel and staring blindly into the shadows. She wondered what was preoccupying his thoughts. Another yawn threatened, but she swallowed it and quietly said, "Think I'm gonna call it a night, sir."

Jolted out of his contemplation, he cast her a fuddled look, then nodded. "Yeah, it's late."

"I've made some progress though," she assured him. "Once Daniel's worked out the location of Asdad, we'll be good to go."

"That easy?"

"I didn't say it would be easy." She leaned against the doorjamb. "Sir? When Quadesh gave you the blueprints, did he say what they were for?"

O'Neill shook his head. "He just said they were what we were looking for."

Tired, she scrubbed a hand over her eyes. Maybe it was because it was late that this didn't make sense, but, "How did he know what we were looking for?"

The colonel stared at her for a moment, thoughtful behind his dark eyes. "Crawford."

"Crawford?" A queasy feeling seeped into her stomach. "How did he—"

"Apparently he'd been doing a little eavesdropping."

Sam shook her head. "The slimy little bast—"

"My thoughts exactly."

She moved closer, perching on the arm of the sofa next to Daniel's socked feet. "Why would he tell Quadesh?"

"He didn't." The colonel sat forward, the light from the hallway catching his face. He looked uncomfortable and tense. "He told Damaris. Quadesh overheard them talking."

"So that explains why she was so suspicious. She knew we had a motive."

"And she was right, wasn't she?" Guilt gleamed in his dark eyes, out of place and grim. He hated this, she realized. He hated the deception.

"Why do you think Damaris didn't say anything?" she asked. "Why not confront us with what she knew?"

"Because that's not how she works. You don't throw away the ace up your sleeve; you wait and play it when it's going to do the most damage."

A buzz of anxiety hummed in her chest, growing with every thud of her heart. "You think she'll come after us?"

He nodded, studying his folded hands. "Her and Crawford. They're up to something. I can smell it."

A nervous laugh escaped. "That could be Daniel's feet, sir."

The joke didn't do much to ease the tension, but at least it provoked a brief smile. He looked up, gratitude and something warmer shining in his eyes, before his face sobered again. Standing, he glanced briefly at Daniel, still sleeping, and nodded her toward the kitchen.

Once inside he asked, "You've scanned all the blueprints into your computer, right?"

It was hardly the sort of information that usually interested Colonel Jack O'Neill. "Yes sir. Well, actually they're on a CD. Why?"

"The less evidence we have hanging around the better."

"You want me to destroy them? I could put them in the furnace if you–"

"No. No, I'll handle it." His hands dropped into his pockets and she could tell he was deliberately not looking at her. Deliberately hiding something.

"Sir?"

He glanced up. "Carter?"

"What's going on?"

The flat look told her it was a stupid question. "You mean other than us working on these *stolen* alien plans without Hammond's knowledge?"

She shrugged to acknowledge the point. "Something else has happened, hasn't it?"

O'Neill stared at her, lips tight. Considering. She didn't think he appreciated being rumbled, but what could she do? After seven years, she knew him too well. He frowned and headed over to the kitchen counter and started making coffee. At four in the morning? "Crawford," he said as he fiddled with the coffee percolator. "He's back, by the way. Saw him a couple of days ago. And he knows about the blueprints. He knows we have them." He stopped moving. "He told Hammond."

The news dropped like a stone into water, radiating ripples of anxiety. When she spoke, Sam's voice was taut. "Why hasn't he done something?"

"Because I denied it." The colonel was in motion again, pulling out the cold filter and looking about for the trash can. It was a distraction, she realized, a way to undermine the weight of his words. "I lied."

"To Crawford? That's no big–"

"To Hammond." He dropped the filter into the trash with a soggy thud. "He asked me point blank, and I lied."

And what the hell do you say to that? "Wow."

"Yeah."

Of course, he hadn't exactly had a choice. "If you'd told the truth…"

"Kinsey would be kicking our butts all over town."

"And Henry Boyd wouldn't get home. That's why we're doing this, right?"

He sighed, both hands spread on the kitchen counter, bracing himself. "That's what Daniel said."

"He's right."

"He's not military." His shoulders straightened and he turned to face her. "The point is, we need to watch our backs. And we need to get rid of those blueprints."

"What are you going to do with them?"

He said nothing, just smiled a dangerous smile that reminded her anew of the years he'd spent in Special Operations. It made her shiver.

CHAPTER TWELVE

In the far-from-opulent VIP quarters of the SGC, Bill Crawford returned from the bathroom and sat down in front of his laptop. To his irritation the security screen hadn't come on; it was set to lock after a minute's inactivity and he felt uneasy at the thought of a passing airman having glanced at what stood bright on his screen. *Never show your cards,* his father had always told him. *Never give anything away.* In general it was wise advice. But not today. His father, after all, had never held all the cards.

He smiled, staring at his laptop with a quiet sense of pleasure. Before him was his completed report on SG-1 and its leader, and he had no doubt his conclusions would make easy reading for Senator Kinsey. And Councilor Damaris. Of course, he had no actual proof that O'Neill had taken the stolen plans from the Kinahhi traitor, Quadesh, but the circumstantial evidence was compelling. Aside from the overheard conversation between O'Neill and Carter, the fact that he'd gotten his team – his injured team! – arrested the very next night was damning. That and the footage of Quadesh obviously going in search of SG-1 made the conclusion inescapable: O'Neill had taken the plans and was lying about it to his CO. And this time there was no world to save – no excuses – to justify his insubordination.

Crawford couldn't repress a quiet chuckle as he clicked 'print.' For seven years Kinsey had been trying to get O'Neill out of the SGC, and he, Bill Crawford, was going to get the job done.

"Mission accomplished, Senator." Picking up the crisp white sheet of paper, he snapped it straight in front of him and began to read. The final paragraph, he thought, was especially powerful and deserved to be heard aloud. Clearing his throat, he began to pace as he read.

"Throughout the mission, Colonel O'Neill demonstrated a persistent lack of judgment in his behavior toward alien dignitaries, on occasion even resorting to verbal abuse. Despite two of his team members being seriously injured, he led an illicit venture into the city against the express wishes of the planetary authority.

His decision resulted in the arrest of his team. Evidence points to O'Neill having been contacted by a Kinahhi traitor and taking possession of stolen technology during this escapade. Although O'Neill denies this charge, I am confident that a full investigation will support my assertion. It is therefore the recommendation of this report that Colonel Jack O'Neill should be relieved of his command pending the results of a formal investigation into the allegations of behavior unbecoming to an officer, theft, and deception of a senior officer."

It was perfect; O'Neill didn't have a leg to stand on. Gathering the rest of his papers together, Crawford set off in search of General Hammond. He was looking forward to seeing the look on the man's face when he gave him a little sneak-preview. It would be rightful compensation for enduring more than a week cooped up in the bowels of the military establishment while the Kinahhi considered whether or not to resume negotiations for their security technology. Personally, he was indifferent to the success of the discussions. If they failed, it would be just another nail in Jack O'Neill's coffin.

The solution, when it came, was blindingly obvious. So obvious, in fact, that Daniel suspected that he'd been deliberately ignoring the links that sat right before his eyes. They were all there, in a neat little row, and the only leap he'd had to take was one of pronunciation. Given the interstellar reach of these diverging cultures, a little allophonic shift was inevitable, hardly a leap at all in fact.

He closed the book and sat back in his chair, staring into the quiet space of his office. He'd left Sam's house the day before, feeling the need for the ordered chaos of his own surroundings as he pieced together the clues and came to the obvious conclusion. He knew where Asdad was – in truth he'd known all along. He just hadn't wanted to believe it.

Exhaling, he reached for the phone. No point in delaying the moment, and he knew Sam and Teal'c were itching to know. Well, Sam was. Itching was hardly the right word to describe Teal'c's passive impatience, but impatient he was nonetheless. Jack on the other hand… Thinking about it now, Daniel realized that Jack had probably guessed long ago and, like him, hadn't wanted to be right.

He hit the speed dial and listened to the phone bleep its tuneless numeric melody, muttering to himself. "Life sucks."

"Sometimes." The unexpected reply came from the doorway, and Daniel put the phone down before it could ring.

"Jack." What the hell was he doing on base?

"Couple of things to do," Jack said, in answer to his unasked question. "And Hammond wants to see me. Something important, apparently." He nodded at the books sprawling across Daniel's desk. "So…?"

"So," Daniel agreed. He sat forward, fingers steepled, feeling slightly nauseous. No time like the present, and yet he found himself fervently wishing that he could delay this little piece of news indefinitely.

Stepping further into the room, Jack tensed. It was subtle, as if his skin had suddenly drawn tight around him. "Found something?"

Daniel just met his friend's wary gaze with a steady one of his own. Eventually, Jack looked away, his jaw moving as if he might have been contemplating words. After a long, long moment he spoke. His voice was very quiet, "I swore to myself I'd never go back there. Not ever."

"No one would expect you to."

If Jack heard, he didn't react. But Daniel could guess the path of his thoughts. No one would expect him to go back, no one except Jack O'Neill. He was harder on himself than he'd ever be on the rest of his team. Daniel was about to make the point when Jack abruptly snapped out of his thoughts, shaking his head slightly and plastering on an all-too-bright look.

"I gotta go see Hammond," he said. "Fill in the others. I'll see you back at Carter's."

Knowing that arguing was futile, Daniel just nodded and watched as Jack turned and stalked from the room. *He doesn't deserve this*, Daniel thought angrily, *he doesn't damn well deserve this*. He slumped back in his chair, shoved the piled books to one side, and glared at the unoffending wall of his office. "Life sucks."

Sparks flew and the air was thick with heat and solder as Sam crafted the impossible from materials she'd scavenged from the base. Sometimes, she thought with a flash of pride, she actually did pull an all-singing, all-dancing rabbit from her hat.

Before her, on the makeshift bench, the anti-gravity device was taking shape. No doubt less elegant than the original, but equally serviceable. So she hoped. But it was hot, detailed work and after four hours her eyes were beginning to feel the strain. With a muted groan, she pulled the soldering mask off and blew a cooling breath up onto her face, making her hair flutter. It didn't do much to cool her down. What she really needed was a drink. A beer would be nice, but under the circumstances she should probably stick to lemonade.

Rolling her shoulders to loosen cramped muscles, Sam turned toward the stairs – only to find Daniel on his way down, with Teal'c close behind. The faces of both men were grave. Suddenly, she felt sick. "What's happened?"

"Daniel Jackson has located Asdad," said Teal'c, as they reached the bottom of the steps and came to stand awkwardly before her.

Sam's eyes moved to Daniel's sober face. "I'm pretty certain," he said, "that Asdad is a corruption of Ashdod. On Earth, Ashdod was one of the ancient cities that formed the Philistine Pentapolis. What makes it significant is that Ashdod was also one of the chief seats of worship for Dagon."

"Dagon?" She bit her tongue, resisting an O'Neillish urge to ask Daniel to cut to the chase.

"Dagon was an ancient Mesopotamian god. And also, apparently, the father of–" He faltered, glanced at Teal'c and took a deep breath. "The father of Baal."

Mind whirring, still gazing at the morose features of her friends, Sam wasn't entirely sure she'd understood his point. "So you're saying that Asdad is actually this place, Ashdod? On Earth?" If that was true then–

"No," he corrected her. "It's not on Earth. Uh, well actually there is a city in Israel called Ashdod but I–"

"Daniel!" Her patience was wafer-thin.

He cleared his throat. "Ashdod is a Hebrew word. It means a place of strength and power – a fortress."

Fortress. Sam's heart thudded once, hard, then skipped a few

beats. "As in Baal's fortress?" The place they'd spent days searching for while the colonel was being tortured to death over and over
and over…

Daniel nodded.

"Does he know?"

"Yeah."

She could think of nothing to say, but her chest ached with compassion. She knew the colonel too well to imagine that he'd let
them handle this without him. "He can't go back there."

"O'Neill will endure this trial as he has many others," Teal'c
assured them both. "He will not succumb to fear."

Sam cast him a hard look. She doubted Post Traumatic Stress
Disorder featured much in Jaffa folklore, but surely even Teal'c
didn't imagine that anyone could survive that level of cruelty
without some kind of psychological damage. "He's only human,
Teal'c."

"Do not undervalue your strength, Major Carter. I do not know
a stronger race than the Tauri."

She smiled, barely. But she couldn't shake a deep feeling of disquiet. She'd seen how tense the colonel had been on Tsapan. How
much worse would it be to go back to the place where he'd suffered so
much? She looked from Teal'c to Daniel and back again, voicing a
thought she hated to admit, even to her closest friends. "What if he
can't handle it? What if he loses it while we're there?"

"Is that not what you feared on Kinahhi," Teal'c reminded
her, "when you attempted to hide Baal's involvement with the
planet?"

She shrank from the memory of the colonel's anger and, worse,
his sympathetic reprimand. *I understand why you didn't tell me
about Baal. I appreciate it, but it can't happen again.*

Daniel sighed and began polishing his glasses. He was obviously uncomfortable with the situation too, but seemed resigned to
the inevitable. "Jack can handle a lot, Sam," he assured her quietly.
"More than you might imagine." And then he shrugged and slid his
glasses back onto his nose. "Either way, it's a moot point. I can't
imagine anyone, or anything, keeping him from coming with us."

"Relieved of command?" Jack spat the words out like sour fruit.

"Are you kidding me? Sir."

Hammond leaned back in his chair, unhappy. "I only wish I were, son."

It was impossible! "On what grounds? Crawford, that son of a–"

Wordlessly, Hammond pushed a staple-bound document across his desk and Jack snatched it up. It was Crawford's report to Kinsey. The rat-bastard. Skimming the words, he quickly found the bullet-points and felt some of the wind drop from his sails. Crawford might have a point about their arrest and the verbal 'abuse,' if you ignored the fact that the Kinahhi were peddling George Orwell's worst nightmare. Not to mention Baal had built his own private resort in their backyard! He dropped the report on the desk. "Has Kinsey seen this?"

"Not yet. But I'm sure it's on its way as we speak."

"It's just a recommendation," Jack pointed out. His mind had shifted now, away from Crawford and thoughts of revenge, toward his other obligations. His team. And Henry Boyd's team. "Do you have to act on it right away?"

Hammond's eyes narrowed and his fingers came to rest across his ample belly. "Officially, I haven't seen it. I think Crawford wanted to–"

"Rub our noses in it?"

A faint smile touched the general's lips. "Jack, it's only going to be a matter of days."

"Days is long enough."

"Long enough for what, son?"

For gating to Baal's god-awful House of Horror, for stealing the power unit Carter needed to make her device work, and for getting Boyd and SG-10 home. "To prepare my team, sir."

"Prepare your team?" Hammond's skepticism was as thinly veiled as Jack's lie.

It was enough to prick his conscience. He grabbed a chair and sat down, leaning over the desk and talking low. "Sir, you've always given me a certain…latitude to get things done. Have I ever let you down?"

"No, but I can't–"

Jack snatched the report from the desk and scrunched it into a ball. "You didn't see this. What's Crawford going to say? That he gave it to you before Kinsey? I don't think so." He paused, seeing an easing in the lines around the general's eyes. He was winning. "Just one mission, sir."

"Off world? Jack, I–"

"It's important." For a long moment he held Hammond's gaze, not just as a fellow officer but as a friend. Jack couldn't tell him more; the more the general knew, the more trouble he'd be in when the truth inevitably came out. His only card was the trust they'd built up over the seven insane years they'd served together on the galactic front-line.

It was enough. "One mission. But if I hear officially from Washington before you leave, then I'll have no choice but to stand your team down, Colonel."

Jack was on his feet in a second. "Understood, sir. And thank you."

Hammond nodded, but remained silent as Jack turned on his heel and headed for the door. Just as he opened it, the general spoke again. "Good luck, son."

Luck? Where they were headed he'd need a damn sight more than luck. A miracle would come in handy. Or maybe two.

Dusk was falling by the time O'Neill's truck pulled up in front of Major Carter's house. For a long time after the vehicle stopped it simply sat, the golden sunset reflecting off its smoked windows. From inside the house Teal'c watched until, at last, the truck door opened and O'Neill stepped out onto the sidewalk. Sunglasses hid his eyes, but Teal'c saw a weary slump to the man's shoulders as the colonel turned toward the house and took a deep breath. There was a brittleness to his strength that spoke of a man who knew what it was to be broken. And there was fear there, where there had not been before. Fear of failure, fear of weakness. That was the burden O'Neill now carried, that was the demon he must vanquish.

Teal'c moved away from the window, opening the front door and waiting for his friend.

"Expecting the pizza guy?"

"I believe Daniel Jackson has ordered Chinese."

"Again?"

"Indeed."

O'Neill harrumphed and eyed Teal'c warily as he stepped inside and closed the door. Teal'c knew he was wondering if he'd been told the location of Asdad. "Major Carter and Daniel Jackson are concerned," he said, unwilling to sport with his friend's intelligence. "Returning to Baal's fortress will be difficult for you."

Despite O'Neill's shrug of indifference, the hardness in his eyes gave him away. "Right now, that's the least of our worries." In response to the curious lift of Teal'c's eyebrow O'Neill simply nodded toward the living room. "They in there?"

They were, and Teal'c followed O'Neill through the house to find the rest of their team sprawled out on the sofa. At his entrance, both Major Carter and Daniel Jackson sat upright like startled marionettes. "Sir," the major said, nodding nervously.

"Hey Jack," came Daniel Jackson's equally uneasy greeting.

O'Neill stopped dead in the middle of the room. He fixed them both with a flat stare and turned slowly to extend it to Teal'c. "Okay, kids," he began, "I'm only going to say this once, so listen up. Yes, this Ashdad...dod...whatever, turns out to be Baal's happy place. Yes, we have to go there. And yes, it sucks. But we're *all* going, and, no, I don't want to talk about it. Okay?"

Major Carter blinked, Daniel Jackson cleared his throat and an uncomfortable silence settled over the room. A silence O'Neill felt obliged to fill. "So here's the deal," he continued. " Crawfish's report to Kinsey wants me relived of command pending–"

"What?" Major Carter was on her feet. "No way. They can't–"

"Easy Major," O'Neill waved her back down. "They can and they will. But until that report hits Kinsey's desk and bounces back to Hammond, we have some time." He thought for a moment. "Not much time. Actually, hardly any time. We have a mission scheduled for fourteen-hundred tomorrow to a convenient dustbowl. From there we'll 'gate to Baal's..." He hesitated over the word, and a flash of frustration crossed his face. "Baal's fortress. We'll do what we have to do, get the hell out and go bring Henry Boyd home. Any questions?"

Major Carter sat forward, anxious. "Sir, the device needs to be mounted on a ship. I thought we'd have more time – maybe enough time to contact the Tok'ra. I don't know where we'd find a ship at such short notice."

O'Neill appeared unperturbed. "We're going to Baal's secret *fortress*, Carter. We'll find a ship. Anything else?"

She shook her head, but Daniel Jackson hesitantly lifted his hand. "Ah, Jack, we have no idea what will be waiting for us on Asdad. I mean, a whole army of Jaffa could be camped at the 'gate."

"I don't think so. There wasn't much left of the place when I... left."

"If that is so," Teal'c warned, "it is possible that the device we seek may have been destroyed."

"Or removed," Major Carter added. "If Baal abandoned the fortress after Yu's attack he might have taken it with him."

"True, Major Glass-Half-Empty. Or we could go there, find what we're looking for and bring home four good people who don't deserve to be left behind to die." O'Neill spread his hands. "Look, I know there are risks. Huge risks. And if any of you want to back out, that's fine. You know that. None of this is official, I can't give any orders here. But I've come too far to give up. I won't give up, whatever the risks."

Teal'c felt a stirring of pride at his friend's words and took a step closer. "I do not intend to give up either, O'Neill."

"I appreciate that, T."

Daniel Jackson stood, pulling his glasses from his face and pinching the bridge of his nose. "I, uh, was translating some of the writings I photographed on Tsapan yesterday. I don't know, but I may have found something interesting. Reference to a shrine..."

O'Neill raised his eyebrows. "Daniel?"

"No, no, it may be important. I'll, uh, go compare it with the Tok'ra maps of the fortress." He offered a brief smile. "Trust me."

"Don't I always?"

Major Carter hid a smile and glanced at her watch. "I'd better get back to the basement. If I pull an all-nighter, I should be able to finish by morning. I hope."

"You will," O'Neill assured her. "That's what you do, Carter."

She cast him a wary look in response. Teal'c had often wondered to what extent O'Neill's determined confidence in the major's ability to solve the impossible was a burden to her, rather than an honor. But they all had their troubles to bear, and as Major Carter and Daniel Jackson left the room the colonel returned his attention to Teal'c. "Career on the line, facing impossible odds and almost certain death... Is it just me, or have we been here before?"

"Several times, O'Neill."

"Kinda getting old, don't ya think?"

Teal'c met his friend's words with silent amusement. He knew as well as O'Neill that neither of them would choose a different life. To live was to struggle, to fight and to triumph. To give up was to die, if not in body then in spirit.

O'Neill nodded, as if in agreement with Teal'c's unvoiced thoughts. But all he said was, "I need a beer."

CHAPTER THIRTEEN

It was a subdued SG-1 that assembled in the 'gate room, thought
General Hammond as he stood watching them from the control
room. Every so often the colonel would cast a quick glance in his
direction with obvious, but controlled, impatience as he waited
for the final member of his team to arrive. But there was none
of the usual banter to kill the time, just a steady sense of purpose that ran icy fingertips down Hammond's spine. Whatever
his people were doing, they were not venturing on a standard
mission of exploration to the desert moon of P6M-832. If nothing
else, the incongruous black BDUs gave that much away.

You know this is wrong, George. The voice was his own, loud
in his head as he watched his flagship team waiting to embark. It
was wrong, and by rights he should be demanding answers from the
obstinate colonel. But as Jack had pointed out the previous day, the
latitude he habitually granted the man had always – *always* – paid off
in the past. Fact was, O'Neill and his team had fought and, in at least
three instances, died for the principles and people they were sworn
to protect. The niggling niceties of bureaucracy might demand that
Hammond stop them in their tracks, but his gut and seven years of
trust told him to give the colonel the leeway he needed. God knew,
when they came back Kinsey's Rottweilers would be straining at the
leash to rip into the man and his team. And it made General George
Hammond sick to his stomach to think that, while SG-1 were out
there putting their lives on the line, he couldn't protect them from the
machinations of a creature like Kinsey.

"Sir?" The voice behind him belonged to the young Lieutenant
Ashley. Mousy and timid, she offered him three pages of white paper,
neatly stapled at the corner. Even upside-down he could recognize
the congressional seal. "An urgent fax came in, sir. From Senator
Kinsey."

Talk of the devil and he doth appear... Hammond eyed the treacherous document as if it were a spitting cobra. He had no doubt at all
what it was, and once he'd read it he'd have no choice but to act on its
content. From the fax his gaze moved back to the 'gate room where

O'Neill was looking up at him again. It was almost as if the colonel could sense Kinsey's malevolent presence.

Clearing his throat and meeting Jack's gaze, Hammond said, "Thank you, Lieutenant. Please put it on my desk."

"Sir, it's marked urgent."

"I'm aware of that Lieutenant. Put it on my desk."

He didn't look at her or the fax, his attention still locked on O'Neill, who was turning to watch the final member of his team stride into the 'gate room. Whatever Major Carter had in her overly-large pack, it was not standard issue. But Hammond was already in too deep to question what it might be. Instead he nodded to Sergeant Davis, "Dial the 'gate, Airman."

The Stargate started to spin and the tension ratcheted up a notch as the first chevron locked. A phone rang behind him, but Hammond ignored it. The second chevron locked, then the third. Someone answered the phone but he tuned out the voice. The fourth chevron locked.

Then the fifth.

Down in the 'gate room O'Neill said something to Jackson, who smiled faintly and nodded. Major Carter shifted her pack, which looked unusually heavy, but was focused on the spinning Stargate. The sixth chevron locked and–

"General Hammond, sir?"

He twitched at the sound of the voice behind him. Ashley, again. "What is it, Lieutenant?"

"Sir, Senator Kinsey is on the line."

Damn it. "Tell the Senator I'll call him back."

There was a pause. Hammond could hear the tinny rant leaking from the phone behind him as Sergeant Davis announced, "Chevron seven, locked."

Thank God! The event horizon erupted into the 'gate room, casting everything in its opalescent light.

"Sir," came Ashley's fraught voice, "the Senator says–"

Hammond ignored her and leaned over to speak into Davis's mike. "SG-1," he said, feeling almost gleeful, "you have a go."

O'Neill turned and offered a sloppy acknowledgment, somewhere between a salute and a wave, before he nodded to his team and they strode as one up the ramp toward the Stargate.

"Good luck, Jack," he muttered under his breath as he watched SG-1 step into oblivion. "And Godspeed." Davis must have sensed the import of his words, because he glanced up curiously. Hammond had no desire to reveal more and turned away. "Shut it down, Sergeant."

"Sir!" Lieutenant Ashley stood behind him, still clutching the phone and seeming close to tears. He didn't blame her; Kinsey had a nasty bark. Almost as bad as his bite.

Offering her a reassuring smile, he took the phone and reluctantly put it to his ear. "This is Hammond," said smoothly. "No, sir, I haven't seen your fax." He smiled at the Senator's next words, "SG-1? They're off-world, sir. Won't be in contact again for at least forty-eight hours."

The Senator exploded and as he held the phone away from his ear, Hammond let himself bask in a smug sense of satisfaction. Perhaps, this once, he had been able to protect his people from the vipers after all. He just hoped that when O'Neill came back he'd pull another SG-1 miracle out of his a– out of the air to save his own skin. Because, as sweet as the moment tasted, Hammond knew it was only a temporary respite. Kinsey smelled blood, and wouldn't be content until he'd tasted it.

'Dustbowl' had been exactly the right word to describe P6M-832. Tumbled-down ruins scattered from the Stargate, half buried in drifting sand. The wide gray desert beyond slowly encroached over the remains of the civilization that had once existed here, and the wind never ceased, tugging hard at jackets and threatening to snatch Jack's cap from his head. He yanked it off and stuffed it into his pocket, just in case.

"Nice place," he muttered, pulling his sunglasses on to keep out the sand.

Around him, the rest of his team stood waiting, expectant and nervous. And the contents of his stomach were congealing into a hard lump of dread. The last time he'd gated to their next destination he'd been a passive observer of his body's actions – until it had been too late, and he'd had his mind peeled away piece by agonizing piece. This time, he told himself, would be different. This time he was in control, and he'd blow his own brains out before he let Baal take him alive again.

Readying his weapon, he turned to Carter. "Teal'c and I go first, you and Daniel wait thirty seconds then come in low. We'll cover you."

"Yes, sir."

She wouldn't say anything about where they were going, or how he might react, not after what she'd done on Kinahhi. He was grateful for that, or at least he knew he should be grateful. Professionalism was what he'd demanded from her. And yet a part of him regretted her discretion; a part that needed a reassuring smile; a part he routinely ignored.

Silently Teal'c came to stand at his side, his steady presence as reassuring as the weight of the gun in Jack's hands. "We will succeed, O'Neill."

"Yeah," he agreed. "Sure we will."

Slowly the 'gate spun, his guts churning in matching circles. He swore he'd never go back... Mouth suddenly dry, he held tight to his P90, screwing his fear and anger together into a tight wad of adrenalin. He could do this. He could damn well do this!

All too soon the 'gate spewed forth its liquid light. But Jack didn't move. His legs seemed rooted to the ground, his heart hammering insanely in his chest. He was going back there. He tried to take a deep breath, but found it hard to suck air around the cold hard lump in his chest. What if he couldn't move from this spot? And then Teal'c shifted at his side, resting the butt of his staff-weapon firmly on the ground. Out of the corner of his eye Jack saw Daniel and Carter come to stand with him. No one spoke. No one needed to.

Straightening his shoulders, he forced words through his dry throat. "This is it, guys, last chance to save your careers."

Daniel cocked an eyebrow. "Last chance to save Henry Boyd."

"We'll be right behind you, sir." Carter's glance spoke volumes. She might not be able to say it, but he knew what she meant – *this time I'll be there for you.* They all would.

Suddenly he could breathe again. The fear didn't subside, but that didn't matter. He had his team with him; he had a fighting chance. "Okay kids, let's go kick some Goa'uld ass."

Sam hit the ground in a roll and was up on her knees, weapon raised, before the chill of the 'gate had eased. Braced for an assault, it took her a moment to realize that none came. Around her a blackened forest was struggling into new life. Stumps of trees reached raw and shattered limbs into the dark, overcast sky, their shapes blurred by a thin mist and the timid growth of a season. Life persisting against the odds.

But there was no bird song, just a flat, heavy silence. Certainly no Jaffa, which was a plus. To her right, Daniel was mirroring her posture on the other side of the 'gate, scanning his surroundings with the professional eye of the soldier he'd been forced to become. He glanced over and caught her eye, shrugged but didn't speak. Behind them the blue light of the 'gate fizzled out of existence and they were alone in a silent world of death and gray mists.

Carefully, Sam stood and did a slow three-sixty. Nothing in the devastated forest moved.

"No welcoming party." The voice, close to her ear, was the colonel's.

She almost jumped out of her skin. "Sir!" Where the hell had he been hiding?

There was a glint in his eye that might have been humor, but was probably an over-dose of adrenalin and fear. Not that he'd ever admit as much. "Teal'c's doing a quick recon."

Sam peered through the mist. In the distance she could see the dark shapes of buildings, and hoped they were as ruined as the forest. "Looks like Yu did a pretty thorough job on the place, Sir."

"I can't take all the credit, Carter."

She resisted the temptation to roll her eyes at the old joke. Given where they were, and what had happened here, even his lamest wise-crack was welcome.

"Jack, Sam!" Daniel's low call drifted flatly through the deadening mist. They both turned and saw him a couple of meters from the 'gate, crouched over something in the undergrowth.

O'Neill nodded her toward him, but made no move himself. His fingers, Sam noticed, still held his weapon ready for use; he was stretched as tight as a tripwire.

Picking her way through the brush, she soon saw that Daniel was studying a cracked stone that lay half exposed on the edge of a shallow crater. The site of the blast had slowly filled in with water, and the stone hung like a derelict diving platform over the muddy hole below.

"Seems like we're in the right place," Daniel said, his fingers tracing a faint inscription on the stone. "I think we've found the origin to Teal'c's bedtime story."

"On there?"

He nodded. "Looks like it used to be part of a temple at some point – it probably housed the Stargate. Most of it I can't see, obviously. But this line," he tapped at the obscure script, "this is talking about the Thunder god being punished. Something, something… 'torn asunder and thus rendered impotent'. And here," he indicated the next line, "'Fleeing to his father's home.'" He looked up when Sam didn't respond, sliding his glasses back up his nose. "Ashdod. Asdad. It's definitely here."

"Question is," said Sam, watching Teal'c emerge from the trees and head toward the colonel. "Is the power unit here? If Baal's abandoned the fortress…"

Daniel pushed himself to his feet. "Guess there's only one way to find out."

As if he'd been listening, O'Neill beckoned them over. "Looks like we're not alone," he whispered as they approached. "Teal'c found some tracks, so keep your heads down. I'll take point; Teal'c, watch our six." Without further conversation he moved out silently through the trees.

Sam followed close behind, Daniel at her heels. Slowly, through the mist, Baal's stronghold came into view. Windowless and gray, it stood ugly and industrial amid the shattered beauty of the forest. As they drew closer Sam saw black fissures gaping toothlessly in its side, and realized that the complex was crumbling. Her spirits rose – perhaps Baal had abandoned the place completely?

Gradually the trees began to thin and O'Neill slowed his pace, eventually raising a cautionary hand and crouching low behind a fallen tree. Sam crept forward, stopping at his side. Ahead of them stretched a wide, ravaged expanse of nothing. Blasted tree stumps and mud-filled craters pocked the barren landscape between them and Baal's looming fortress.

"I remember it being bigger," the colonel murmured.

"If there are Jaffa within the complex," Teal'c cautioned, "our approach across the expanse will be observed."

"Fish in a barrel," Daniel agreed.

Teal'c raised a curious eyebrow. "I do not–"

"Never mind." He waved it away. "So what do we do?"

Sam glanced over at the colonel. He'd pulled out his monocular and was scanning the complex. "I don't see any movement. Nothing on the roof or inside."

Daniel shifted. "Teal'c? The tracks you saw – were they Jaffa? Maybe there's a native population here?"

It was a good point, and Teal'c inclined his head in thought. "They were indistinct. I cannot be certain."

"We're not here to make friends with the locals, Daniel." The colonel pocketed his monocular and slid lower behind the tree. "And I'm not in the mood for a picnic in the woods."

"It would be safer to wait for nightfall, sir," Sam suggested carefully. "If we're spotted out there–"

"The place is a ruin, Carter. Look at it! Nobody here but us chickens." The last comment prompted an odd, bitter laugh from him that was cut off almost before it began. He moved again, crouching with a wince and favoring his right knee. "Let's just get this thing over with."

Daniel's eyebrows were climbing into his hair as he exchanged an alarmed glance with Sam. "Ah, Jack, is that wise? That's a lot of empty space and we're only talking about a few hours here."

"I'm not hanging around in the woods to be–" He cut himself off sharply. "There's no one there." It sounded more like an affirmation of faith than anything else, and before anyone could object O'Neill had vaulted over the dead tree.

"Sir, wait…!" Too late. He was already running.

"Damn it," Daniel muttered, scrambling to his feet and heading after the colonel. Teal'c wasn't far behind, leaving Sam to watch their backs as they headed out over no-man's land, expecting the lancing blast of a staff weapon at any moment.

Sam cursed. One more stunt like this and she'd have to consider relieving him of command. For all the good that would do on a covert, unsanctioned and highly illegal mission. But at least it might keep him alive long enough to get home. Maybe.

CHAPTER FOURTEEN

He couldn't stay still. He couldn't just sit there and wait for them to come for him, not this time. He had to keep moving. Crouching low, Jack skirted the edge of the trees until he spotted a rise of slightly drier land amid the mud-filled craters surrounding Baal's fortress. Gun clutched close, he darted out into no-man's land and waited for the shout or the weapons fire.

Nothing. He ran on, and behind him he could hear the sodden footfalls of his team. A twinge of self-reproach snapped at his heels, but it wasn't enough to puncture the incessant need to keep moving, to keep in control. Last time he'd been fleeing through these trees... Alien memories of hitting the cold wet forest floor made him shiver, and he ran on. Ahead of him gray walls loomed high through the mist, but all on the ground was silence.

Slowing as he approached a wide trench of black, sucking mud, Daniel caught him up. Teal'c and Carter were close behind. "Now what?" Daniel muttered breathlessly, glancing at the quagmire before them. "Through or around?"

"Around." Who knew how deep that stuff was? Last thing he wanted was to lose half his team in a swamp. "Keep low."

The detour was long and soon the mud was creeping over the tops of his boots, its grasping, sticky fingers threatening to keep hold of his feet with every yank of his leg as he struggled on. Behind he heard no murmur of complaint, although he could sense a waft of disapproval in the air. Most likely either Carter or Teal'c were the source. He ignored them, and thanked all the gods he could think of that they weren't taking enemy fire; stuck in the mud as they were, they really would have been fish in a barrel. Or sitting ducks. Or any number of other threadbare clichés. A greenhorn lieutenant would have known better. Great call, O'Neill.

But at last the ground began to firm up and his pace quickened. He led his team through the remains of the mired forest toward the shattered walls ahead. Lumps of rock scattered the ground now, providing some cover as they crept closer to the dark and silent fortress.

He stopped, mud seeping coldly through the legs of his pants, and ducked behind a large chunk of fallen wall. The rest of the team joined him, all filthy and wary.

"Doesn't seem like there's anyone there," Carter noted in a tone that hovered between rebuke and relief.

"At least no one who's watching," Jack agreed, squinting up through the mist. Looking at the dark face of Baal's stronghold was easier than acknowledging Carter's guarded concern.

Daniel cleared his throat. "Let's hope our luck holds."

"Let us hope we do not need to rely on luck, Daniel Jackson."

Teal'c's quiet reproof earned a wince from Jack. But he didn't comment, focusing instead on the obstacle ahead. He nodded toward a gaping hole in the wall to his left. "That looks good." And dark. He wasn't afraid of the dark. It was the white light that terrified him, over and over and–

"Sir?" Carter was frowning, as if she'd had to repeat herself.

Disturbed by his own lack of focus, he frowned back at her. "What?"

"I said, we should be careful when we go inside. The structural integrity of the building must be shot."

"Ya think?" He rose to his feet, ignoring the tight expression on Carter's face. "Daniel with me, Teal'c watch our backs." Carefully they moved out from behind their cover, edging closer to the cave-like entrance. "Daniel," he whispered as they began to scramble over the rubble, "does this look anything like the map?"

There was a pause, the sound of feet slipping on loose rocks, and then, "Ah, maybe. I'll know more when we get inside."

That was debatable, Jack thought, as he climbed over the lip of the opening and crunched down into the silent room beyond. Mist crept in after him, adding a damp opacity to the fire-damaged room. Slip-sliding down the debris behind him, Daniel came to stand at his side. He glanced up, eyebrows raised. "That doesn't look good."

Above them half the ceiling was missing, and through the hole Jack could see up and up into darkness. No white light, no sign of life. Thank God. On the other hand, it seemed as though a stiff breeze could bring half the complex down on their heads. "Move out," he whispered, looking around for a door.

"There," Teal'c offered, pointing with his staff weapon. He crossed the small room in two strides and began to examine the controls of a sealed door.

Meanwhile, Carter scrambled over the wall and into the room. She was moving awkwardly, and Jack realized he'd forgotten the extra weight she was carrying in her pack. The device she'd constructed in her basement wasn't exactly portable. "You okay?"

"Yes sir," came the standard response. And then, after a pause, "How about you?" There was a definite subtext of 'Are you going nuts yet, sir?'

"Just peachy, Carter. Nothing like a little nostalgia trip to bring back all those good times." Well, ask a stupid question… "Teal'c," he called in a low voice, "how's it coming with the door?"

Irritation flickered over the Jaffa's face. "I believe I shall need your assistance, O'Neill." Not so long ago, when Junior had still been in residence, Teal'c could have probably prized the door open with one hand tied behind his back. Jack knew his friend found this human weakness difficult to bear at times, and so he resisted the urge to comment. Instead he silently crossed the room and set his hands next to Teal'c's, leaning all his weight back as he pulled. The doors cracked and Daniel wedged the butt of Teal'c's staff weapon into the gap, levering it open.

Beyond was more darkness. Jack slipped through the narrow opening, weapon at the ready. Behind him came Teal'c, Daniel and then Carter. There was a muted quality to sound beyond the door, and when he flicked on his flashlight he saw that they were in a long, horribly familiar corridor. He froze, fighting a sudden urge to run. *They all look the same. All Goa'uld corridors look the same.* It didn't mean they were anywhere near his cell. Or the other place… He swallowed, hard. "Any ideas which way?"

From his left came a rustle and a new beam of light joined his. "Uh, according to the map," Daniel said, "the stronghold is based on a design of concentric circles with interconnecting corridors – like a spokes on a wheel."

"The power unit is likely to be at the center, in a control room," Carter chipped in.

"So I guess we need to head that way." Daniel peered up and squinted at the flat wall ahead of him. "Uh, if we can find a door."

"Maybe there's a ring device?" Carter suggested. "There must be, in a place this big. It could take us right to the control room."

"If it's working."

Jack glanced at his watch. Time was slipping by and they only had forty-eight hours before their scheduled sit-rep; if they failed to check-in, Hammond would be forced to start looking for them. The consequences of that could be very bad for him, them and Henry Boyd. He made a decision. "Teal'c, Carter – you go left. Keep in radio contact, and if you find anything – a door, a corridor – yell. Daniel, with me."

With a nod of acknowledgement, Carter and Teal'c moved off into the shadows. When their footsteps had faded, Jack cast a cautious glance at Daniel. He was studying his boots, as if contemplating saying something he didn't quite know how to phrase. Jack forestalled him. "I still don't want to talk about it."

The feigned look of innocence was almost comical. "Huh?"

"Let's just find what we're looking for and bug out. Okay?"

Daniel shrugged, pushing his glasses up his nose. "Suits me."

"Good. Stay sharp." And with that they headed out, following the beam of his flashlight as it danced ahead of them like a treacherous will o' the wisp.

Teal'c carefully measured his stride to keep pace with that of Major Carter, encumbered as she was by the device she carried in her pack. He had considered offering to relieve her of the burden, but he had learned long ago that Samantha Carter disliked any allowances to be made for her gender. And in everything but brute, physical strength, no allowance was required. However, he did not wish to anger or embarrass her and so said nothing as they walked through the silent corridors of Baal's former stronghold.

Had Teal'c been a man prone to open displays of emotion, he might have smiled; it warmed his heart to see anything Goa'uld reduced to rubble and dust. One day, he hoped, rubble and dust and the memories buried beneath would be all that remained of the species.

"It's kind of creepy, don't you think?" Major Carter's words took him by surprise.

"I do not," he told her truthfully. "The demise of any Goa'uld is a matter for celebration."

"Except Baal's still out there," she pointed out. And then in a hesitant voice she added, "I was kinda surprised that the colonel didn't wait for nightfall to do this."

He glanced over in time to catch the tight-lipped expression that accompanied her words. "His decision appeared rash. Even for O'Neill."

She looked up, face strained. "Do you think he's handling it, Teal'c? Seriously. Maybe we shouldn't have let him come?"

"If O'Neill did not consider himself fit for duty, do you believe he would have participated in the mission?"

It was intended to alleviate her concern, but it did not. "To be honest, I'm not sure how clearly he's thinking. He's so intent on getting Boyd home, he might have underestimated the impact coming back here could have on him." She shook her head slightly. "We all might have done that."

Her fears were disconcerting. "Perhaps," he said, "we should ensure that we spend as little time here as possible?"

Major Carter nodded. "And I think we should try and find the power unit without the colonel needing to–" Abruptly she stopped. At first he did not understand why, but then she nodded further along the corridor. On the inside wall the remains of a door gaped open, but from within came a distant glow of golden light.

She cast him a look. "There's power."

He nodded, and said what she had not. "And, perhaps, the enemy."

Grim-faced she toggled her radio. "Carter to Colonel O'Neill."

After a squawk of static, O'Neill answered. "What's up, Carter?"

"Sir, we've found a doorway. Should we proceed or hold position?"

There was a long pause during which Major Carter stared steadily at the faint light ahead of them. And then O'Neill spoke. "Proceed with caution, Carter. We'll finish the loop and catch up."

"Understood, sir." She straightened her shoulders and turned back to Teal'c. "Ready?"

He was not. "Major Carter, you neglected to mention the presence of light and power in your report."

"I did?"

He did not deign to answer and she buckled under the weight of his gaze.

"Okay, I just think we should try and find what we need without the colonel having to see any more of the complex than necessary. If he had to see the place where Baal– We don't know how he might react."

"When O'Neill arrives at the doorway, he will see the light for himself."

The major flashed him a quick smile. "Yeah, but by then we'll be on our way out with the power unit. Right?"

His only response was the doubtful lift of an eyebrow. On occasion, Major Carter could be as stubbornly optimistic as O'Neill himself.

Given the nature of their work, days and nights at the SGC often blurred together. Teams came and went according to the dawns and dusks of alien worlds, and the hum of activity in the concrete corridors was constant. And yet, somehow, General Hammond always knew when Earth's small sun was setting far above the mountain. He could almost feel the shadows lengthening and hear the collective sigh of those to whom evening meant home and hearth. Or perhaps it was simply his age. By six o'clock, home and hearth sounded darn appealing.

Stifling a yawn, the general stepped into his office and closed the door. His run-in with Kinsey was still playing on his mind, and the initial sense of triumph was giving way to a nervous agitation as he waited for the other shoe to drop. Not this evening, he told himself. It wouldn't drop this evening. Collapsing into the chair he reached for his briefcase and hefted it onto his desk; he'd take a few reports home to compensate for his early departure. Lifting the pile of papers from his inbox he–

Knock-knock

He stifled a curse. "Come in."

The last person he wanted to see pushed open the door.

"Mr. Crawford." Hammond kept his face even. "I thought you'd gone back to Washington."

"I had. I understand Senator Kinsey spoke to you today, regarding my report on SG-1?"

"He did." And Hammond was darned if he'd elaborate further. "Is there something I can help you with, Ambassador?"

A tight smile tugged at the little man's mouth as he handed over a sheet of white paper. "My orders," he said, "to return to Kinahhi and conclude the negotiations for their security technology."

Hammond didn't bother to look. Lounging back in his chair, he stared up at the young man. Crawford's eyes were hard, like black diamonds. "I once got a piece of advice from an old friend," Hammond told him, "and I've tried to live my life by it ever since. 'You can judge a man by the company he keeps.'" He nodded to the slick, expensive suit. "Kinsey might take you where you think you want to go, son, but at what price?"

The orders fluttered down onto his desk. "I don't need lectures in morality from a man who's made a career of legalized murder, General." He jerked his head in the direction of the Stargate. "Do what you have to do, I'm leaving first thing in the morning."

Hammond bit back his anger as he rose slowly to his feet. "Son, men like me – men like Colonel O'Neill – have given their lives, over and over, to protect the freedoms Kinsey's willing to trade for the price of a ticket to the White House." He took a deep breath and picked up the orders, glancing at them once. "I have no choice but to follow these. You do. The technology the Kinahhi are offering is not what this country is about."

"I think," Crawford replied, "that's something for the *elected* representatives of the people to decide. We're not a military junta yet." He smiled coldly. "Now, follow your orders like a good little soldier."

"Now you listen–"

"First thing in the morning, General." And with that he turned and was gone, leaving Hammond steaming silently as he stared at his open office door. The upstart little son-of-a– Blowing out a deep breath, he abruptly flipped open the top of his briefcase. He'd had enough for one day. He was going home to a cold beer and a hot shower, and then– What the devil?

There, stuck on the inside of the briefcase lid, was a bright yellow Post-it note with two words scrawled across it in O'Neill's brash handwriting. *Investigate Crawfish*.

Hammond felt his anger mutate into something very close to satisfaction. "My pleasure, son," he murmured, peeling off the note and heading for the shredder. "My pleasure."

For the most part, they walked in silence past doorways and

empty chambers, all dark and lifeless. Occasionally Jack stopped and slashed his flashlight across a room, but it revealed nothing but the broken remains of startled flight. It seemed as though Baal's Jaffa had withdrawn in a hurry, presumably during the firefight with Lord Yu. It wasn't exactly the *Marie Celeste*, Daniel thought, but there was a similarity in once sense. "Where are the bodies?"

"Huh?"

"The bodies – the dead Jaffa. Were are they? Looks like they pulled out in a hurry. They wouldn't have had time to retrieve the bodies too, would they?"

Jack shrugged, but it was a stiff gesture. "Maybe."

Or maybe they didn't pull out? Goose bumps prickled across Daniel's skin. Maybe there were still Jaffa deeper into the complex who had disposed of their fallen comrades? Mind obviously bending in the same direction, Jack picked up his pace. "We should hook-up with the others and–"

Twisting, grinding metal shrieked deafeningly above them, followed by an earsplitting crash that rippled through the floor like an earthquake. Daniel yelped, flinging his arms over his head. Even Jack ducked as a puff of dust drifted through the cracks in the ceiling, floating on the echo of falling masonry.

Then all was silence once more. Dust kept sifting down, pattering on the arms and shoulders of Daniel's jacket.

"I might be wrong," Jack said after a moment, brushing at a sleeve, "but this section may not be entirely stable."

"Not entirely stable?" Daniel echoed, coughing.

Jack's response was lost in the squeal of his radio. "Colonel, come in," came the urgent voice. "Sir, did you feel that? Are you guys okay?"

"Dusty," he replied. "You?"

"We're fine, sir." There was a pause before she spoke again, and when she did Daniel had the distinct impression that she was being gently coerced. "Sir, we've discovered a ring transporter. It's got power and I think I can configure it to take us to the center of the complex. Permission to proceed, sir."

Jack was moving as he spoke, urging Daniel forward with a nod. "Negative. Hold your position, Carter. You'll need back up."

"Yes sir." Her frustration translated well through the radio. Jack obviously picked it up too and scowled; it was clear to both of them that Sam had hoped to complete the mission alone. It was equally clear that there was no way Jack would let her get away with it.

Hurrying to catch up, Daniel pulled out his map and studied it under the bobbing flashlight. Sam was assuming that Baal had used the Kinahhi power unit to power the fortress. However, Daniel was less convinced. Baal's weapon seemed to hold an iconic value in the myth, which might indicate that its role was more ceremonial. This would be especially true if, as the inscription on the buried stone near the 'gate had revealed, Baal's power had been 'rendered impotent.' Powerless, literally? Before they'd left Earth Daniel had studied the Tok'ra map in detail and identified a number of chambers that might well have been used for worship or ceremony. His bet was, if the power source was still here, it was held and protected in one such room. Like a relic.

After another half hour of walking through the dark corridors, the silence occasionally broken by the moans and shrieks of stone and metal under stress, Jack dropped his pace and reached out a hand to slow Daniel. With the tip of his gun he motioned toward a gaping door a few meters ahead of them, from which spilled a faint yellow light. Edging back into the deep shadows of the corridor wall, he dragged Daniel with him. Even in the gloom Daniel saw the alarm in his friend's face. "Someone's in there," Jack whispered. His fingers grasped his gun so hard the knuckles were turning white. Daniel had never seen him so spooked.

"Maybe it's just a light?" he suggested. But then, in the silence, he heard the tread of booted feet approaching from the dimly-lit corridor.

Jack lifted and aimed his P90 at the door in a single, fluid motion. He was as still as stone, every muscle bunched. Slowly Daniel also raised his weapon, casting an eye around at the limited cover available. Darkness was their biggest ally. The footsteps drew closer and Daniel felt his own tension tighten into a band of pressure across his chest.

"Don't let them take you, Daniel." It was a rasp, angry and afraid.

The footsteps slowed and a large, shadowy figure appeared in the doorway. His staff weapon was silhouetted against the dim light, held easily and ready for use. He turned and glanced once down the corridor as the yellow light glinted dully on the golden brand on his forehead. Then two things happened at once: Daniel recognized Teal'c and Jack pulled the trigger.

"NO!" Without thought he shouldered into Jack, knocking him hard against the wall. The single bullet scorched through the air and Teal'c dropped.

"What the hell–" Jack cursed.

"Teal'c! It's Teal'c!" Abandoning Jack, Daniel raced across the corridor to the Jaffa. Teal'c's hands were clutched to the side of his head and all Daniel could see was blood oozing through his fingers. Panic deafened him to everything, narrowing his vision to a single point as he pulled his friend's hands away from the side of his head. Gradually, gradually, reality unfolded. Teal'c glanced up at him, confused. He looked at the blood on his fingers, returned them to the side of his head, then looked again.

Daniel grabbed his face, turning it. "Let me see." Blood welled from the nick in the top of Teal'c's ear. His ear! Thank God, thank God…

"I do not understand," Teal'c said at last, pulling his head out of Daniel's grasp and rising to his feet. Daniel rose too, turned and saw a shell-shocked Jack O'Neill slumped against the wall, his arms limp at his sides. He was staring at them in absolute horror.

"He– We, uh, thought you were the enemy." Daniel's words were swallowed by the silence.

Teal'c glanced at him, and Daniel saw no anger, only a deep concern. "I believe this is known as a 'friendly fire' incident, is it not?"

Daniel struggled for a smile. "Uh, yeah. I guess. Right Jack?"

Jack didn't respond. His face was in shadows, but his stillness was disturbing. Still was one thing Jack O'Neill didn't do except in extremis. Still and quiet, that's how Daniel remembered him in his cell, toward the end. Still and quiet and without hope. Like now.

"We must make haste," Teal'c said, ignoring the blood dripping from his ear. Probably didn't want to draw Jack's attention to the wound. "Major Carter is waiting at the ring transporter. She insisted that I come and direct you to the correct corridor."

Still Jack didn't move, and Daniel took a step toward him. That, it seemed, was enough. With an effort Jack lunged into action, his steps heavy, almost drunken. As the shadows crept back from his face, Daniel saw the devastation there. He recognized the expression of self-loathing, he'd seen it on Abydos many, many years ago. "Let's go," he growled as he moved past them. "And Teal'c, put something on that ear before you bleed to death."

Daniel exchanged a troubled glance with Teal'c. If he hadn't knocked the gun out of line there was no way Jack would have missed his target. Teal'c would be dead, and they both knew it. "It was a mistake," Daniel offered softly.

Teal'c said nothing, simply bowed his head in silent acknowledgment of the truth.

But Daniel couldn't forget Jack's words as they'd waited in the darkness, *Don't let them take you, Daniel.* He just hoped Jack could hold it together long enough to get the hell out of this place. Sam had been right, coming back here was a very bad idea: they should never have let it happen.

CHAPTER FIFTEEN

Hiding next to the door, Sam lowered her weapon as the colonel prowled into the room, trailed by Daniel and Teal'c. They all looked shaken.

"What happened?" she asked, stepping out of her hiding place. "I heard a gunshot."

The colonel barked a harsh laugh, circling the room with a face as hard as cracking stone. "You did. I shot Teal'c!"

"What?"

Daniel made a face. "It was an accident." He waved at Teal'c, who was fixing a dressing on his ear. "We thought he was, uh, one of Baal's."

We? She could read between the lines, and what she saw there turned her cold. The colonel didn't make that kind of mistake. Ever.

"So, what say we find this damn gizmo and get the hell out of here?" O'Neill snapped. "Turns out I really, really, hate this place."

"Yes, sir." Disturbed, Sam dragged her attention away from Daniel and returned to the transport rings. "I think I have it configured for the center of the base, sir. If it's anywhere, that's where the power unit will be."

"Okay, great. Let's go." The colonel moved to stand in the middle of the ring-pattern on the floor, but his hands stayed away from the gun that hung limply across his chest. And his eyes stayed away from Teal'c.

Sam risked a glance at Daniel. He was frowning. "Ah, actually, I think what we're looking for may be somewhere else."

"*May* be?" O'Neill didn't seem in the mood for debate. "Where else?"

"Well, if I'm right and the inscription on the tablet we found near that 'gate indicates that the shield was broken – and that *neither* part worked – it's possible that the power unit could have been used ceremonially. In which case–"

"Ah!" O'Neill cut him off roughly. "Too many ifs, buts, and maybes, Daniel. We'll try Carter's idea first."

And that was that. Daniel pressed his lips together in an expression that drifted between irritation and resignation, but he held his tongue. With an apologetic shrug toward him, Sam moved to the controls. "I can set it to activate remotely."

"Come on, come on," the colonel muttered. "Just do it."

Quietly, Daniel and Teal'c joined him. Sam activated the transport rings and darted into range just as they whipped down around them. In a blur of motion they were gone. The disorientation of instantaneous travel lasted only a moment, and Sam soon found herself training her weapon around a brightly lit, empty operations center. Two doors, at right angles to each other, led out into dark corridors beyond and she eyed them warily. Dark mouths to dark caves, hiding who knew what. But they couldn't hold her attention for long amid the soft hum and whir of technology in action. Jackpot!

Cautiously she moved away from the ring transporter. "This looks like it," she murmured as she approached one of the terminals. There was definitely naquadah there, she could almost taste it. But, for once, that wasn't what she needed.

"Looks like this place is still occupied," Daniel said from behind her, trailing fingers over the dust free machinery.

"It is possible that Baal has retained a skeleton force in order to protect his stronghold from looting by other system lords," Teal'c suggested.

The colonel said nothing, but she could sense him prowling the room. He wanted to be gone. Gratefully propping her heavy pack against a wall, Sam slid beneath a console and started searching.

"Daniel," O'Neill said suddenly. "Watch that door. I'll take the other one. Teal'c…" There was a long, uncomfortable pause. "Take a load off."

But Teal'c had other ideas. "I shall watch with you, O'Neill." The colonel didn't reply and the awkwardness of his silence filled the room. Doing her best to tune it out, Sam started work. They needed to get out of here, fast. And not just because of lurking Jaffa.

But as the minutes ticked past she felt her frustration rise along with the tension in the room. Despite her best efforts, she could find nothing that matched the intricate technology of the Kinahhi plans. After half an hour of fruitless searching, she pushed herself out from beneath the console in a flash of exasperation. "You know, maybe you're right, Daniel. Maybe it's not here."

O'Neill didn't move from his position by the door, but she could see his back stiffen. "Not here?"

"I'm sorry, sir. I thought it would be. This is the control center for the whole base. But I can't find anything."

Daniel shifted, turning toward her. "It's possible that the power unit won't work without the other half of the device. It would explain why the System Lords let Baal keep it. In which case, as I was saying before, it might have a ceremonial function. I've identified a number of–"

"*Get down!*" The colonel's yell ripped through the air as he swung away from the door. The blast of a staff weapon flashed past him, exploding into the wall behind Sam. She hit the deck, hard. "The other door!" O'Neill ordered. "Go!"

The colonel flew across the room, as close to real panic as she'd ever seen him. Teal'c was already backing up, his weapon primed and ready for use.

"Carter, move it!"

As she tried to rise, another bolt of plasma scorched overhead. She was in direct sight of the approaching Jaffa. On her stomach, she worked her way behind the meager cover of Daniel's discarded pack. A third blast skimmed so close she could smell singeing hair as she pressed her face into the cold, hard floor. "Daniel!" she yelled. "My pack, get my pack!" It sat just to the left of him, unharmed, and contained everything Baal needed to put his shield back together. If they let it fall into his hands… "Go!" she shouted, still pinned down behind Daniel's pack. "You have to get it out of here!"

Daniel dragged her backpack into the corridor, Teal'c and O'Neill laying down covering fire. "Come on!" the colonel yelled at her. "You can make it!"

They were twenty feet away, no more. But the air was full of weapons fire and she could hear the stump, stump, stump of heavy boots approaching from the corridor beyond. Edging across the floor she flinched with every explosion, until a voice bellowed, "Jaffa! Sha'lokma'kor!"

Gunfire rattled in response. "Carter! Run!"

Scrabbling to her feet, she launched herself toward the door. Now or never. Now or– A blast caught her in the back. She was falling…. Someone yelled, not her. Gunfire filled the air until she couldn't breathe, and the floor came up to meet her with a bone-crunching thud that smashed her into darkness.

Hiding in the shadowed doorway, Jack watched as Carter hit the floor. The zat blast caught her in the back and she fell like a stone, cracking her head and lying motionless as the blue light danced across her body. Behind her, Jaffa flooded into the room. One paused and turned her over with the toe of his boot. Jack felt his stomach dissolve as the man dropped to one knee and lifted her head by the hair. He was going to kill her. "Kree'ta!" barked another, followed by something unintelligible. The Jaffa holding Carter glanced up, shrugged, and let her head drop back to the floor.

"Jack, we have to go," Daniel whispered urgently, pulling on his arm. "I've got Sam's pack."

"And they've got Carter!" His weapon spewed another round, sending the startled Jaffa scattering. But more were filling the room, a fire storm of staff-blasts scorching the air. It looked like a whole damn platoon.

"We cannot defeat them here, O'Neill." Teal'c's voice boomed through the chaos. "And we must not permit Major Carter's device to fall into Baal's hands."

Screw the device. Jack's mind was red with panic. "We can't let Carter fall into Baal's hands!" *Acid, daggers, cold white death again and again...* Never. "We can't–"

A staff-blast exploded into the wall behind his head, showering them with jagged, biting debris.

"Jack, we'll come back!" Daniel yelled, hefting Carter's pack over one shoulder. "But we have to get out of here. Now!"

Fight or flight? His mind was torn between the two, slowly pulling apart like a fraying rope. *Don't let them take you!* He'd blow his own brains out before he'd let them drag him back to that hell. But would he blow her brains out to save her from the same nightmare? His weapon dipped. He'd killed her before, once. He knew he could do it. He'd killed her to save her.

His finger tightened on the trigger.

"Jack!" Daniel grabbed his gun, horrified. "What the hell...?"

Reality slammed home, his weapon snapped up. Oh God... Keeping his eyes on Carter, he started to back away. "Fall back," he barked. "Fall back!" Scanning the ceiling and walls of the control room, he took aim at an illuminated sconce and fired. "Kill the lights. We have to hide."

Daniel and Teal'c understood, and as the lights shattered he watched Carter fall into shadow. "Go," he hissed to his friends, grabbing Daniel's arm to keep from losing him in the darkness. Together, in pitch black silence, they fled into the depths of Baal's fortress.

He was leaving her behind. He was leaving her in hell.

Bill Crawford stood before the Stargate, laptop in one hand and briefcase in the other, staring at the stubbornly inert 'gate. A scattering of soldiers – or whatever they were called in the Air Force – decorated the edges of the room, all studiously avoiding his gaze and doing a good job of blending into the gray walls of the 'gate room. He'd been there for twenty minutes and his patience was evaporating. There was nothing he hated more than being made to look a fool.

At his side Lieutenant Ashley stood stiffly, staring through the empty Stargate as if she was wishing herself light years away. As well she should. He turned on her, glaring. "Five minutes, you said. Where the hell is he?"

Ashley flinched. "On his way, sir. General Hammond is– He had some urgent business to attend to before–"

"Urgent business my ass!" From the flush on her face he knew he was right. Hammond was yanking his chain, making him look a damn fool in front of the silent, sniggering men. Oh yes, he knew they were sniggering behind their impassive soldier faces. Sniggering at the suit outwitted by the uniform. Showed what they knew; when it came to real power he held all the cards. He turned on Ashley, coming nose-to-nose with her. "I've had enough," he hissed, carefully setting down his laptop and briefcase. "You tell Hammond that he's violating direct orders and I'll see him in a court martial for this act of–"

"I don't think so, son." The slow Texan drawl came from the doorway behind him.

Turning, Crawford saw the general march into the room. He wasn't in his usual uniform, but instead was dressed in the same drab greens that O'Neill and his team had worn on Kinahhi. And he appeared to be armed. Behind him followed four other men, similarly dressed and clutching ugly guns. "What the hell are you doing?"

"Following orders, Ambassador." Hammond turned and looked up at the control room. "Dial the Kinahhi home world, Sergeant."

Crawford gaped as the 'gate began to spin. "You're coming with me? Why?"

Hammond smiled. "To investigate the allegations in your report. You've accused my people of a serious offense, sir. I intend to get to the bottom of it."

"But–"

The general took a step closer, head cocked slightly to one side. "Unless there's some additional information you'd like to share that might save me the trip, Ambassador?"

Swallowing his anxiety, Crawford jutted out his chin and followed his father's advice. *Never look weak.* "You know everything I do, General. I have nothing to hide."

"Is that so?" Hammond asked quietly. Before Crawford could answer the Stargate burst open, startling him with its wild blue flare. At least he stayed on his feet this time. The general gestured to the four men behind him. "Colonel Tyler, proceed at your discretion."

The colonel, yet another mook in uniform, nodded to Hammond and waved his team forward. "Allen, Kendall, with me. Barker, stay with the general."

As the soldiers stepped up onto the ramp, Hammond moved to follow. "After you, Ambassador," he offered generously, and with a smile added, "I don't get to do this nearly enough."

Suppressing his irritation, Crawford picked up his laptop and briefcase and strode up the ramp. Hammond was just a soldier – what did he know about the intricacies of diplomacy and politics? The only thing he'd find on Kinahhi was the evidence to condemn his precious SG-1. And with that cheerful thought Crawford set his jaw and stepped into the icy vortex of the wormhole, praying that this time he wouldn't lose his breakfast when he emerged on the other side.

He'd blow his own brains out before he'd let them drag him back to that hell. But would he blow her brains out to save her from the same nightmare? His weapon dipped. He'd killed her before, once. He knew he could do it. He'd killed her to save her.

The memory twisted like an over-wound clock spring, turning and turning until his mind was too tight to move. He sat locked in rigid immobility, watching as the scene played over and over in his head. He'd been ready to kill Carter. He'd been ready to kill her to save her from his own nightmare. What the *hell* had he been thinking? A terrified laugh bubbled up in his throat and he sucked it back down hurriedly. Quiet. He had to be quiet. Teal'c and Daniel were resting, sleeping after the hours they'd spent creeping through the ruined fortress with the Jaffa snapping at their heels. Not wanting to be trapped, he'd insisted they make camp in this cold, damp corridor that hadn't seen life for months. Water and the icy night air were seeping in from somewhere, and a soft light that might have been cast by a moon followed where they led. It was cold, but better that than being trapped like rats in a room with no way out. A room that twisted and turned, upside down and right side up. He shivered.

The image of Carter's body, sprawled lifelessly on the floor, bled into his mind. But he pushed it away. He refused to think about where she was, what they were doing to her. He couldn't bear to; it threatened to cut the last few strands binding body and soul together. He just prayed that Baal wasn't there, that she wouldn't have to see that slick, careless face as the knife cut into her–

Memory erupted as keen as a blade. He jerked so hard that water sloshed from the canteen he was clutching and splashed coldly onto his leg. His damn hand was shaking.

"Jack?" It was Daniel, roused from a half-sleep.

"It's nothing."

But Daniel wasn't stupid. "Did you hear something?"

"Go back to sleep."

"I wasn't." He pushed himself upright and rested his back against the wall next to Jack. He shivered. "It's cold in here."

"Air conditioning courtesy of Lord Yu."

A soft grunt was his answer, and they drifted into a silence interrupted only by Teal'c's deep breathing. Odd to see him sleeping, Jack thought. He wondered what he dreamed about. Did he have nightmares? Did he relive all that he'd been forced to do in the name of Apophis? Had he ever ripped a man's soul from his body, piece by piece? Life by life. Endlessly, hopelessly–

"Jack?"

The canteen in his hand was shaking so hard water was dripping from his fingers. Not just his hand, he realized. His whole body. It must be the cold. Daniel was right; it was freezing and–

"I'm sorry."

"For what?" Damn, his teeth were chattering.

"I shouldn't have let you come back here."

Jack snorted. "And it was your decision how?"

In the faint ambient glow of their makeshift campsite, Jack saw light flash against Daniel's glasses as he stirred. "I was there, Jack. I know what happened. I saw what Baal–"

"Stop!" He couldn't hear this. "Just stop it."

But Daniel was relentless. "No one could go through that without being… damaged. It's not surprising that you–"

"Damaged?" The word escaped like steam from an engine. "So now I'm a basket case?" A shivering, pathetic basket case willing to kill a friend in the name of his own fear.

"No!" A firm hand on Jack's wrist accompanied the word. "Jesus, Jack, anyone who'd been through that would have some kind of reaction to being back here! You're only human."

"Am I?" *His weapon dipped. He'd killed her before, once. He knew he could do it. He'd killed her to save her.* He yanked his arm out of Daniel's grasp, still shaking. He damn well couldn't stop shaking.

"Yes, you are." Daniel's words were calm and even, spoken with such faith that Jack almost bought the fiction. "He couldn't take that from you."

The bloody, pulped face of a dead Jaffa seemed into his memory, his own hands slick with blood. He shivered. "You sure?"

"He didn't break you, Jack. You protected Shallan. You saved her!"

But he was wrong. "I was lucky, that's all. Without you…" – he laughed, the sound scarily on the edge of hysteria – "…and without Yu, I would have talked. I almost did. You know that. I was *this* close to it." He sucked in a shivering breath. "Why else would you offer me ascension?"

"To save your soul, Jack." There was a pause. "Maybe I was wrong?"

"You were a Higher Being, Daniel. How could you be wrong?"

Daniel shifted again, moving close enough that Jack could feel the faint warmth of another human being through the chill air. But it didn't stop him shaking. "I was wrong just now."

"What?"

Daniel's head leaned back, landing softly against the stone wall. "Sam didn't think you should come back here. She thought it would be too difficult. She wanted to protect you. And for a moment there, I thought–" He sounded like a kid at confession. "For a moment there I thought she was right."

Jack looked away, staring down at the dim outline of the canteen clutched in his still shaking hand. He'd aimed his gun right at her head, finger tight on the trigger. "She was right," he rasped. "You should've listened to her."

"No. Think about it. Why are you here?" When Jack didn't respond, Daniel answered his own question. "To save Henry Boyd and SG-10. You're not here for revenge, or because you're following orders. You came here to save people, *knowing* how hard it would be. Knowing you'd probably be fighting more nightmares than Jaffa."

Jack just stared down at the canteen. His fingers were freezing. "So?"

"Don't you get it? If Baal had broken you, if he'd destroyed what makes you human – what makes you Jack – then you wouldn't be here." His tone warmed, a trace of a smile on his lips. "Come on, who else but Jack O'Neill would be this stupidly brave?"

Brave? "Wrong again, Daniel. Scared stupid, maybe. Not brave." If he was brave he wouldn't be so afraid he could hardly breathe, so traumatized that even the thought of *seeing* that room again made him want to vomit. So screwed up that he'd considered putting a bullet in Carter's head.

"It is you who are mistaken, O'Neill." Teal'c had woken up, or perhaps he'd never been sleeping at all. "There is no courage without fear."

For crying out loud. "I *shot* you, Teal'c! I could have damn well killed you. If Daniel hadn't–" His voice choked on humiliation. "I was afraid. Scared shitless. And it nearly killed you."

"And yet you are still here," Teal'c observed calmly. "You have not given up on Henry Boyd. Or Major Carter. A lesser man would retreat in the face of such overwhelming fear."

"Don't think I don't want to!" He surged to his feet, control slipping. He tried to hold onto it, but it flailed away like a rope cut under tension. "Don't think I don't want to run for it and never, ever set foot in this stinking hole again!" He stopped, turning and pressing his forehead against the cold wall, sucking in a raw breath as the truth leaked out quietly and shamefully. "Don't think I haven't thought about giving up. On Boyd and Carter."

Teal'c rose fluidly to his feet. "The fact that you do not, O'Neill, is testament to the man I am honored to call brother. Our choices, not our impulses, define us."

"He's right," Daniel added, also standing. "Whatever you feel, you'd never abandon them. I know you, Jack. You're a better man than that."

He closed his eyes, forehead knocking gently against the cold stone. "Am I?"

"You're still here, aren't you?"

He supposed he was. Despite the nauseating sense of dread coiling in the pit of his stomach, he was still here. He blew out a shaky breath and felt it reflect off the wall, wafting an ephemeral warmth against his face. *I'm still here. I'm still alive. I'm still Jack O'Neill.*

And Majors Boyd and Carter still needed him. No one gets left behind.

He didn't move, forehead still resting against the wall. "Daniel? Where do you think the power unit is?"

Daniel's back came to rest next to him. When he spoke, his voice was deliberately matter of fact. Businesslike. Jack could have hugged him. "I've identified a couple of ceremonial chambers in the complex. My guess is one of those. Perhaps an altarpiece, a focus of worship."

"Can you find it?"

"I think so."

With both hands, Jack pushed himself away from the wall and turned. All he could see of Teal'c was the faint gleam of moonlight reflecting off the brand on his forehead. Just like the moment he'd nearly shot him. He swallowed hard and pushed past the memory. "Carter said we need a ship. If there're Jaffa here, there must be a Tic-Tac around someplace."

Teal'c cocked his head in a moment of pointed silence. "There is likely to be a tel'tak close to the fortress. Most probably a landing platform on the roof."

"Good. Go with Daniel to find the power unit, then head to the roof and get yourselves a ride. A fast one."

Daniel moved again, glasses flashing in the dim light. "What about you?"

"Me?" Standing up straight, Jack squared his shoulders and took a deep breath. It was steady. He wasn't shaking anymore. "I'm going to find Carter."

CHAPTER SIXTEEN

Sam woke slowly and groggily, her head aching and nerves jangling with the familiar, slightly toasted sensation of a zat blast. Must have been at close range, she figured, to keep her out this long. She knew it had to have been a while because she found herself staring up at a low, unfamiliar ceiling.

Without much hope she reached for her P90 – it was gone, as was her Beretta, her zat, and even the dive knife she carried. No radio either, but at least the flashlight was still in her vest. Slowly standing, she switched on the light and glanced around the odd-looking cell. It was long and rectangular, with a ceiling she could almost touch. At the far end, molded into the wall, were what could have been benches if the wall had been the floor. As it was, she couldn't guess their purpose and turned her attention to the other end of the long cell, where a hefty metal grate covered the square entrance.

Cautiously she approached, ears open for any sounds. But all was silence. The grate itself was heavy, dark and roughly made. A low hatch had been cut through the metal, secured by a very crude-looking bolt. Had her hands been smaller, and her arms about a foot longer, she could have reached through and opened it; not exactly the kind of technology she'd expected from Baal. It was curiously makeshift. It occurred to her that the cell might once have been secured by a force shield that had been disabled during Lord Yu's attack. Her heart did a little nervous skitter as she considered the possibility that this was where the colonel had been detained.

Banishing the thought, Sam tucked her flashlight into her belt, curled both hands around the bars and gave them a good shake. Nothing – didn't move an inch. Standing back, she leveled a hefty drop-kick at the center of the grate. It reverberated with a satisfying clang, but achieved little more than a substantial jarring of her knee. Improvised it might be, but the door to her cell was as impenetrable as any force shield.

Swallowing a growing sense of frustration and panic, she pressed her face against the grate and tried to see farther down the corridor. She angled the head of her flashlight through the bars, revealing a row of open, square doorways just like hers. Except hers was the only one barred; all the rest were dark and empty.

"Hello?" she called, her voice echoing thinly back to her. No answer.

She tried to take it as a good sign; at least the rest of her team must have escaped. She fervently hoped they'd taken the Kinahhi anti-grav device with them. At the very least, she hoped they'd destroyed it. The idea of Baal turning Earth's sun into a black hole with the aid of a weapon built by her own hands was an irony too bitter to contemplate. Kinsey would love it.

Pulling her flashlight back into the cell, tugging as its crooked neck wedged in the square confines of the bars, she turned off the light and stood for a moment to let her eyes grow accustomed to the dark. There was nothing she could do. She hated that. Retreating to the rear of the cell, she slid to the ground and leaned her back against the wall. All she could do was wait, for rescue or for the Jaffa. Both were coming, of that she was certain. Her fate would depend on who arrived first.

"You know what first attracted me to archeology?" Daniel Jackson asked, as he tramped at Teal'c's side through ankle-deep water that pooled icily in the dark corridor. "The weather. Egypt, South America, maybe Italy and Greece, North Africa… *That* is where I expected to be spending my days." He shivered. "Ironic, huh?"

Teal'c considered his reply. He was consistently surprised by the human ability to disguise true feelings with inane babble, a tactic reminiscent of a battlefield feint. O'Neill was a master of such deception, but it seemed that all his friends shared the trait to a greater or lesser degree, especially when under stress. Teal'c refused to be distracted by such behavior, and so simply said, "I believe your dissatisfaction has less to do with the temperature than your fear for O'Neill and Major Carter."

Daniel Jackson frowned. "I'm trying not to think about that."

"Both O'Neill and Major Carter are formidable warriors. They will triumph."

It was Daniel Jackson's turn to be silent. For a while the only sound in the corridor was the quiet sloshing of water as they walked. When he did speak again, his voice was much softer. "Some battles aren't fought with guns, Teal'c."

"O'Neill will not succumb," he insisted, "wherever the field of battle. He will be victorious, or die in the attempt."

His friend slowed, head shaking. "That's exactly what I'm afraid–"

"Aray Kree!"

The young voice boomed out from behind, arresting them both mid-step. Teal'c's hand tightened on his staff weapon as he glanced over at Daniel Jackson; they both knew that surrender was impossible. "If you leave now," Teal'c called in response, back to the owner of the voice, "I will spare your life."

"Has'shak!" The voice was closer now, youthfully arrogant.

"No," Teal'c replied as he turned to face the young Jaffa. "You are the fool." It was a child's face, a boy only a few years older than Rya'c.

The boy's eyes widened when he recognized the brand of Apophis upon Teal'c's brow. "You are the Shol'va!" He swung his staff weapon up, eager for use. "My God will reward me for your capture."

Teal'c shifted his stance, ready for the fight the boy offered. "Your god is false."

"And your lies are well known!" The boy's lunge was marred by his anger and easily parried in a half turn. Using his momentum to carry him around, Teal'c swung the butt of his weapon up into the boy's chest and sent him sprawling. With a deft twist, he had the head of his weapon open and pressed against the boy's throat.

"Tell your master that he will not go unpunished for his crimes. Tell him that the Jaffa will rise from beneath his fist, and that we will soon rid the galaxy of the scourge of the Goa'uld! Tell him to fear us."

The boy's mouth opened and closed, angry and disbelieving. And perhaps, beneath it all, there was a glimmer of hope. But not enough.

"Daniel Jackson," Teal'c said, without looking away from the Jaffa's face. "Now is the time."

From his left he heard the electronic fizz of a zat'nikatel opening. The young Jaffa's head turned, mouth open in shock, as Daniel Jackson fired a single shot. He jerked as the energy danced across his body, then lay still. Teal'c stood straight, staff weapon coming to rest on the ground. Just a boy, he thought, lying cold in the water.

Daniel Jackson cleared his throat. "You, ah, couldn't have changed his mind."

He turned to his friend; Daniel Jackson seemed to possess the uncanny ability to see into the hearts of all men. "He is much like my son."

"I know. And you freed Rya'c. One day you'll free them all."

Teal'c nodded, returning his gaze to the unconscious face of one of his own. One day all Jaffa would be free and the Goa'uld would be dust in the wind. But not this day. "We must leave quickly. The shot from the zat'nikatel will have alerted others."

"It's not far from here." Holstering his weapon Daniel Jackson peered down the dark, wet corridor. "If I'm right, there should be a door somewhere on the left." He made a face and glanced up at the ceiling. "Let's hope the room's still standing."

Jack crouched in the shadows, contemplating the dim light emanating from the cross-corridor. The electronic compass on his watch indicated south-southeast. And who knew where the hell that was on this godforsaken planet, but as long as he was still heading toward the center of the complex he was going the right way. After Carter had been taken they'd fled, heedless of direction, into the outer rings of the fortress. But he knew Carter would be at the heart of the stronghold, close to Baal. Close to that room…

A tremor ran through him, and he ignored it.

The question was, whether to head toward the light or away from it? Light meant power, which meant Jaffa. Jaffa might also mean Carter. Or capture. Gritting his teeth he repeated Teal'c's homily – there is no bravery without fear. There is no bravery without fear. At this rate he'd be the bravest sonofabitch in the galaxy.

Silently he stepped out into the corridor and crept toward the light, keeping to the shadows, every sense straining for the enemy. There was more warmth here, at least, and the corridors were increasingly ornate. More like he remembered from his previous stay at Baal's Pleasure Palace. But he wasn't thinking about that.

He was thinking about Carter, and getting her the hell out of there before they flung her against that damn spider web that sucked you down into– Damn it! Think of something else. Cold beer. His dock, at dusk. Fishing. Fishing with–

A door hissed open ten feet ahead. Pressing himself against the reliefs carved into the walls, he held his breath as booted footsteps clanked into the corridor and headed... away from him. Slowly, he peered from his nominal hiding spot and saw the backs of three Jaffa marching toward the light. Thank God.

Dry-mouthed he crept after them, passing the doorway on his right. Two doors that would open automatically as you approached and–

He was half-carried, half-dragged down the corridors, a Jaffa on each side, fingers digging into his arms. Gut and legs liquid with terror, he let them haul him through the doors and out into the bright corridor. He knew where they were taking him. It was only moments away, but it wasn't now. Not now. It didn't hurt now. He was still himself, he was still Colonel Jack O'Neill, serial number–

Jolted back to the present he found himself standing frozen and alone in the corridor. Staring at the door. An innocuous door. But his mouth tasted like bile and his head spun. He forced in an urgent breath, but it ratted in his dry lungs and made him cough. His knees gave way and he slid down the wall, trying to stifle the sound. He knew where he was. He knew *exactly* where he was.

And somewhere in the back of his mind an alarm started to blare.

Booted feet, the jangle of armor. The bark of a voice. Getting closer. Coming for him! Adrenaline pumped him to his feet, mind ultra-sharp and everything suddenly playing in cut-glass clarity. There was only one place to hide.

P90 clutched to his chest, he turned to the door and watched it hiss open. Light from behind him flooded the dark corridor beyond, casting his shadow long and thin. But even in darkness he would have known this place; the walls were soaked with the stench of his despair. Without pause he stepped inside and the doors slid shut behind him. The corridor faded into gloom, but enough illumination seeped inside to outline shapes. Square black shapes, the openings of the anyway-up cells; his had been the third on the left. On rigid legs he walked past it, unable to keep his eyes from turning and fixing on the object of a thousand nightmares. It was dark and empty; just like him.

Ahead there was a noise, someone moving. Wrenching his morbid gaze away, he crouched low and crept forward. The cells didn't seem to be working. As soon as Yu had knocked out the power generators, the gravity-twisting had stopped and the cells had become nothing but long, dead-end corridors with open mouths. That's all they were still. He crept closer to the sound of movement, peering through the increasing gloom, not daring to use his flashlight.

He forced himself to concentrate on the differences from last time – the lack of light or power, the mildewed scent of decay. The hefty metal grate covering the entrance to one of the cells. That was new. And unique; no other cell was barred. His heart jumped with a beat of hope. Carter?

Licking at dry lips he crossed the corridor, still keeping low as he started to run toward the locked cell. A little C4 should get the grate off. With any luck they'd be back out and hiding in the rabbit-warren fortress before the alarm could be raised. And from there–

Light hit him from behind. He flinched and dodged into the shadows of a cell. Trying not to think about where he was, he crept deeper into the blackness as heavy footsteps reverberated down the corridor behind him. Three Jaffa passed the cell door – Larry, Moe and Curly – big and brutally armed.

They stopped, as he'd guessed they would, outside the locked cell.

"Your friends have abandoned you," a voice announced, imperious and gunmetal cold. "You are alone here."

"Haven't caught them yet, huh?" Her bright, spirited response danced through the darkness and filled Jack's heart with pride. Creeping toward the entrance of the cell he risked peering around its lip. The Jaffa who had spoken stood close to the grate, his face hidden in the murky light. Jack could see nothing of Carter.

"They hide like rats in the sewers. But they will be caught," Curly replied. "And if you do not answer our questions, they will watch you die. Slowly."

"I don't think so."

"Your bravado is foolish. If they come for you, we will be waiting."

"Like I said, you haven't caught them yet." But Jack detected a tremor of uncertainty in her voice, and shared it. The Jaffa was right; the trap was set and she was the bait. Just peachy.

Curly must have detected the same tone of disquiet, because he leaned closer to the bars. "Tell me now what I wish to know, and your end will be swift and painless."

There was a long pause, and then, "My name is Major Samantha Carter, United States Air Force. Serial number 638–"

"Shel kree!" The Jaffa snapped, turning away. "Bring her."

The screech of a bolt being drawn set Jack's teeth on edge as he ducked back into the shadows. Three Jaffa. He could take them; he had the element of surprise and a faster, more deadly weapon. Carter would hit the deck as soon as she heard the first shot, and the guards would be down before they knew what had happened.

Crouching in the darkness he readied himself. He was close and the targets were large enough to compensate for the lack of visibility. He switched his weapon to single shot and settled the sight against his eye. The Jaffa leader, Curly, was the first to walk past his hiding place, head bare and inviting a bullet. Jack's finger tightened on the trigger, waiting for Larry and Moe to come into view before he made his move. And then there were three, one on each side of Carter, fingers biting into her arms. She looked frightened, but was doing her best to hide it.

Good night assholes. His finger squeezed the trigger and–

Light flooded the corridor. "Shor'wai'e!" A voice barked the words from the corridor beyond. Jack froze.

Chastened, Curly turned back to the men escorting Carter. He didn't look happy. "Tal'shak," he muttered. "Yas!"

Picking up the pace, they dragged Carter forward and out of Jack's line of sight. Slowly he lowered his weapon, thankful for his luck. If he'd taken the shot a second sooner the new arrival would have walked right in on their escape and raised the alarm. He and Carter would have been trapped like rats in the proverbial trap. As it was, he still had a chance.

Galvanized, he crept out of his hiding place as the doors at the end of the corridor slid shut. Breaking into a run he sprinted toward them, then stopped and made himself count to five before stepping through and peering out into the corridor. He just caught a glimpse of Carter's blonde hair as she turned a corner to his left; darting to the opposite wall he followed her in a low run.

It was only then that he realized he'd run right past his former cell without a backward glance. Nothing like a little action to keep a guy distracted; he hoped all his ghosts would be so easily appeased.

Half-right, Daniel thought as he shouldered open the narrow door and pushed his way into the room. The door was wedged shut by half the ceiling and the contents of the room above, and he was forced to climb up onto the rubble as he squeezed inside. He sniffed; the stench in the air was grossly unmistakable. He moved the beam of his flashlight carefully across the floor until it touched the armored arm of a long-dead Jaffa buried beneath the debris. Water dripped from the ragged hole that was once the ceiling, trickling through the wreckage and adding its own scent of damp decay to the putrid reek of rotting flesh.

"Is this the place we seek, Daniel Jackson?"

Teal'c's flashlight darted about, glinting against golden walls and coming to rest on two pillars which stood at the center of the room. Reaching from the ceiling to the floor, each was of different design – one shimmering a soft gold, the other simple stone. Approaching the golden pillar first, Daniel ran his fingers over the characteristically Phoenician engravings of the sun god and his sun-horses. Then he circled the pillar, flashlight held close to his face as he studied its unblemished surface, until his questing fingers found what he sought. A raised cartouche, bearing the legend Meleq. Professor Kelly would be green! Smiling to himself, he turned to the stone pillar. A relief of Baal, wielding a lightning bolt, dominated the pillar. It was primitive but beautiful, and the design was clearly Canaanite – almost identical in composition, in fact, to the mosaic ceiling on Tsapan. Above the image, inscribed in the little darts and triangles of Ugaritic cuneiform, was a line of text. He spoke slowly as he translated, "Verily Baal has fallen to the earth, Dead is Baal the Mighty." Then he crouched, fingers tracing more words beneath the image. "Baal the Conqueror lives; the Prince, the Lord of the Earth, has revived." He glanced over at Teal'c. "A reference to his defeat at the hands of the system lords, perhaps?"

"Perhaps," Teal'c agreed. He looked around the empty chamber, and when he spoke again his voice carried a shade of doubt. "I do not believe the power unit we seek is in this chamber, Daniel Jackson."

"No," Daniel agreed, pushing back to his feet. "There should be more. An altar, a place of worship." Slowly he circled the stone pillar again, fingers trailing over its rough surface until he found the cartouche that corresponded with the golden pillar. It too was raised, and dirt had settled into the deep crevasses of the carving. He blew gently and a little puff of masonry dust circled up into the air. The name within the cartouche was also written in Ugaritic script, but it did not spell Baal. Instead the name was Re'ammin. He ran a finger over the word, nudging a clump of stone dust from the top of the first letter, pressing a little harder than before. "It could be that–" Beneath his hand the cartouche slid slowly and irrevocably inwards with a soft grating sound of stone-on-stone. Daniel froze. "Uh-oh."

Teal'c's eyebrow rose curiously, just as the ground beneath Daniel gave way. With a yelp he fell, hit something hard and went tumbling down and down.

Back in the cells, Sam could have sworn she'd felt eyes on her. Not unfriendly eyes, but her skin had crawled with the sensation of being watched. Perhaps she was clutching at straws, but the fanciful part of her mind hoped that she'd felt her team watching her. That they were there, waiting in the shadows, to free her.

The practical part of her mind hoped she'd been imagining things, and that her team had hightailed it back to the 'gate with the anti-grav device – that they'd gone to beg Hammond for reinforcements before they tried to spring her.

The realistic part of her mind told her that was bull. The colonel would make at least one rescue attempt before calling for backup. She knew him too well to doubt that. If he didn't come, the only explanation would be that the Jaffa had gotten to him first. And that was a scenario she really didn't want to consider.

Pushing such demoralizing thoughts from her mind, she fixed her attention on where she was going. They'd taken a right from the doors at the end of the cell block, then a left approximately twenty meters further on. They'd been walking along this corridor for a good three minutes, and she'd seen several other Jaffa march past. It must be the heart of the remaining occupation of Baal's stronghold; something to remember on the way out. PMA – positive mental attitude. She remembered it from the Academy's survival training. Colonel Kirk Greenberg had taught it, a brick-house of a man with a neck as thick as his head. Positive Mental Attitude, the first rule of survival.

Her memories were disrupted when her guards stopped abruptly and she was yanked around to face another anonymous door. She went hot and cold simultaneously, realistic enough to imagine what awaited inside. Or at least to try. The colonel's eyes came starkly to mind, haunted and blank as he'd stumbled through the 'gate with the strange woman's wrist gripped in his hand. He'd said nothing, just stood there shaking with adrenaline until Doctor Fraiser had gently coaxed him toward the infirmary. He'd refused to lie on a gurney. He'd refused to let her touch him.

Something had done that to him. Something here. Something, in all likelihood, through those doors. If it had driven the colonel to the edge, what the hell would it do to her?

She tried to swallow, but her throat was dry. Panic pulled at the edges of her mind and she ruthlessly ignored it. Fear was dangerous, fear was the enemy's weapon and she wouldn't do their job for them. Instead she forced herself to recall everything she'd been taught about resisting interrogation. Colonel Kirk Greenberg trooped back into her thoughts.

Anger, that was vital. And she had it in spades, especially when she remembered O'Neill's return and the fragile weeks of recovery afterwards. She wouldn't let the bastards get the same satisfaction from her!

Faith. She had that too, faith in herself and her team. If there was a chance, she'd take it and be out of there in a flash. She only needed a single chance. And if not, her team wouldn't leave her behind. No one gets left behind; that was the whole reason they were here in the first place. Her team would come for her; she just had to hold out long enough to give them a chance.

In front of her the doors hissed open and a hand pushed her into a brightly-lit room. There was an acrid scent in the air, an acidic mixture of steel and blood. A Jaffa she didn't recognize was waiting for her inside, a tall bullish-looking man who wore his armor like a second skin. "Over there," the Jaffa ordered, nodding toward a large metal grate. It was dark, rusty brown, like a huge metallic spider's web. Beyond it a corridor led off into black oblivion. She walked toward it curiously. They hadn't tied her. She'd been expecting that, arms behind her back, legs bound into a stress position. Maybe a blindfold. There was none of that, and her spirits began to lift. Perhaps her imagination had gotten the better of her? Perhaps without Baal's malevolent presence they wouldn't resort to his methods?

Turning to face the Jaffa she saw that he'd moved to stand behind a control panel on a low platform not far from the metal grid. Nodding over her shoulder she said, "What is it?"

He didn't answer, but he met her gaze with the lifeless eyes of a shark as he reached out to touch the controls. And suddenly she was falling. The impossibility of it hit her at the same time as she crashed painfully against cold, hard metal.

Spread-eagled against the grate, she struggled to remember which way was up. She'd fallen back and now lay crushed beneath at least ten Gs. *Baal still uses gravitational technology.* Daniel's words sprang vividly to mind, spoken that afternoon in her house with the spring sunshine outside and the whiteboard keeping the room in semi-darkness. *No floating cities or ships. It's much–* He'd stalled, swallowed something bitter. *It's on a smaller scale.*

A smaller scale. Like this. Gravitational manacles. She couldn't move a muscle, couldn't lift a finger. The panic that had been fluttering on the periphery of her mind took hold with a vengeance. She couldn't move. She couldn't fight. She was totally helpless! A claustrophobic scream expanded in her chest and sweat broke out on her forehead, trickling coldly down the side of her face. Only her eyes could move, and they fixed on the slowly approaching Jaffa. In his hand he held the dive knife she always carried off-world. He held it toward her, and like magic it lifted – or fell – until the point was leveled at her shoulder. "I am Hadat, servant of Baal," he told her. "You are Major Samantha Carter, of the Tauri. My master only wishes to know one thing from you." His other hand lifted and his thick fingers held her GDO. "The code to open the shield across the Tauri Chappa'ai."

Sam stared at the knife. She'd only ever used it for bivouacking or emergency repairs to her kit. But she knew it was sharp; it could cut sinewy wood like butter. It would cut sinews like butter too. The muscles in her arms bunched helplessly, rising panic painting a thousand nightmare images. If she could only move. If she only had a fighting chance!

"If you do not cooperate," Hadat continued, "I will bring your worst imaginings to life. Do you understand me, woman?"

Woman? She clung to frail shreds of outrage and forced herself to answer. Her voice was dry, but she'd be damned if she let it shake. "Serial number 63–" The knife fell, plunging into her shoulder like ice on fire. She couldn't even move enough to flinch. Air hissed through her teeth, but she refused to cry out.

Hadat smiled, a pitiless parting of lips over dark, stained teeth. "This is just the beginning." He sounded eager.

Closing her eyes, Sam fled to the back of her mind, miles away from the pain, and forced herself to wonder how Daniel had known about Baal's gravity tricks. It was a puzzle; she liked puzzles. She'd figure it out, and really everything else that was happening didn't matter. She could ignore the pain and figure out the puzzle. When she was done she knew her team would be there to free her.

Then she'd kick this bastard all the way to hell. And leave him there to rot.

CHAPTER SEVENTEEN

Instinctively, Daniel wrapped his arms around his head as he tumbled, bumping and bashing every single part of his body until, with a final thud, he came to rest on a cold, hard floor. Gravel and small shards of stone rained down after him, and he lay curled into a protective ball until it had stopped pattering against his jacket. At last everything was still and he risked uncurling. His right hip protested vigorously. But he could move his leg and the pain lacked the fire of a broken bone. No doubt he'd be turning sunset shades of purple in the next few days, but he could live with that. At least he could walk. Dust swirled in the air as he pushed himself to his feet, making him sneeze. Loudly. He winced at the noise echoing around him. Echoing…?

His flashlight lay on the floor a foot or two away, and as he bent to pick it up, Teal'c called down. "Daniel Jackson?"

"I'm okay." He waved the light up toward Teal'c. "I think I've found something."

The chamber was large by the standards of the fortress, the largest room they'd seen so far. Narrow pillars stood in familiar concentric rings, glinting with gold as the beam of his flashlight flitted across them.

"Daniel Jackson." The voice was startlingly close and Daniel almost jumped out of his boots.

"Teal'c!" Heart thudding, he peered at his friend. "How did you get down here?"

The Jaffa raised an eyebrow. "There are stairs," he replied. "The trapdoor you opened revealed them."

Daniel winced and shifted the weight off his bruised hip. "There were stairs?"

"Perhaps the opening mechanism was not intended to be activated from the position in which you were standing?"

An O'Neillism instantly sprang to mind, but Daniel simply shrugged. "I guess not." Stairs and bruised hips couldn't distract him for long. "Look at the architecture," he said, indicating the pillars with his flashlight. "Remind you of anywhere?"

Teal'c considered for a moment. "It reminds me of all Goa'uld palaces."

"No, no, the pattern of the pillars," Daniel prompted, wandering off into the small forest of gold. "Look at them. It's an exact copy of the shrine in Tsapan."

Teal'c followed, his own flashlight crossing Daniel's. "So it appears."

"And," Daniel added, his excitement mounting, "at the center of the Tsapan chamber, we found the Kinahhi anti-grav device. I knew it looked out of place! The Kinahhi must have devised their own power supply once Baal had been driven out. It was originally a *shrine*, not a control center. It was the center of Baal's power, literally as well as figuratively. The center of his religious power and the center of his physical power."

He moved on through the pillars. "But unlike the shrine on Tsapan, this is symbolic, not functional. So we're looking for an altar, possibly Canaanite, which would be a–" He stopped as his flashlight touched it. "A large stone platform. Ideal for offering sacrifices to your god." A god whose image was immediately before them.

Teal'c circled the altar from the other direction, the attention of both riveted on the golden statue that rose from the center of the dais. About three feet in height, it was a stylized image of Baal – or Re'ammin – complete with lightning bolt raised in one hand and thundercloud in the other. Its skin was gold, the tall Canaanite headpiece glittered red, with rubies or an alien equivalent, and its loincloth had the mellow off-white tinge of ivory. It was beautiful, but Daniel left all such details fluttering around the edges of his mind as he focused on one single fact.

"Its eyes glow."

Jack pressed himself against the inside of a small storeroom as dual footsteps clanked down the corridor outside. He listened carefully; definitely two men, one with a longer stride than the other and both heavily armored. They would do. Ideally he'd have preferred one opponent, but time was running out and he was taking too damn long creeping down the corridors of Jaffa Central. He needed to move faster; more than that, he needed an exit strategy. And this was it.

Pulling his zat from its holster he peered quickly into the corridor.

It was empty aside from the two Jaffa walking away from his hiding place. Readying himself, he stepped out behind them. "Hey."

The Jaffa spun around, startled.

He strolled forward, striving for nonchalance. "Is there a Krispy Kremes around here? There has to be one, right? I could kill for a Dulce de Leche."

The taller of the two raised his weapon and barked an order to his sidekick. "Jaffa kree!"

"Kree?" Jack repeated, still walking closer. "What is that? I mean, seriously – kree? No one's ever–" He fired. The first went down in a quivering tangle of limbs. The second just had time to ignite his staff weapon before he joined in his friend's involuntary break-dance on the floor.

Jack prodded the first with the toe of his boot. Out cold. Holstering the zat he grabbed the man's ankles and hurriedly dragged him back to the storeroom. The second man was heavier. "Too many damn Krispy Kremes," Jack grunted as he lugged the Jaffa's deadweight out of the corridor, his back protesting with every step.

Once they were lying side by side, slack-jawed and silent in the small room, Jack ran his eyes critically over the taller of the two. A little on the big side, but better that than too short. With a grimace, he squatted close to the man and fumbled for the straps of his armor. "Trust me," he muttered as his fingers encountered warm, sweaty flesh, "this is a hell of a lot worse for me than it is for you."

Daniel stood before the idol, staring at its softly glowing eyes. It was a beautiful face, actually, and bore little resemblance to the man he'd seen here, peeling Jack's soul from his body as mechanically as you'd peel the skin from an apple. Yet there was something of Baal's inhumanity in the frozen features of the statue. It was a mask, no different from a host's body, behind which true evil hid, dark and incomprehensible.

"Daniel Jackson?" Teal'c interrupted his musing with mild impatience. "Do you believe this is the power unit we seek?"

Slowly Daniel nodded. "It has to be. Something's making its eyes glow. And its location here, at the center of the worship of Re'ammin, is obviously significant."

"Then we must take it and leave," Teal'c declared, stepping up onto the stone dais. "We have still to locate a ship and–"

"No, wait!" Too late. A bright flare sizzled through the air as Teal'c reached for the statue, flinging his arm harshly backwards and sending him stumbling from the platform. Daniel winced. "It's, uh, shielded."

Teal'c flung him an accusatory glance and shook the pain from his hand. "So it appears."

"We need to cut the power," Daniel decided, circling the altar again. "There has to be a control panel somewhere."

Turning, Teal'c sent his flashlight crisscrossing the forest of pillars. "We do not have much time, Daniel Jackson. O'Neill and Major Carter will soon require a tel'tak for their escape."

Their escape? Daniel envied Teal'c his optimism. If they were doing to Sam what they'd done to Jack…? He was clinging on by his fingernails; what would it take to finally tip him over the edge?

"They will be waiting for us on the landing platform," Teal'c insisted. "We must hurry."

"Yeah," he agreed, forcing himself back to the here and now. He returned his attention to the image of Baal. "It's a good bet the controls to the force shield will be in one of the pillars nearby." He gestured behind him. "I'll take this half of the room."

With a nod, Teal'c turned and disappeared into the shadows on the other side, the beam of his flashlight tilting and bobbing as he moved. Daniel approached the first pillar. He couldn't shake the feeling that someone was watching him, and glancing over his shoulder he saw the baleful eyes of Baal's statue staring at him out of the darkness.

He stared back for a moment, willing the icon to reveal its secrets. But it remained silent and still. With a shiver, Daniel got down to work.

The droplet hung in the air, suspended in front of her like a moment in time. She stared at it, unable to move her head as the bead of liquid trembled above her right eye.

"The acid," came the voice of Hadat, her tormentor, "will eat through the soft tissue of your eye. And, from there, through the optic nerve and into your brain. Such a shame, to ruin a pretty face."

She closed her eyelids. At least she could do that. And if she couldn't see it, it wasn't there. Daniel. She brought him to mind instead, sitting earnestly in her living room, talking about Baal's gravity technology. How had he known? Was it possible that the colonel had told him about this? She didn't think he'd ever spoken to anyone about it, beyond the terse statement in his report: *I was interrogated for several days regarding the Tok'ra mission.* His clothes and Janet Fraiser's tight, appalled face had told a different story. But not one she'd ever heard in detail. Was it possible that–

"The code, Samantha. A few numbers to save you this torment. Such a pretty face. Such pretty eyes." Reluctantly her eyelids peeled open. Behind the tremulous drop of acid his killer eyes were bright. "A few numbers, Samantha. Or an agony you can't begin to imagine." He shook the knife from which the drop was suspended, making it tremble, and she wrenched her head sideways with an involuntary whimper. Damn it! She hated giving him that much. Even though she knew it was only the start. "Just give me the first number," he suggested. "Just the first one and I won't have to ruin your pretty–"

The door hissed open. "What is this?" Hadat growled angrily, turning toward the interruption. The knife fell to his side and the acid dripped onto the step of the dais, sizzling and burning its way through the stone. Sam felt sick, imagining her flesh bubbling in the same way; jaw clenched, she lifted her gaze to the distraction in the doorway. A single Jaffa stood there, face obscured by his helmet. He seemed to be staring at her. "Ya'ol'wa?" demanded Hadat.

Abruptly, and with a swiftness and economy of movement that seemed familiar, the newcomer raised a hand and pointed. "Jaffa," he said, his voice muffled by the helmet, "Kree!"

"Shak'ti'qua?" Hadat frowned.

The helmeted head nodded and said something else. Sam wasn't sure, but it sounded a lot like 'cappuccino'. She watched with hope beating hard in her throat. That voice, the way he moved…

Hadat circled the intruder, gesturing impatiently at the Jaffa's weapon. "Shel nor-ak." He looked nervous, glancing around for a weapon of his own. The knife he held, her knife, was pitifully inadequate against a staff weapon. *Not quite so confident, when your victim isn't pinned out like a lab rat, huh?*

The newcomer glanced down, lifted his staff weapon in both hands and said, "You want this?" Hadat blinked once, opened his mouth to answer, and was met with a savage blow from the butt of the weapon under his jaw. He fell back, blood gushing from his nose, and hit the ground with a brutal crack to the back of his head. Sam's knife fell from his limp hand and skittered across the floor. Then the electronic zing of a zat blast jerked Hadat into stillness and the doors to the room slid shut.

No one spoke. Her rescuer was just staring at her, as if transfixed. Sam stared back, half-delirious with relief and adrenaline, her mind running in circles. A laugh, lurking on the borders of hysteria, bubbled up as words sprang unbidden to her lips. "Aren't you a little short for a Jaffa?"

It broke the moment, and in a flurry of movement the helmet retreated into the armor to reveal Colonel O'Neill. His face was at once ashen and flushed, jaw tight and eyes bright. "Carter." It was little more than a heartfelt murmur, spoken as he stepped over the inert body of Hadat and cautiously came toward her. Compassion, dismay, relief and other, less defined emotions, darted across his guarded features as he drew nearer. "I should have gotten here sooner. I shouldn't have–"

"Don't get too close!"

He froze, glanced down at the floor and up again.

"Sir? The control panel. On the platform."

Nodding, he was up there in two strides, staring in confusion at the controls. She could see his lips moving as he muttered to himself, hands hovering indecisively over the alien device. "Any ideas, Carter?"

Not really. "The power switch should be one of the larger controls."

He glanced up, shrugged slightly, and pressed something. An invisible rock slammed into Sam's chest, compressing her lungs until she could barely draw breath. "No!" she hissed desperately. "Not that one!"

The colonel's head shot up. "Which one Carter? I don't wanna–" His gaze moved past her, down into the blackness behind the grate. And she had the sudden, horrifying sensation of being suspended over an abyss by nothing more than a treacherous spider's web.

She fought for another gulp of air. But it wasn't enough. "Sir…" A whole cosmos of pin-prick lights were prancing through her spinning head. The world was fading to gray at the edges.

"I don't know which one!" O'Neill's voice was muffled and far away. The gray was turning to black, the stars were winking out, and she was falling and falling and falling into darkness.

Daniel stood staring at the pillar in front of him, his flashlight glinting softly on the gold leaf that covered the stone. Upon it, in the same Ugaritic characters as on the pillar in the room above, was a name cartouche. "Baal-Gad." He said the words quietly to himself, searching briefly for the meaning. "Lord of Good Fortune." Who said the Goa'uld didn't have a sense of humor? He ran his fingers over the inscription and pressed gently. But there was no sliding of stone-on-stone, and no static hiss as the force shield dropped. He turned and moved on. The next pillar was plain, the next decorated with a stylized lightning bolt. The third, however, bore another cartouche. The name in this one read, "Baal-Hammon." Lord of Wealth. That, at least, was appropriate. Again, he pressed the cartouche to no effect.

"Daniel Jackson!" Teal'c's voice drifted from the other side of the room. "I have found a cartouche upon a pillar. The language is not Goa'uld, however. I am unfamiliar with its origin."

Daniel turned and squinted through the gloom. "It's Ugaritic Cuneiform, from the city state of Ugarit about 12000 BC. Whether it originated there, however, or somewhere off-world is anyone's guess. But Baal was a principal deity in Canaan so—"

"Daniel Jackson," Teal'c interrupted, "do you believe this inscription is of use to us?"

"Ah, maybe," Daniel mused, nodding. "I've found a couple over here too. Looks like all of Baal's epithets. Baal-Gad, Baal-Hammon." He moved along, flashlight searching for the next cartouche, "Baal-Meon. That means Lord of the Dwelling... Ah, here's an appropriate one – Baal-Ze'bub. Lord of Flies. Flies and disease." He chuckled darkly. "Beelzebub, or Satan – very apt."

"Did not Sokar adopt that persona?"

"Sokar was the Egyptian version. I guess there's no monopoly on absolute evil." He concluded his circuit around the dais and came to stand with Teal'c. "Plenty to go around."

"Without doubt," Teal'c agreed, then indicated the pillar before him. "The inscription is here."

Daniel looked. "Baal-Peor," he translated. "Lord of the Opening."

"Opening?"

"Too obvious," Daniel assured him as he touched the carving. "I mean, that would be tantamount to saying Open Sesame and–" Beneath his fingers the stone moved inwards. Daniel flinched, braced for either himself or the ceiling to fall. Neither happened. Instead, at the foot of the pillar, a small door slid back to reveal the glowing crystals of Goa'uld technology. Eyebrows raised, he glanced ruefully at Teal'c. "Open Sesame."

"Sir…" Carter's voice whispered through the room, her eyes rolling back.

Panic rising, O'Neill stared at the incomprehensible control panel in front of him. The lights and buttons blurred into a chaotic mosaic, a jumble of meaningless color. He had no clue. No damn clue! The gray of Carter's lips was seeping up into her face. She wasn't breathing. There was no time! Standing back he leveled the staff weapon at the control panel and fired. Sparks and flame flared high into the room, electrical wiring fizzed, and the lights on the console gutted and died. A bloom of acrid smoke filled his lungs, choking him as he raced down the steps and back toward the gravity wall. For an instant he panicked; Carter was gone. The grate had opened, plunging her into death and– Then he saw her, crumpled at its base. The gravity field was dead.

Heart pounding, he rolled her onto her back and pressed his fingers to her neck, bending close to her mouth until he felt a tickle of air against his skin. Thank God! A steady pulse and good breaths. Sitting back, he took her chin between his fingers and started to shake her gently. "Carter, wake up. We gotta go."

She stirred groggily and groaned.

"Carter!" The fire in the circuitry was crackling nicely, and he knew it could only be minutes – maybe moments – before Larry, Curly and Moe came to investigate. "Come on! On your feet."

Her eyes opened, disoriented and afraid for an instant. Then recognition and memory surfaced and she was back with him, pushing herself up from the floor. "What happened?"

"I couldn't find the off-switch." Offering her a hand up, he glanced toward the door. "We need to get out of here."

"Wait," she said, letting him pull her to her feet, but resisting his tug toward the door. She was staring at the sprawled body of the Jaffa who'd been interrogating her. *Interrogating?* What a wonderful euphemism. "Sir, may I use your zat?"

Normally he wouldn't have hesitated, but her serene tone unnerved him. "Carter?"

"I promised myself I'd kick his ass to hell." She sounded positively icy, so restrained she might as well have been still pinned against the gravity wall.

Jack shifted, uncomfortable with seeing so much of himself in that oh-so controlled demeanor. "Consider it kicked, Carter. Come on, we gotta–"

"He's not in hell yet." There was a plea in her voice that he couldn't ignore. He couldn't give in to it either.

"In cold blood, Carter?" She held his gaze, but rage flickered behind her polished military façade. "That's not who you are." That was the kind of thing he'd do, not Carter. "You're better than that."

She shook her head, a hand pressing against the wound on her shoulder. It needed to be dressed. "How many people do you think have been through here?" she asked distantly "How many more will be?"

"Killing him won't change that." He knew it for a fact. "And it won't make you feel any better."

Carter turned away, staring at the grate and studying it closely. He followed her gaze, tracing the hated contours with his mind. It was an abomination. The whole room was an abomination.

Suddenly he knew what he had to do, what he'd wanted to do since the day he'd stumbled home with Shallan in tow. Feeling oddly disembodied, as if acting on a some kind of divine plan, he stepped in front of Carter. The dissipating smoke swirled around the dark metal of the gravity wall, and he could almost see his own blood mingling with Carter's on its bars. Breath motionless in his lungs, the retching stench of acid and fear in his mouth, he raised the zat and fired. And fired again. Then, without pleasure or pain, he fired for a third time. The monstrosity blinked and shimmered out of existence, leaving only the yawning blackness beyond. From inside the Jaffa armor Jack pulled one of the two concussion grenades he'd retrieved from his vest. "Carter!" She turned and he tossed it to her.

"Do the honors."

Her expression was curiously blank as she yanked the safety pin and slipped her finger through the pull ring. She stepped closer to the pit, the one he'd fallen into too many times to remember. Silent words fluttered over her lips before she tugged the ring and hurled the grenade with enough power to send the damn thing to hell.

The detonation shook the entire room. Smoke and dust belched from the pit like a parody of an opening Stargate. And if that didn't raise the alarm he didn't know what the hell would. Jack didn't plan to find out. Activating the helmet on his armor he cursed as his vision narrowed to the impractical slit through which the Jaffa viewed the world. How the hell did anyone ever fight in these things? Fumbling for the staff weapon he grabbed Carter's arm and pulled her toward the door. "Time to go, Major. Try to look defeated." It wouldn't be hard.

Stepping out into the corridor, he could already hear the clanking of running men in armor. Hoping for the best, he pushed Carter ahead of him and leveled his staff-weapon at her back. Head bowed, she gave a damn convincing performance as the cowed prisoner.

"Let's go," he hissed. And together, with nothing but a thin disguise between them and catastrophe, they marched into the face of the enemy.

CHAPTER EIGHTEEN

General George Hammond disliked Councilor Damaris from the moment she glided into the large, white conference room at the heart of the Kinahhi government complex. Her gaze drifted up and down his uniformed length with a disdain she didn't bother to hide, and she pointedly addressed her words to Crawford.

"You bring more soldiers, Ambassador? After the actions of Colonel O'Neill you cannot imagine that is acceptable."

"I–"

Hammond didn't give him time to finish. "Ma'am," he said, stepping forward, "my name is Major General Hammond. I'm the leader of Stargate Command, and as such am the commanding officer of Colonel O'Neill and his team. You have made some serious allegations about my people, and I'm here to investigate."

So quick you'd miss it if you hadn't spent a decade in close company with politicians, Damaris flicked a glance at Crawford that made him square his shoulders and stand straight. Almost at attention, and definitely edgy. His reaction gave him away; compared with the Kinahhi he had all the subtlety of a Goa'uld. "There is nothing to investigate," Damaris said smoothly. "Ambassador Crawford, I believe, has shown you the evidence of Colonel O'Neill's guilt?"

Hammond shook his head. "The stolen blueprints in Colonel O'Neill's possession is the only evidence that will convince me, or any court of law in the United States." He paused. "I gather you searched SG-1 before they left, and found nothing?"

"Lack of evidence does not prove their innocence," Damaris stated. "We know the plans were put into their possession."

"Where I'm from, Councilor, that's just not good enough. Your allegations can't be ignored, but your evidence is lacking. I'm here to find out the truth." He looked over at Crawford. "I'm sure that's what we all want."

Crawford jutted out his chin. "The truth," he said, "is already in front of you. You're just too stubborn to see it. This little masquerade won't save your people, General. They've gone too far this time."

"We'll see." Hammond turned back to the cool face of the Kinahhi councilor. "I'd like to see SG-1's accommodation while they were here," he said. "Just in case there's something your people missed."

Narrow-eyed, Damaris nodded to a weather-beaten soldier, not far from O'Neill's age. He broke rank and fell in at Hammond's side. "Commander Kenna, please escort General Hammond to plaza 101," she told him. "Offer any assistance he may require, within reason."

"I appreciate your help, ma'am," Hammond began, suspicious of her easy capitulation, but refusing to sacrifice good manners. "I'm sure–"

"Ambassador?" Damaris's attention left him, a deliberate snub. "Have you brought the treaty documents? The Security Council is keen to finally sign the agreement with your people."

"Your wisdom and patience are much appreciated, Councilor," Crawford oozed, turning his back on Hammond. "And I trust this will mark a fresh start in the relations between the Tauri and the Kinahhi…"

Warily, Hammond watched them walk away. He didn't give a damn about the woman's good opinion, or Crawford's, but he was beginning to wonder if she was less subtle than she imagined. Her pointed rebuff spoke of anger, and in his experience the root of all anger lay in fear. The question was, why was Councilor Damaris afraid of him? What was she hiding? And did he have an ice cube's chance in Houston of finding out?

With a determined sigh, he turned to the man at his side – Commander Kenna. As reserved as Damaris, a soldier hid behind the man's alien eyes and Hammond knew he was looking at a kindred spirit. Politicians were anathema to all good military men the galaxy over, or so it seemed.

"Please follow me, General," Kenna offered, quite properly keeping his thoughts to himself.

"Thank you, son." Hammond braced himself for another tour through the endless white corridors of Kinahhi bureaucracy.

Small wonder Colonel O'Neill hated this place; it was like the Pentagon in triplicate.

Teal'c crouched before the control panel, eyeing the glowing crystals and wishing for Major Carter's knowledge. Shutting down the power should be a simple task, but he knew the tricky minds of the Goa'uld and feared that any tampering would either raise silent alarms or mete out arbitrary punishment, most likely in the form of sudden, painful death.

"What if we pulled them all out?" Daniel Jackson suggested, peering over Teal'c's shoulder. "Would that work?"

"It may," Teal'c agreed. "Or it may cause the device to self-destruct, killing us both in the resulting explosion."

There was a pause. "So maybe not. How about the green one? Just pull the green one out and see what happens."

Teal'c threw a glance over his shoulder. "Do you wish to do this yourself, Daniel Jackson?"

His friend backed off a step. "No. No, I was just… You know. Trying to help."

"Your silence," Teal'c observed, "would be most helpful."

Eyebrows climbing, Daniel Jackson opened his mouth to answer. Then closed it and offered a sheepish smile. Then frowned, clearly thinking of something else and again opened his mouth to speak. Just then, a distant explosion rumbled through the complex, dislodging some of the rubble above them and sending it tumbling down the stairs in a cloud of rocky dust. Daniel Jackson flinched and glanced up. Another noise was chasing the heels of the explosion, a screeching sound of failing metal. It was much, much closer. "That doesn't sound good."

Teal'c followed his friend's gaze to the mosaic ceiling. In the room above something large and heavy thudded to the floor – more masonry, he suspected. Dust motes sifted through the small tiles, one of which fell, tinkling to the stone floor. It did not bode well.

"We'd, ah, better hurry," Daniel said calmly, gaze flicking up to the ceiling and back.

Without further conversation Teal'c turned back to the crystals. His fingers hovered, and eventually landed on the green one. "Daniel Jackson, I will–"

Thunder detonated above him. The air turned thick and choking and something heavy slammed against his back. It knocked the breath from his lungs and smashed him hard into the floor. A crushing weight pressed him down, heavy and growing heavier. Breathing became arduous. A waterfall of rocks fell just feet from his blurring eyes, suffocating the room with dirt. His lips and mouth were coated.

"Teal'c!" Daniel Jackson was yelling his name. "Teal'c!" Suddenly the weight on his chest lifted a fraction. He could breathe more easily. But he could not move. Had he still possessed the power of his symbiote... But no, even now, he would not regret its loss. Better to die free than to live as a slave.

As the avalanche abated sounds resurfaced. The closest were soft grunts of effort. He strained to turn his head and saw Daniel Jackson with his shoulder wedged under the broken pillar that pinned Teal'c to the floor. In the hazy beam of his flashlight he could see the strain on his friend's face as he braced it, his human strength the only thing between Teal'c and crushing suffocation.

"Go!" Teal'c managed to say. "I cannot move."

"No!" Daniel grunted. "Not leaving."

Teal'c coughed, but there was no room to draw adequate breath and he felt his lungs begin to spasm. He plunged down into his own mind, a journey well paved by years of kelnoreem, and took control of his body, coaxing his lungs to relax. Air trickled in, and slowly his eyes opened. He found them resting on a dull, red light mere inches from his face. It was one of the Goa'uld crystals. It must have fallen free when the pillar fell. "The force shield," he asked, dismayed by the wheeze in his voice. "Is it deactivated?"

"Can't see," Daniel grunted in response. "Teal'c, you gotta move. I can't hold this forever."

"Then go," Teal'c growled. "Take the power unit. Find O'Neill and–"

"I said no!" Anger flared in his friend's voice. "Now help me!"

Stubborn. As stubborn as O'Neill. With a grunt of effort, Teal'c pressed his back up against the pillar, forcing his arms to push up, struggling to create enough space to get his legs beneath him. Muscles shaking, something sharp cutting into his shoulder, he pushed up and into the pillar.

"Yes!" Daniel Jackson hissed. "It's moving."

Teal'c roared his frustration as he pressed up, arms screaming in pain. At last he got a knee under him and leaned his back into the endeavor. Above him Jackson was snarling with his own effort. "Get out!" he gasped. "I can hold it!"

Muscles trembling with the effort, Teal'c squeezed from beneath the pillar, tearing flesh and clothing as he slithered over the jagged, broken stone.

With a final yell, Daniel Jackson jumped free and the pillar crashed into the floor. He was breathing hard and dabbing curiously at a scratch on the side of his face, glasses opaque with grime and slightly askew.

"I am in your debt," Teal'c gasped.

"I thought we quit keeping score years ago." Daniel Jackson sneezed and glanced up at the collapsed ceiling. The worst had fallen between themselves and the staircase to the room above. Had they been beneath it, they would not have survived. "We were lucky."

Teal'c acknowledged the truth silently.

"On the plus side," his friend continued, turning to look behind him, "the force shield is down."

Teal'c stared at the mound of rubble that now covered the altar. "It appears we shall have to excavate the statue."

"I guess we'll be needing an archeologist then..."

Teal'c didn't comment, although he noted the glint of humor in his friend's eyes. Instead, he simply followed him to the place where the icon had once stood and began helping him to pull away the rubble with his bare hands.

Sam tried not to react as six Jaffa hove into view around a bend in the corridor. Smoke curled from the open doors of the torture room behind her, and she hoped it would be enough to distract them.

"Pa'kree?" barked the Jaffa leader, slowing the pace of his men.

Sam slowed too and every muscle in her body coiled in anticipation. Three-to-one odds, only she wasn't armed and her shoulder thrummed with numbing pain, leaving her left arm hanging virtually useless. Still, they'd faced worse and–

The startling jab of a staff weapon in her back sent her stumbling. "Kree!" snarled the colonel, one hand seizing her good shoulder and roughly urging her forward. With the staff weapon he gestured back toward the smoke. "Tauri!"

The Jaffa seemed unsure, but O'Neill simply ignored him and shoved her forward again. Fate balanced like a blade standing on its tip. Sam decided to give it a push in their favor. "You bastard!" she growled at the colonel, breaking free of his grip. "You'll never win against us! You'll never–"

The colonel slapped her face, hard. Reeling back, hand over her split lip, she tasted blood. But O'Neill didn't pause. Grabbing her arm, he hauled her away from the Jaffa.

"I'm gonna make you pay for this!" she yelled for effect, twisting in his grip just far enough to see the troop of Jaffa turn and start jogging back toward the smoke. Then suddenly she was being yanked around a corner and they were out of sight. Thank God. O'Neill loosened his hold on her arm, but didn't speak or let go. Less than twenty meters further on he stopped outside a small, nondescript door. With a brief glance either way he opened it and pulled her inside.

Two Jaffa lay trussed and semi-conscious on the floor, alongside the colonel's tac vest and half his kit. Including a P90. The sight of the gun made her fingers itch for her own lost weapon; she felt naked without it.

This hiss of the Jaffa helmet opening drew her attention back to O'Neill. He looked concerned as he gestured toward her face. "Sorry about the lip. How is it?"

Painful, she thought, running a light finger over the swelling. "Fine. You fooled them."

"Yeah." He started unbuckling his armor. "You need to see to that shoulder. There's a med-kit in my vest." He lifted the heavy breastplate from his shoulders and dropped it with obvious relief on the floor. "Gah!" he muttered, sniffing disgustedly at his T-shirt.

Ferreting through the vest, she found the med-kit and lowered herself to the floor. She could feel bruises running the length of her back and legs, an imprint of the grate she'd been compressed against. With her good arm, she dragged the med-kit into her lap and found a sterile dressing. Pulling down the neck of her T-shirt she winced as the fabric plucked at the wound beneath. The ragged edges of the gash opened like bloody, swollen lips. Gritting her teeth she slid the dressing over the top, pressed down and wondered how to reach the adhesive bandage.

"I'll get it." The colonel crouched in front of her, now free of the Jaffa armor, sweat-damp and carefully avoiding her eyes. "I should have gotten to you sooner," he muttered as he slid the bandage under her shirt and around her shoulder, binding it tight enough to staunch the bleeding.

He felt guilty? "Sir, you couldn't–"

"You need a shot of antibiotics," he added, tying off the bandage with a professional twist. "God knows who else that knife's been in."

Sam smiled bleakly, trying to forget the image of it suspended above her like the executioner's blade. "It was mine," she said quietly. "My dive knife."

O'Neill grunted and prepared the antibiotic shot, lifting the syringe to the light until a tiny drop of liquid beaded on its tip. Sam shivered as she stared at it. "He dipped it into acid," she heard herself say. "When you came in, he was going to drop it into my eye and–"

"Don't." Jaw clenched, he stared at the needle for a moment. Far away.

Sam closed her eyes, the sickening truth turning her hot and cold; he had lived the very nightmare she'd escaped. Lived through it over and over again, each time knowing what was to come. And no one had rescued him. No one had saved him. Dear God, how the hell had he stayed sane? "Sir, I wish–"

"Don't," he said again, more softly this time. "It's over. It's done." With that, she felt the sharp jab of the needle in her arm and the firm pressure of his thumb over the pin-prick wound. "We need to get moving."

Looking up, she nodded. "Thanks, sir."

Half a smile touched his tense face. "For the shot?"

"For coming after me."

He stood, hefting his vest and stuffing the med-kit back into a pocket, once more avoiding her gaze. "What else was I gonna do,

Carter? Run away and leave you here?"

Maybe, she thought, catching the note of self-reproach in his voice. It told her more about what he'd suffered here than anything else. That he'd come after her anyway, despite the demons riding him, reminded her that nothing she felt about this man's courage and loyalty was unwarranted. She rose, ignoring the sudden light-headed tilt to the room. "Let's get out of here, sir."

For a moment he met her eyes, a tiny acknowledgement of the truth. Then he slipped on his tac-vest and reached for the P90. "Daniel and Teal'c should be waiting for us on the roof. With the power unit and a getaway car."

She smiled. "A fast one?"

"It'd better be." He tossed her his zat. "Let's go."

"That's it!" Beneath the rocks and rubble Daniel saw the glint of a ruby encrusted headpiece. It had taken half an hour of finger-bleeding digging to reach the statue, the whole time conscious that the rest of the ceiling could land on their heads if they so much as sneezed. But at last, there it was, as coldly beautiful as before.

Teal'c worked uncomplainingly at his side, although Daniel suspected he must have cracked a rib, or worse, when the pillar landed on him. Not that he'd ever complain. Teal'c meant 'strength' and his parents had named him well.

"You pull," Daniel suggested as he pushed and shoved the stones out of the way. A golden face came into view, and to Daniel's absolute relief its eyes still glowed soft yellow. The cave-in hadn't damaged the power unit. Teal'c wrapped his large hands around the statue's head and leaned back with all his weight; not really the recommended method of excavation, but in a pinch anything would do. Teal'c pulled, Daniel pushed at the rocks, and little by little the statue emerged until the whole thing was freed and it lay prone amid the rubble. An ignominious fall for a god.

Squatting in front of it, Daniel ran his fingers over the smooth lines of the sculpture. It was truly a piece of art.

"The power unit must be concealed within," Teal'c said, standing above him like the voice of reason.

A trickle of dirt pattered down onto the broken pillar behind them. Daniel wondered what exactly was holding up the ceiling, then decided it was better not to wonder. With a sigh, he rolled the heavy statue over. But the back was as smooth as the front – so where the hell did you put the batteries? He let his fingers explore, touching, twisting, and experimenting as he looked for something that might trigger a release mechanism. But there was nothing. "Help me stand it up," he said after a while, his frustration growing.

Once on its feet, he cupped its face with both hands and explored lightly along the jaw line. In the back of his mind he heard the warning note in Teal'c's voice, "Daniel Jackson..." but ignored it. Finally, his questing fingers found an anomaly on the smooth metal skin. The tiniest of lumps, one on each side of its neck. Eyes still fixed on the statue he pressed down hard. For a moment nothing happened, and then he heard a slight hiss.

"Watch out!" he yelled. Jerking his hands free, Daniel jumped back as a thin green mist shot from around the statue's neck. Extending no further than three feet in radius, it fell to the floor like rain, hissing against the stones.

"Poison," Teal'c observed.

"Nice." Climbing to his feet, Daniel wiped his hands on his pants. "Look," he said, nodding at the statue. The light was fading from its eyes in a slow parody of death. Carefully, Daniel reached into a pocket and pulled out his bandana. He approached the statue cautiously and wrapped its headpiece in the cloth. It only took a gentle twist for the section to come loose, and he lifted it carefully and set it on the floor. Keeping his distance, he peered inside. A silver cylinder sat within the body of the figure, emitting a faint violet light. "Take a look," he invited Teal'c, glancing up over the tops of his glasses. "Does that look Goa'uld to you?"

Teal'c shook his head. "It does not."

"Bingo!"

An eyebrow cocked in response.

"Bingo. You know, B.I.N.G.O?"

The eyebrow climbed higher.

"Never mind." Binding a hand in his bandanna, Daniel reached in warily and touched the alien device. Nothing happened. More confidently, he slipped his fingers around it and pulled. It slid free with a smooth click. Twelve inches long, it was beautiful in its simplicity, and as he carefully laid it on the floor he could see familiar markings engraved on its metallic surface. "Derigo chao," he read, glancing up at Teal'c. "To bring order to chaos. It's written in Ancient."

Teal'c considered for a moment. "Those are not words of war."

"No," Daniel agreed, carefully wrapping the soft cloth around the device. "Wouldn't be the first time the Goa'uld have used peaceful technology to wage war." And not just the Goa'uld. He glanced up. "We need to get this to Sam."

If she's still alive. The thought popped out of nowhere, chilling him. Swallowing hard, he emptied MRE's out of a pocket in his tac vest and settled the power unit snuggly inside.

"We must hurry," Teal'c said quietly. "O'Neill will be displeased if we are tardy."

Tardy? Daniel shook his head, amused by the choice of words, and rose to his feet. "Come on," he said. "Let's go steal a ship."

CHAPTER NINETEEN

The stairs seemed endless, marked only by the dimming glow of his flashlight and the rhythmic throbbing of his right knee. Carter climbed ahead of him, head bowed and silent. Her injured left arm hung limply at her side, the zat clutched tightly in her right hand.

She hadn't said much since they'd left the storeroom, but he could feel her tension like static in the air. He'd rarely seen her so on edge. Not that he blamed her. The image of her plastered across the landscape of his own nightmare lurked dangerously in the back of his mind. Had he looked that vulnerable? Had he looked that frightened? The thought churned around and around, a noxious mixture of anger and panic. Only a few times in his life had he been truly helpless, and each one had threatened to unravel what passed for his sanity. He suspected each one still could, if he let himself think too much.

"Carter?" He spoke more to distract himself than because he had something to say.

She turned and glanced back at him. "Sir?"

"Let's take a breather. My knee's killing me."

She said nothing, just watched as he unhooked a canteen from the back of his belt and handed it to her. After a couple of mouthfuls, she handed it back.

"When did you last eat?" he asked.

"Not sure. I'm not hungry, sir."

"Come on, Carter, you know better than that." You ate when you could, not when you were hungry. Delving into a vest pocket, he pulled out a couple of Mainstay bars. "Mmmmm," he enthused in his best Homer Simpson, "artificial vanilla flavoring…."

It earned him a glimmer of a smile as she took the rations from his hand. "Mouth watering."

He peeled open his own bar and took an unenthusiastic bite. "You know, seriously, my knee is going to give up the ghost if we don't get to the roof soon."

Carter nodded and nibbled at the end of her ration bar, staring up the stairs in silence. For a moment he thought he'd lost her, that she was back down there with the knives and the acid. Clearing his throat, he was about to yank her out when she spoke. "I think I can see some light, sir."

"Really?" Stepping up level with her, he lowered his flashlight. After a moment his eyes adjusted and he could see what she meant. A very faint halo of light was glowing on the right-hand wall. "That's it. That's the roof."

"There'll be Jaffa up there."

"Nothing we can't handle Carter."

"Last time–"

"Last time was last time." He stuffed the remains of his Mainstay bar back into his vest. "We've taken knocks before, Carter. It's no different." Only it was, and they both knew it. But he wasn't about to admit that. He needed her focused. "Finish up and start moving. You know how Teal'c gets if we're late."

"Yes, sir." Tucking the barely-touched rations into the pocket of her pants, she took a deep breath and started climbing. He followed, and they walked in a silence that seemed to deepen with each step.

Slowly the light brightened into strips that ran beneath a set of double doors and in a line down their center. As they drew near, imperceptibly at first, they began to slow. *She* began to slow. It put Jack on edge; she was reminding him too much of himself. By the time they were ten steps from the door they'd stopped, and Carter was staring at it like it was the enemy.

"I'll be back in a minute," he told her carefully, taking the remaining steps two at a time – much to the outrage of his right knee – and pressing his ear against the door. Beyond, he heard the scuff of booted feet, a muffled order, and the quiet whine of engines at rest. Their luck had held.

Trotting back to Carter, he kept his voice low. "Sounds like we're in the right place. I can hear engine noise and movement. But I don't think the party's started yet."

"So we wait?" She sounded doggedly normal.

"We wait." Moving closer, he whispered, "Carter, you hanging in there?"

"What do you mean?"

"I mean, are you okay?" He knew she understood everything that little word encompassed.

She flashed him an angry smile. "I'm fine, sir. Ready to kick some Jaffa ass."

Oh, *so* not fine. "Carter–"

"Sir. I'm not going to let you down."

"I know that." What else could he say? He knew what she was feeling, he'd been there and bought the T-shirt. Repeatedly. There was absolutely nothing to say. So he changed the subject. "You don't have a vest. When it goes down, try to stay behind me."

"Yes, sir." But he doubted she would. Behind her eyes and the automatic reply lurked something dark. Like him, she knew there were things worse than death. Capture being the worst of them.

Daniel stared at the bank of ring devices in astonishment. Ten rows of ten, all neatly aligned in a grid, each set of rings was only large enough to hold two men: a death glider flight crew.

"Many Goa'uld fortresses and Ha'taks have such facilities," Teal'c told him, circling the control panel. "It enables the speedy deployment of fighters in case of surprise attack."

He eyed the smoke-damaged, waterlogged room dubiously. "Are they still working?" He doubted any Jaffa had been scrambled from here since Lord Yu had brought the place to its knees.

Teal'c didn't answer immediately, concentrating on the controls. When he looked up, there was a hint of triumph in his face. "We have been fortunate, Daniel Jackson."

Blowing out a slow breath, Daniel reached for his gun and moved to stand inside one of the rings. "You know we're going to have a welcoming committee up there, right?"

"I do. We must be prepared to defend ourselves."

"Right." That easy.

After touching the controls, Teal'c moved to stand next to Daniel inside the set of rings. "I will secure the area behind us," he said, readying his staff weapon. "You concentrate on the area before."

"Got it," Daniel nodded. "Front. I can do that." And it wasn't a lie. Who'd have thought, when he entered grad school, that a decade and a half later he'd be wielding a gun like a pro? Certainly not him, not in a million years.

"Standby." Teal'c ducked into a defensive crouch. "Three, two, one–"

Whap, whap, whap.

Short and dizzying, the experience was almost more disorientating than 'gate travel. As the rings whipped up from around them, Daniel found himself standing on a windswept, blast-damaged rooftop, with gray clouds scudding overhead and at least a dozen astonished Jaffa staring at him.

For a moment, no one moved. Then someone yelled, "Shibio diu!" and all hell broke loose.

The sounds of a firefight bled through the doors, along with the welcome rattle of a P90.

"Party's started," the colonel murmured, heading up the stairs. "Let's go join the fun."

Stomach twisted into a knot, Sam nodded but didn't answer. Speaking required effort, and she had none to spare from the struggle to keep her anger at bay. It was like a live thing, frightening and unpredictable. That single drop of acid hovered before her mind's eye, waiting to fall. All she could think about was how many times it had dropped and burned into the colonel. How many times he'd screamed. And how she hadn't been there to save him. Not one time. It made her want to howl with rage, at herself and the bastard who had tortured him. *And you*, a quiet voice reminded her, *they tortured you too*. She silenced it. She didn't care about that. Certainly not enough to make her this afraid.

Afraid? The word caught her unawares and she stumbled, causing Colonel O'Neill to glance at her uneasily.

Ignoring the look, she kept on climbing. *Not afraid*, she corrected herself. *Angry.* She was angry. Angry at what the colonel had endured. She reminded herself of that fact with every step as she followed him up the stairs and watched him listen at the door.

"Sounds like they're on the other side of the roof," he whispered. "Get the doors open, Carter. And stay sharp."

The controls were simple. Her fingers slid over them mechanically and obediently the doors drew back to admit a blast of cold air and a flood of thin light. She squinted, pressing herself flat against the wall while her eyesight adjusted. The colonel was on the opposite side of the door, and as her vision cleared she watched him cautiously peer around its edge. Following his example she saw a dozen Jaffa arrayed around a huge landing platform dotted with burned-out death gliders. They were harrying two familiar figures. Daniel ducked behind the remains of a rusting glider, raking the Jaffa with gunfire, while Teal'c raced headlong for a serviceable looking tel'tak that sat halfway between him and herself.

"Go!" O'Neill hissed, slipping out of the door.

Heart hammering, she followed and did a swift three-sixty. No one behind them, all attention was fixed on Daniel and Teal'c. Silently, the colonel signaled her toward the tel'tak while he crept up on the Jaffa who had Daniel pinned down. He took cover behind the ruined walls of what might once have been a storage facility. Running at a low crouch, Sam was almost at the tel'tak when O'Neill opened fire. Single shots. Three Jaffa went down.

With angry yells, the remaining men turned their weapons on the new threat, blasting chunks of stone as the colonel dove behind the crumbling wall.

"Hey!" Daniel yelled, breaking cover and opening fire in a wide arc, sending more Jaffa sprawling to the ground. Sam kept running, her wounded shoulder pounding with each step, until she was within the shadow of the tel'tak. Keeping low, she searched for the doorway, creeping silently, each movement focused and controlled. It was all about control. Control your anger, control your fear. She was almost there, almost inside the ship where she could–

"Stop!" The business end of a staff weapon jabbed into her ribs and she froze. "Disarm, or die where you stand." The fingers on her weapon went slack as, slowly, she turned her head. A young Jaffa, almost a boy, stood staring at her through hate-glazed eyes.

They mirrored her own, she suspected.

Caught between the Devil and the deep blue sea, Jack thought as the last of the Jaffa fell to Daniel's gunfire. They hadn't stood a chance once he'd come in on their six. Bad tactics; always cover your ass. High on adrenaline and victory, he vaulted over the blasted stone wall and strode toward Daniel. The air was ripe with the battle-scents of ozone, gun-powder and blood, and he couldn't help a feral grin that spread across his face. They'd done it again!

"You're getting good with that thing," he called as Daniel emerged from behind the rusting glider. "They're gonna have to start paying you more."

"They pay per scalp these days?" Daniel's uncomfortable glance only briefly touched the fallen Jaffa, before skittering away toward the tel'tak. Hopefully Teal'c and Carter were safe inside.

"Them or us," Jack reminded him. But Daniel's distaste served to puncture his battle-high, bringing him slowly down to Earth. Or wherever.

"Talking of which," Daniel said, "I saw Sam with you. Is she okay?"

Good question. He shrugged slightly, avoiding his friend's inquisitive gaze. "She will be."

There was a long pause, and he knew damn well what Daniel was wondering. In the end, being Daniel, he came out and asked. "Did they hurt–"

"Yeah." Jack looked away, out across the cloudy, rain-sodden sky. He heard Daniel's muttered curse, snatched away by the wind, adding another half-turn to the guilt that twisted inside. He should have gone after her right away, not hidden in the dark like a kicked dog. A whining dog. A whining–

Daniel's head snapped up. "Did you hear that?"

He did. A distinct whining sound, growing louder. Turning into a roar… "Get down!" Flinging himself at Daniel, they hit the ground in a tangle of limbs. A blast detonated a foot from their position, showering them with plasma-scorched stone. Death gliders. One screamed overhead, a second on its tail, strafing the ground. The first banked high, coming back around for another pass. Scrabbling behind the frail shelter of the grounded glider, Jack grabbed for the radio on his shoulder. He knew damn well what their target would be. "Teal'c! Carter! Scramble!"

Half on his back, Daniel raised his P90 and fired uselessly as a glider tore across the sky on its second pass. Shrapnel and smoke scorched the air, the noise so loud Jack barely heard the static squawk of his radio. "O'Neill." It was Teal'c. "Major Carter is not aboard. "

"What?" He risked a glance over the rusting metal. All he could see was the bulk of the tel'tak. "Where is she?"

"I do not know, I have not–"

Damn it. "Go!" he yelled. "Get airborne. Now!"

Teal'c didn't reply. But the tel'tak roared into life, taking off at an impossibly steep angle, twisting up into the sky with a scream of its own. Jack's radio crackled again. "O'Neill, hold fast. I shall return."

And with that, the tel'tak sheared off into the low clouds, drawing the death gliders behind it like a high-tech Pied Piper.

Jack felt a tug on his arm and shifted his attention from the sky. "Ah, Jack, I see Sam."

He spotted her instantly. She stood at the far side of the roof, revealed now the tel'tak was gone, eye-to-eye with a Jaffa who held her at the end of his staff weapon. Neither was moving.

Jack glanced at Daniel, then back toward Carter. His heart sank. "Crap."

Clouds whipped past the window as Teal'c pushed the tel'tak into a steep climb. The planet's wind buffeted the ship and its engines protested their misuse. But he paid their howls little mind; he knew their capabilities.

At last the clouds became ragged, their tattered edges fluttering as he emerged into bright sunshine above. He still did not soften the climb, heading beyond the blue to the dark of space. The tracking screen showed two gliders pursuing him, and he allowed himself a moment of satisfaction. His friends would be spared until he could return for them. Had the tel'tak been armed, disposing of his opponents would have been easy. But the Goa'uld disliked any but their most trusted Jaffa to wield weapons, and so cargo ships such as this went unarmed.

Unarmed, but not unprotected. It was shielded, and if he so wished the tel'tak's stealth technology would render it invisible. However, his role as decoy would not be served by invisibility. Destruction, not evasion, was his mission. A sudden blast from his pursuers rocked the ship, jarring him hard against the controls and reminding him that it was a mission he shared with his enemy.

Just then, the atmosphere began to thin, shredding before his eyes until the bright stars and black void of space surrounded him. He felt more comfortable out here, away from the pull of gravity and buffeting of the atmosphere. He banked the ship up, tipping it backward into a loop and opening up the view of the pursuing gliders. The lead ship twisted up and back, rolling over as it headed straight for Teal'c, cannons firing. Fast, maneuverable and well armed, the death gliders were more than a match for the lumbering tel'tak. Strategy, not firepower, would win this battle. But Teal'c had an advantage over all his adversaries; he had served for seven years with O'Neill. He knew the value of unorthodoxy.

"I've seen him before," Daniel said, as he and Jack cautiously approached the Jaffa holding Sam hostage. It was the boy he'd encountered on the way to Baal's shrine. Disheveled and afraid, he radiated the anger and humiliation that defined adolescence; Teal'c had knocked him down like a child, and now he was out to prove himself. Sam, it seemed, would pay the price.

Jack cast Daniel an urgent glance. *Deal with it.* But he kept his P90 raised and his gaze fixed on the boy as he took a cautious step to his right. The kid was watching, and moved to keep Sam between them. "Come no nearer," he shouted. "Or she will die."

Carefully, Daniel raised his hands, keeping them clear of his weapon. "You know, this isn't going to work. Why don't you just let her go and we'll all walk away?"

Quick brown eyes flashed to his. "You are the enemy. No one will walk away."

"We're not your enemy," Daniel insisted. "We're not the enemy of the Jaffa."

"Ha!" the boy spat. "Then why do twelve of my brothers lie dead at your feet? Your words are as empty as those of the Shol'va."

Jack shifted. "You couldn't do it, you know. You make one move to fire that thing and you'll be joining your brothers over there."

The kid puffed out his chest. "Kalach shal'tek!"

"Victory or death," Daniel translated quietly; this could be going better. And then, just when he thought it couldn't get worse, it did.

"Those the only options?" The words came from Sam, clipped and bitter. "You know, I could have sworn there was another one. It involves knives. And acid. And a sarcophagus."

The Jaffa turned back to her, rattled. "Silence!"

"Or what?"

"Or this." The head of the staff sprang open, jabbing hard into her chest.

"Drop it!" Jack dodged sideways, looking for a clear shot. "Drop it now!" But the kid compensated, pivoting around Sam to shield himself from Jack.

The moment balanced on a pinhead. Even the wind seemed to still. Until Sam shattered it. "You little piece of shit."

"Carter…"

She ignored the warning. Instead, her hand shot out and seized the end of the weapon, muscles bunching as she pushed it up from her chest. She only succeeded in lifting it to her face, but didn't seem to care. "Let me go," she hissed in a voice Daniel barely recognized. "Let me go, or I'll kill you."

Fear and fury flared. "You are a fool! You cannot–"

"Can't I? You wanna see? You wanna see what I can do?"

"Carter, I can't get a shot!" Jack warned, urgently. "Back off."

Sam didn't seem to hear. "Why don't you see what happens when you don't have your victims pinned out like lab rats? You little piece of–"

"Has'shak!" The boy tried to wrench the weapon from her grasp, but she was too strong.

"Major! Back off!"

The staff weaved in front of her face, like a snake about to strike. "SAM!" Daniel yelled.

He was too late.

CHAPTER TWENTY

Bill Crawford sat next to Councilor Damaris at the wide, white conference table and immersed himself in a rare feeling of satisfaction. SG-1 were as good as taken care of, the treaty with the Kinahhi was signed, sealed and only waiting for him to deliver it to Senator Kinsey. Between those two events he had enough brownie points to ride all the way into the White House on Kinsey's ample coattails. Despite the irritations and delays, his time here had been profitable. His father would have approved. *Time is money*, he had often said. *Spend it wisely*.

Now all that remained was to dispense with the final irritation and he could return home, to a world where the coffee was sweet and the food didn't send his stomach into spasms.

The final irritation chose that moment to present itself, quick eyes belying the avuncular features. Crawford rose as General George Hammond strode into the room, his uniformed lackeys trailing him like unappealing bridesmaids. "General," he smiled. "Any luck?"

"I'm not looking for luck, son."

Which is fortunate, Crawford thought, *because you're fresh out, George*.

Councilor Damaris remained seated as she spoke. "Then I trust, General Hammond, that you are now satisfied with our evidence and that you will hand over SG-1 once they have returned to your planet?"

Hammond's face darkened, only serving to accentuate the sharpness of his eyes. "I'm afraid you can trust no such thing, Councilor. So far, I've seen no evidence whatsoever linking the stolen plans to SG-1. And I can assure you, even if I had, I would never hand over my people to you. We deal our own justice."

Oh, it was a joyous moment. Clearing his throat, Crawford turned to Damaris. "If you will allow me, Councilor?"

She graced him with a fleeting smile and granted permission by the slight inclination of her head.

Pushing the slim document across the table toward Hammond,

Crawford could barely contain his satisfaction. "I'm afraid, General, that under section 3.4.1 of our treaty with the Kinahhi, any criminal offense that takes place within Kinahhi jurisdiction is to be subject to Kinahhi justice. And vice versa, naturally."

Hammond's expression turned thunderous. "Tell me you're not serious."

Crawford just smiled and revealed the winning hand. "It's a standard extradition clause, General. When SG-1 returns home, you'll be obliged to send them to Kinahhi to face the consequences of their crimes."

The look of outraged shock on the general's face was priceless. Crawford enjoyed it almost as much as he was anticipating a similar look on O'Neill's arrogant features. It would be like watching the wheels fall off the Homecoming Queen's float.

He was going to relish seeing them flounder in the mud.

The arid surface of the planet's single, lifeless moon swept beneath Teal'c as he raced for its far side. The gliders were still in range, their continual bombardment rattling his teeth with every jolt of the ship. It would not be long before the shielding gave way. He must act now, or not at all. Sending a silent prayer into the void, he reached out and engaged the stealth device. Cloaked in invisibility, he dipped the ship into a steep dive toward the moon's surface, skimming along close enough to see its rocky craters before pulling up steeply and climbing out of its weak gravitational field.

The death gliders were banking, frustrated at having lost their prey. Soon they would return to base. He needed to keep them occupied for his plan to work. He slowed the ship, bringing it to a halt above the moon's gray surface, then slid from his seat and hurried toward the escape pods. Sealing one of the four, he hit the release and ran back to the cockpit. As the pod dived toward the moon, Teal'c fired his engines and came around in a slow circle. One of the gliders fired a few speculative shots at his last position, but, as he'd hoped, the other went in pursuit of the pod. Teal'c followed.

With a small puff of dust the pod hit the surface of the moon and the glider slowed, hovering like a vulture awaiting a kill. A brief, ironic smile twitched at Teal'c's lips. Carefully, he lowered the tel'tak over the glider, just getting close enough for his plan to work.

Freeing his zat'nikatel from its holster, he once more left the cockpit but this time headed for the ring transporter. While a transporter usually needed a corresponding set of rings to function, the tel'tak could retrieve matter located immediately below it as long as it was within the physical range of the ring mechanism. He hoped he was close enough.

Readying himself, he activated the transporter and found himself holding his breath. In seconds the rings returned, depositing a section of glider canopy and its pilot in a jumbled heap on the floor.

"Na'binim–?" the pilot began, pushing off the canopy and staring around in bewilderment.

Teal'c raised the zat and fired, sending the Jaffa twitching to the floor. He allowed himself a moment of satisfaction. And, since he was alone, indulged in a little amusement. "Resistance," he told the fallen Jaffa, "is futile."

After hurriedly cuffing his enemy's ankles and wrists, Teal'c dashed back to the cockpit and watched as the glider, fatally breached, nose-dived into the moon's surface. Its mate, however, did not come to investigate its demise. Perhaps its pilot had seen the rings and sought to avoid a similar fate?

Sliding back into the pilot's chair, Teal'c studied the tactical scanner until he found the errant glider. It was far above him, and on a trajectory that would take it right back to Baal's fortress. To his friends.

Throwing the tel'tak into a turn he set out in pursuit. Unarmed, he couldn't bring the glider down, but perhaps he could pull his team out. If he reached them in time.

It happened in slow motion. Carter's face twisted with anger and her hands locked around the end of the staff weapon as it sizzled into life. Daniel screamed her name and the charge spewed from the mouth of the weapon. "SAM!"

Impossibly, she wrenched the staff to one side. The plasma bolt skimmed past so close Jack could smell her singed hair. With a roar of outrage, she yanked the weapon from the boy's hands and swung it viciously into the side of his head. He staggered and fell to one knee.

Stunned, Jack could only watch as she threw down the staff. "Not so tough now," she spat, kicking the Jaffa hard in the chest. He fell, sprawled on his back. Then she was on him, fists flying and rage spilling from her lips. "Not. So. Tough. Now!" She punctuated each word with a blow. "You. Little. Piece. Of–"

"Carter!" Jack lurched into action, grabbing her shoulder and trying to pull her back. But she was lost in a frenzy, reason gone. Straddling the kid's legs, he grabbed both her arms and yanked her back, hard. "Stop!"

Her weight toppled her backward and she landed on her ass, taking him with her. Squirming free, she sprang to her feet with an inarticulate growl and lunged for the Jaffa.

Jack was faster. Tackling her with a move worthy of the NFL, he brought them both crashing back to their knees. Pain exploded in his right leg and he cursed a blue-streak, but didn't let go. One arm clamped around her chest, the other around her midriff, he pinned her arms to her sides. "Don't!" he yelled around the pain. "Carter, stop!"

"Let go! Let me–"

"No." She bucked and struggled – and, damn, she was strong – but he didn't give an inch. "You don't want to do this!"

"Let go!"

Daniel dropped into a crouch in front of them. "Sam, listen to me." His hand hovered between himself and Carter, as if nervous of provoking her with a touch. "Don't do this. You'll hate yourself. He's just a kid."

Her whole body went rigid, and Jack could feel her gasps against his chest. But at least she'd stopped squirming He relaxed his arms a little, but didn't let go. "It wasn't him, Carter," he said quietly, close to her ear. "He didn't hurt you."

Breaths still coming fast and shallow, she shook her head and stared at the ground. Striving for control. When she spoke, her voice shook. "What they did to you…"

To me? Displacement; a classic psychological response, and he should know. Worry about someone else so you don't have to think about yourself. He glanced up, saw Daniel's eyes dancing away from him, and suddenly got it. Displacement or not, something had changed. They both *knew*; Daniel had seen the live broadcast, and now Carter had suffered her own personal taster. They both knew, and he hated how exposed that made him feel. He hated how real it made the memories. He hated how much harder it was to hide the truth. Cold and weary, he released her. She sagged away from him, hands coming to rest on the ground, head bowed. Her back rose and fell as she sucked in shaking breaths.

"It's over, Sam," he told her softly. "Let it go."

She turned, fixing him with a wretched look. "How do you do that?"

Bury it. Ignore it. Deny it. "You just keep going."

He held her gaze, trying to reassure her. She just shook her head and turned away, her eyes falling on the boy who lay bruised and bleeding on the ground. The reaction was instant, as if she was seeing him for the first time. Anger and color fled from her face, shoulders slumping and arms going limp at her sides. "Oh God." A hand pressed over her mouth. "Oh, my God."

Silently, Jack reached out and turned her away, his gaze meeting Daniel's in a mute appeal for help. He couldn't handle this; it struck way too close to home. From the compassionate look on Daniel's face, he suspected that he knew all about it. A wave of shame washed up with the realization; had Daniel seen him crack like this? Had he been a non-corporeal witness to the hatred that had poured through his fists and beaten the nearest Jaffa to a bloody pulp? A witness to the same hatred ebbing from Carter, leaking out with every shallow breath.

Carefully, Daniel took her arm and drew her to her feet, talking softly. Reassuring. Daniel never judged, he always seemed to understand exactly how you felt. Even when you were blatantly in the wrong. Sometimes it drove Jack nuts, other times he envied him like hell. This was one of those times; Daniel always knew the right thing to say.

He stood up, wincing at the pain in his knee. "Find some place to hide," he called after them, falling back on the practical and leaving Daniel to deal with the rest.

Glancing over his shoulder, Daniel nodded. It was more than just agreement; there was a question in his eyes as he indicated the fallen Jaffa. *Is he okay?*

Acknowledging the request, Jack crouched, grimacing slightly at the kid's bloody nose and swelling left eye. Cautiously, he peeled open the other eyelid and saw the eye roll backward in his head. Then he felt for a pulse; it was strong, if a little slow. The kid would be fine, although he suspected his ego had taken a worse beating than his face. Getting your ass kicked by a girl probably didn't rank too high on a budding Jaffa's list of personal achievements. With that thought he stood up. "Let's go, kids, reinforcements won't be far away."

"Sir?" Carter turned, white-faced. "We can't just leave him–"

"No different from a bullet, Major."

"But I–"

"He would have killed you."

Her eyes closed slowly, then opened with harsh determination. "Is he dead?"

"Nope. Not even close. But he'll have one hell of a headache when he wakes up."

Relief washed over her in a shiver. "Thank God."

He actually found himself envying her that comfort. How sick was that? Squinting up at the empty sky, he pulled out his sunglasses and slid them on. The victim of his own fists had never woken up, and he didn't want her to see that in his eyes. She already knew too much. "Now move it," he urged, taking the lead. "We need to find a defensible position until the cavalry arrives."

"Before we go," General Hammond said, placing his fists firmly on the conference table, "there is one avenue of investigation we have yet to cover."

Opposite him, Crawford shook his head. "General, you're really pushing your luck. Councilor Damaris has been very patient, and I think when Senator Kinsey hears of this he will–"

"I'm sure the Senator will understand." And that was a lie as big as the Lone Star State. In fact, he hoped that Kinsey wouldn't understand at all. He bared his teeth in lieu of a smile. "With your cooperation, Ambassador, it won't take long."

Suspicion radiated across the table in waves. "My cooperation?"

Hammond turned and nodded to the man standing discreetly at his left shoulder. "If you'll permit Major Barker to search through your briefcase and laptop–"

"I will not!" Crawford jumped to his feet like a target in a shooting gallery. "How dare you imply that I have any involvement with this sordid affair?" Red-faced, he was spluttering with anger. "You've gone so far over the line I don't even know where to begin with my report to Kinsey. You can kiss goodbye to that cozy office of yours because–"

"Mr. Ambassador," Hammond cut in. "If you have nothing to hide then you have nothing to fear."

"Of course I have nothing to hide!" He turned to Councilor Damaris, as if for confirmation. "This is ridiculous!"

With a slight nod, the councilor also stood. "We have no reason to suspect Ambassador Crawford of this crime, General. And on Kinahhi we would certainly never allow a person of your status to level such an accusation. However –" her glance moved and came to rest on Crawford – "since we have no doubt of your innocence, Ambassador, perhaps it would be expeditious to allow the search to take place?"

Crawford's feathers were still ruffled, but the councilor's assurance seemed to carry some weight. "Very well," he said stiffly, addressing his words to Damaris. "As you say, Councilor, it will hurry things along." He turned back to Hammond. "Frankly, the sooner the SGC gets its nose out of Kinahhi the better for us all."

Hammond felt his own hackles rise. "I can assure you, Ambassador, that for as long as you are using the Stargate, the SGC will be involved with this and every other world we encounter."

A slight, dangerous smirk toyed with Crawford's mouth. "We'll see, won't we?" And somehow, it sounded like a threat.

The Kinahhi Council Chamber was hardly the place for that discussion, however, so Hammond swallowed his anger, filed his suspicion, and turned back to Barker. "Take a look at Ambassador Crawford's belongings, Major. And be thorough."

"Yes sir," came the enthusiastic response; the ambassador hadn't made himself any friends at Stargate Command.

"You're wasting your time," Crawford said, pushing his briefcase and laptop across the table. "You'll find nothing there. In fact, you're just doing my job for me."

"And what job is that?"

He didn't even try to deny it. "Cleaning house at the SGC, General."

Hammond made no reply, returning his attention to Barker, who had emptied all the papers from Crawford's briefcase and was starting to take apart the lining. He just hoped Jack's suspicions about Crawford were right and that he'd find the smoking gun. Because, without it, things were looking pretty damn bleak for SG-1.

Things were looking pretty damn bleak for SG-1.

"Fire in the hole!" Jack hurled one of his two remaining grenades and dived for cover. A barrage of enemy fire burst overhead as the explosion shook the entire building. He held his breath, waiting for the roof to give way and send them plunging down. It didn't, and he almost regretted it. It would have been one way out of their current mess. As it was, they were surrounded on three sides by angry Jaffa. Reinforcements had come, and come with a vengeance. The three of them were crouched in the bombed-out remains of a storeroom, barely keeping the enemy at bay. And unless they did something crazy, it would only be a matter of minutes before they were overrun.

"Sir!" Carter yelled, right on cue. "I've got an idea!"

"Do it!" he shouted back. Whatever the hell it was, it had to be better than the alternative.

"You'll have to cover me."

"You got it. Daniel, take Carter's position."

Daniel moved in a low crouch. "I'm running out of ammo," he warned. "I'm gonna have to start throwing stones soon!"

"Whatever it takes." He risked a glance at Carter. There was some life back in her face, at least. Ironic, really, since death was stalking closer with every minute. "Ready?"

She nodded.

"This gonna work?"

"Maybe."

Good enough. It was Carter, after all. She'd make it work. "On my mark."

"Yes, sir."

A Jaffa showed himself, firing twice before diving back into cover. The blast spat shrapnel up into Jack's face. "Gah!" He flinched away and pressed the back of one hand against his stinging cheek. It came away bloody. "Whatever you're gonna do, Carter, do it fast!" Returning fire he started the countdown. "Three, two, one. Mark!"

As Carter vaulted over the top, Jack threw his last grenade. The explosion knocked her sideways, but she was up on her feet and racing away from the Jaffa within moments. Two of them made her instantly, but Jack took them out with a couple of rapid shots. Then he stood up, presenting a better target. "Hey! Losers! This way."

"Damn it, Jack!" Daniel yanked on his tac vest. "Get down!"

He did, just as a wave of enemy fire exploded overhead. When he peeked over the wall again, Carter was gone.

Sprinting across the roof, Sam kept her eyes on the prize. A plasma bolt hissed past her face, its static heat scorching her cheek. Ignoring it, she ran on. Almost there. The prize was half a death glider tipped up on its back end with its staff cannons aimed skyward. Crucially, they looked intact.

Skidding in beneath the ship's shattered wing, she flung herself flat on the ground and waited. She wasn't taking any fire. The colonel must have taken out the men on her position. She pushed herself to her feet, took a quick look at the smashed canopy of the ship, and started climbing up the outside. Her injured shoulder protested, but she ruthlessly ignored its weakness. Scrambling above the canopy, she wedged the heel of her boot against its edge. A hefty kick sent it screeching open, falling backwards and crashing to the ground. So far, so good.

Boots first, Sam lowered herself into the cockpit and jammed her feet against the back of the pilot's chair. She hit the ignition and hoped for the best.

The best didn't happen; it was dead as a Dodo. "Damn it!" She'd have to resort to plan B. Pulling up every scrap of information she'd ever read about the X301, Sam searched the cockpit. The staff canons mounted on the ship were removable and self contained; she'd once seen one dissected in Area 51 during the retro-fit of Apophis's death glider. They had their own supply of liquid naquadah and a docking port designed for swift exchange by repair crews. Question was, where was the release mechanism?

Instinct told her there had to be a manual release. It wouldn't make sense to leave valuable weapons tied to a dead machine. Her fingers ranged across the controls, down the side of the seat, searching for a lever or a handle. Anything that might–

KABOOM!

The ground detonated with a bone-jarring impact. Chunks of stone exploded up into the air and the concussion knocked her out of the cockpit. A death glider shrieked overhead.

"Carter!" O'Neill's voice barked out of her radio. "Carter, come in."

Feet scrabbling for a hold, she dragged herself back up the side of the glider and toggled her radio. "I'm okay, sir."

"Carter, get out of there!" His voice was taut, the rattle of gunfire almost drowning it out. "We can't hold them. Get back to the 'gate and–"

Another screaming pass of the glider cut off his words. Explosions strafed the landing platform, rocking the wrecked glider until it threatened to topple over entirely. Clinging on with one hand she yelled into her radio. "Colonel? Daniel? Come in!"

There was no answer. As the glider soared up into the sky, she realized the sound of fighting had stopped.

"No." She slipped her fingers over the lip of the wing and pulled herself up far enough to peer over the top. She had a good view of her worst fear. Their position had been overrun. Daniel was on his knees, hands on his head and a staff weapon aimed at his back. The colonel was face down on the ground, a booted foot on his neck as his arms were roughly pinned behind him. He was still struggling. Sam felt sick; she knew what awaited them. And so did they. The colonel might have destroyed the gravity wall, but cruelty was imaginative and could be practiced anywhere. "Not this time," she promised them. "Not this time."

Sliding back down to the cockpit, her mind emptied of everything but the need to save her team. She saw nothing extraneous, focusing entirely on the glider and her memories of the X-301.

The mental map in her mind guided her hands as they skimmed across the console and up to the overhead controls. To the right, and down. A small black lever you hooked with a finger. Heart hammering, she slipped her hand over the damaged upper controls until– There it was! Holding her breath, she slid her index finger under the lever and pulled back. A quiet hiss and click were her reward. *Yes!* Adrenaline pumped hard through her chest as she slithered down the glider to land on the ground with a soft thud.

Pulling her zat from her waistband, she activated it and ducked down low enough to be able to see under the glider's broken wing. The Jaffa were milling around their captives, watching the colonel being dragged to his knees and thrown toward Daniel. He wasn't struggling anymore, but there was defiance in his posture. *Good. Hold that thought, sir.*

The staff cannon was mounted beneath the wing, which meant she'd be in full view when she removed it from the undercarriage. She figured she'd have thirty seconds, pushing a minute, to get it off the glider, aimed and firing. You could do a lot in thirty seconds. In thirty seconds a single drop of acid could burn right through your eye and–

You just keep going.

Orders were barked on the far side of the platform. A search party would be sent to find her any minute. Sucking in a deep breath she slid under the glider and out into the open. Thirty seconds and counting. Her spine prickled, whispering of enemy eyes on her back as she reached for the staff cannon. She ignored the sensation and just kept going.

Twenty-nine, twenty-eight, twenty-seven…

CHAPTER TWENTY-ONE

"This is outrageous!" Crawford was beginning to sound like a broken record as he stared in disbelief at his laptop, lying in pieces on the table.

Hammond wasn't buying it. Arms folded, he watched the young man. "This isn't the first time we've had rogue operatives stealing alien technology." He directed the words at both Crawford and the Kinahhi councilor. "Who are you working for, Crawford? The NID or someone else?"

Crawford's dark eyes blazed. "I didn't do this, General."

Disturbingly, Hammond almost believed him; Crawford was either one hell of an actor or there was truth in his words. But the evidence was incontrovertible. "The blueprints are right here, Ambassador. Inside the lid of your laptop."

"It's a set-up." Crawford glanced over at Councilor Damaris, whose face wore a mask more impenetrable than ever. "You believe me, Councilor."

Damaris inclined her head slightly. "I have no reason to suspect you, and yet here is the evidence before me."

A dark flush stole over Crawford's face. "You can't—"

She stalled him with a curt hand gesture and rose to her feet. When she spoke, her attention was fixed on Hammond. He met her cool gaze with equanimity. "Given that this crime has been committed under Kinahhi jurisdiction, General, I invoke the right under paragraph 3.4.1 of the treaty to detain Mr. Crawford here for—"

"You can't do that!" Crawford yelped, suddenly panicking. "General, this is wrong! I didn't do this. It was O'Neill! He had the plans. He—"

"Silence!" Damaris's voice was sharp as broken glass. Just like her eyes. "You have no choice, General Hammond, but to acquiesce to the terms of our treaty." Then she turned her gaze on Crawford, meeting his appalled expression with one that gave little away. "Justice will be served, Ambassador," she assured him after a moment. "Have no fear of that."

Hammond shifted his weight from foot to foot, nervous and not entirely sure why. This should be a victory, made all the sweeter by Crawford being the architect of his own destruction. And yet, as duplicitous as Crawford was, the idea of leaving him to the mercy of these people jarred with everything Hammond knew to be right. "Councilor, I would like to return to the SGC with the evidence and with Mr. Crawford. We can do tests on the documents to determine who has touched them and who–"

"This matter is nonnegotiable," Damaris informed him, giving a brief nod to two of the soldiers at attention around the room. "Mr. Crawford will be held here while we investigate. We too have our methods of ascertaining the truth, General."

"Councilor, I–"

"She's right, General," Crawford broke in, stepping back from the table, hands raised, as the soldiers came to take him away. "You don't have a choice." The panic had receded, replaced instead with a cold anger. "But remember this; when the truth comes out, you and SG-1 will be buried so deep you'll never see daylight again."

One of the men placed a hand on Crawford's arm, coaxing him away. He shook it off angrily, turning on his heel and stalking toward the door. The two Kinahhi soldiers fell in behind him, leaving Hammond with the distinct impression he'd just made matters a hell of a lot worse.

The staff weapon dug painfully into Daniel's back, a nice counterpoint to the dull throb inside his skull. The head-wound was courtesy of a hefty blow at close range; they might not have the accuracy and fire power of a P90, but when the bullets ran out, the staff had all the advantages.

Jack knelt next to him, bristling with insolence and sporting a large collection of scrapes and bruises to the side of his face. He looked drawn and tense. "You okay?" Daniel whispered.

"Peachy," came the dry reply. "You?"

"Looking forward to getting out of–"

"Silence!" Another swift jab in his back. Daniel made no comment, just glanced over at Jack. His roll of the eyes was eloquent.

Turning away, Daniel glanced around the rest of the platform. Sam was out there, hopefully alive and well and planning a rescue. And Teal'c was out there too, although the return of one of the gliders had ominous implications. What could a tel'tak do against a couple of heavily armed fighters anyway?

"On your feet!" An abrupt yank on his arm dragged him to his feet, his bruised hip sending needles of pain down through his thigh.

Grimacing, he struggled for balance as Jack was hauled upright at his side. "Our rooms ready so soon?"

The Jaffa made no answer, simply pushed them into motion. Daniel's stiff hip wouldn't cooperate, and he staggered, falling down to one knee as he... saw something. On the far side of the landing platform, he saw movement. A flash of blond hair behind the rusted remains of a death glider. Sam! Afraid of betraying her position, Daniel immediately looked away. But a spark of hope ignited as he was dragged back to his feet. His hands were unbound, resting compliantly on top of his head, and he relished their freedom. If Sam was planning something, then he'd be ready.

There was no way to warn Jack, however, without raising suspicions. So he slowed his pace as far as possible, exaggerating a limp and trying to keep half an eye on Sam's position. She'd have to hurry. Ahead of them a set of double doors stood open, leading to a dark flight of stairs. Once they were inside, rescue would be much more difficult. He found himself counting his paces as they approached the doors, waiting and waiting. Hoping.

Something flickered in the corner of his eye. With an instinct born of seven years in the field, Daniel flung himself at Jack. "Get down!" They hit the ground just as a massive plasma blot came blazing overhead, taking out five Jaffa in one fell swoop. Chaos erupted as another explosion sent Jaffa tumbling in bloody agony. A third hit blasted shrapnel high into the air. Orders were barked and a pair of rough hands grabbed at his arm. Letting himself be pulled to his feet, Daniel used the upward momentum to fuel his fist, swinging hard against the Jaffa's jaw and sending him crumpling to the ground. Yanking the staff weapon from his limp hands, Daniel swung around in a swift three-sixty as Jack scrambled to his feet.

"Nice," O'Neill commented, glancing down at the fallen Jaffa. "Teal'c teach you that?"

"He–"

Fire rained from the sky. The glider was back, roaring overhead, guns blazing. The roof shuddered with each detonation, flinging

Daniel back to his knees. But this time it kept on shuddering.

"Oh crap!" Jack yelled. In front of them a huge section of the roof began to fold in on itself. Three Jaffa fell howling into the chasm. And Jack kept shouting, seizing Daniel by his vest, "Get back. Daniel, move!"

Cracks raced across the roof, filigreeing the surface under his feet like the glaze on old pottery. He lurched backwards, still at Jack's side, heading toward the edge of the roof. But they couldn't move fast enough. The network of cracking stone was all around them. Everywhere. "The whole thing's gonna go!"

The glider came in for a second pass, cannon blasts battering the weakened structure. The chasm widened into a huge, black pit as more and more of the roof slid toward the center and fell. Backing up, they were almost at the low parapet that surrounded the roof. There was no where else to go. And then, with a crack, the floor listed steeply. Daniel slipped, his right knee hitting the ground hard. Shards of pain jolted up his leg as he fumbled for purchase on the gritty, undulating ground.

"Daniel!" Jack had his wrist, fingers digging deep. "Grab hold!" He did, clutching at the fabric of his friend's jacket. Bracing himself against the parapet, Jack hauled Daniel to safety. Barely. He'd scarcely grabbed hold of the wall when the roof beneath them collapsed with a deafening roar.

"Hang on!" Jack yelled, flinging both arms over the quaking wall.

Eyes screwed shut, expecting any moment to be dragged down to a pummeling, suffocating death, Daniel clung on for dear life. Everything shook. The whole world was overtaken by thunder and destruction. *Sha're*. Her image slipped into his mind, as it so often did in times of stress, half a prayer and half a promise. He could almost taste her in the air. And he clung to her, fingers scraping against hard stone. *Sha're...*

Slowly the noise and shaking subsided, and she faded. Daniel choked up a lungful of rock dust and opened his eyes. Only a narrow frill of fractured stone remained, crumbling beneath their booted feet.

Jack coughed and spat out a mouthful of dirt. "You okay?"

"Been better." Desperate didn't begin to describe their situation.

All around them the landing platform was funneling into the abyss. Like a black hole, only faster. At its lip he could see dirty, bleeding hands groping desperately as they tried to hold on. Another judder rippled through the structure and the fingers slipped, plunging with a desolate scream down into the depths. Turning away and holding tighter to the wall, Daniel tried not to imagine what was happening to the fallen man. Enemy or not, the Jaffa knew pain and fear just as he did.

"Don't move," Jack warned, shifting slightly until he had a better view of the ruin. On the far side of the chasm the roof was still intact. It might as well have been on the far side of the moon; reaching it was impossible.

On the plus side, they were both still alive. Panting, Daniel gasped, "Could be worse, right?"

Jack didn't answer. His attention was fixed on the horizon.

Daniel peered myopically at a black dot against the gray clouds. "Jack?"

"It's worse."

The death glider screamed toward her. Its weapons were firmly locked onto Daniel and the colonel, clinging helplessly to the remains of the fortress's wall.

"You sonofabitch!" Sam hissed, angling the huge staff weapon up to track the glider's path. Without sights she had to rely on instinct alone. But anger and adrenaline honed her vision, heightening her reflexes. A huge pulse of energy flashed through the staff weapon. The recoil skewed the weapon off its precarious perch, but her eyes never left the plasma bolt as it lanced across the sky and impacted perfectly on the glider's left wing. "*Yes!*"

Banking hard, the ship tried to pull up. But it was too badly damaged. A burst of random fire skimmed harmlessly out into the clouds as the glider rolled over onto its back. Then the engines stalled. For a nightmare moment Sam envisaged it plummeting into the roof, bringing down the whole structure.

It didn't happen.

One wing clipped the building, sparking as it screamed down the outside of the fortress behind O'Neill and Daniel. A plume of fire belched up into the air, marking the glider's death, and forcing the colonel and Daniel to bury their heads in their arms. Leaving the heavy weapon, Sam wiped sweat from her face and dashed across what remained of the roof. Her injured shoulder throbbed, but the pain was miles away, locked behind a wall of adrenaline.

Three Jaffa were trapped close to the stairs which she and the colonel had climbed. The rest were gone, swallowed by the collapsing building. Whatever – and whoever – lay beneath must also be dead. She felt a pulse of angry triumph, knowing that the whole obscene complex would soon be reduced to rubble.

As she reached the edge of the hole, she slowed. Beneath her feet, the ground was shifting like sand on the beach.

"Carter!" The yell came from across the collapsed roof. "Get back!"

Like hell. She needed a rope. Or a miracle. "Sir, I'm gonna try and get back into the complex and find something to–"

A groan shuddered through the building. Another section of roof cracked, tipped and slid down into the chasm, kicking up a cloud of choking dust. Beneath her feet the floor rippled and bucked. Hunkering down, she braced herself with a hand on the floor. It wasn't looking good.

"Sam!" Daniel's yell was desperate. "Get back! That whole section's going!"

Glancing over her shoulder, she saw what he meant. A large fissure had opened up behind her, running out on both sides and inching wider and wider with every second. She began to ease herself backwards. It couldn't end like this. Not like this! But her slight movement was too much. With a lurch, the roof began to move.

Panic seized her. She flung herself toward safety, but she couldn't get a grip. She couldn't hold on. She was sliding, falling... She screamed out her anger and terror. "NO!"

A shadow passed overhead. "Carter!" someone yelled frantically. And then she was plunging toward death, alone in the dark.

The whole section fell away and Carter plummeted into the pit. Jack's heart dropped with her. "Carter!" he bellowed, making an involuntary, futile lunge forwards.

Daniel grabbed his vest and yanked him backward, face ashen. "Jack, you can't–"

Whap, whap, whap.

Goa'uld rings whipped down into the hole, then shot back up in a golden blur. Jack's head snapped up in parallel, heart pounding. A tel'tak loomed steadily above them.

"Teal'c?" Daniel only sounded half hopeful.

Maybe. Maybe not. Slowly the ship moved, its shadow passing over them, low enough that he could see the ring transporter hatch opening. Teal'c or trouble, Jack thought, as the rings stacked around them. Teal'c or trouble.

In a disoriented blink, he found himself standing in the tel'tak's hold, Daniel still clutching his vest. The first thing he saw was a comatose Jaffa and what seemed to be half the canopy of a glider. Then he heard a dry cough, spun on his heel and was knocked sideways by a giddying wave of relief. Carter sat propped up against a wall, pasty white and choking up dust. But alive. Very much alive. He sank down at her side, reaching for her shoulder and struggling for detachment. When he spoke, his voice was ragged. "Carter?"

She nodded, catching her breath, *I'm fine.* But it had been a close call. His hand tightened reflexively on her arm. Way too close.

"O'Neill, Daniel Jackson!" boomed a familiar voice. "Are you well?"

"Teal'c!" He stood up with an elated smile. "Great timing, buddy. You should–" An explosion rocked the ship. *An explosion?* He flung up his arms in exasperation. "*Now* what?"

Teal'c appeared in the doorway to the cockpit. "Come, O'Neill. I believe you would wish to witness this."

Curious, and a touch suspicious of the intensity in his friend's voice, Jack glanced over at Daniel, then Carter. Both looked blank. But Carter valiantly pushed herself to her feet and Daniel reached out a hand to steady her. With a shrug Jack cautiously made his way into the cockpit, the rest of his team trailing behind.

Another explosion knocked him off balance, and he braced himself against the wall. Outside orange tongues of fire swept up and licked at the windows, casting Teal'c's skin in bronze as he pointed through the flames. "There."

Warily moving to the window, Jack peered out. "Whoa." Below him an inferno burned in the pit of Baal's fortress, belching out flares of bright flame and black smoke. It looked like hell, and he should know. Even from this distance he could hear the roar, like a huge beast in pain. He felt a presence at his side and glanced over to see Carter standing with him. Her face was ashy beneath the dirt, but the edginess he'd seen in her before the battle had eased.

"Look," she murmured, drawing his attention back to the fortress. The rest of the landing platform was sagging, the rusted remains of death gliders sliding helplessly into the hellhole below. And then, with a violent quake, the entire roof gave way. The wall he and Daniel had clung to crumbled with it, sending up a plume of smoke and dust so thick and heavy that the whole ship was cloaked in swirling grayness.

He stared out into it, seeing nothing but memories of that place. Acid and daggers, hopelessness and fear; its stench had oozed from the very bones of the building. The smoke swirled, revealing patches of light and fire, the smoldering ruins of Baal's stronghold. The smoldering ruins of his nightmares.

"It's gone." Carter's voice was quietly triumphant.

He turned to look at her. She was still staring down at the inferno beneath. "You okay?" he asked softly.

She offered him a faint smile, a flash of white through the dirt that covered her face. "Much better, sir."

He nodded. "Yeah. Me too."

CHAPTER TWENTY-TWO

Councilor Tamar Damaris stood staring out at the ordered city below. She liked order; it was predictable and safe. Order never left anything to chance, never permitted the unforeseen. Never permitted surprises.

That was why she disliked these Tauri so much. They were without order, reckless and unpredictable. Their minds were undisciplined, their thoughts dangerous. And they brought the unexpected with them, as troublesome as flies on a summer evening.

A soft knock on her door announced the arrival of Commander Kenna, as requested. "Enter," she called, turning from the window as the door opened and the soldier stepped inside, shepherding the Tauri Ambassador before him.

The human's eyes fixed on her, strangely dark. O'Neill and the alien, Teal'c, had eyes of a similar shade. Damaris didn't like them, she preferred the clear-eyed gaze of her own people. These dark eyes were not trustworthy. "You may release his bonds, Commander."

Without question, Commander Kenna followed his orders and retreated to wait discreetly by the door. Damaris turned her attention on Crawford, who stood rubbing at his wrists.

"I hope this is the end of your charade, Councilor," he said at last. "We both know I'm innocent."

She nodded slightly. "Tell me, Ambassador, what were the blueprints to our technology doing in your..." She fumbled for the alien word.

"Laptop," Crawford supplied. "And I told you, it was a set-up. O'Neill must have put them there."

O'Neill. She had been right to suspect him; his aura on the *sheh'fet* had indicated his danger the moment he stepped through the device. "He is resourceful and deceptive," she mused aloud. "A dangerous combination. It is well he is no longer a concern."

Crawford took a step closer, bristling with ill-concealed anger. "No longer a concern? If that's the case, why am I the one charged with this crime and not him? He should be the one rotting in your jail – him and his team."

"We do not have jails, Ambassador, as you well know. And you must learn patience. When the time is right, your innocence will be proven." She offered him a smile, although it was forced. "In the meantime, you are free to enjoy the hospitality of Kinahhi."

He did not appear pleased by the prospect. "When will the time be right? I've already told Senator Kinsey that SG-1 are is of the way."

"And so they are," she assured him mildly. "No doubt they are endeavoring to use the technology to recover their missing colleagues from the planet trapped within the event horizon of a black hole."

Crawford nodded. "And what happens when they get back? Another triumph for SG-1! Kinsey won't like–"

"I can assure you," she smiled, "that their return is extremely unlikely."

To her surprise the Tauri man's face tightened. "What does that mean?"

She lifted her shoulders in a delicate shrug and decided to reveal no more. She had thought his stomach stronger. "Merely that the task they have set themselves is a difficult one. Do not fear. Should they succeed, will it not be apparent that they used our gravitational technology?"

Crawford's brow contracted in thought. "Yeah, I guess it will."

"At which point, you will be exonerated. O'Neill and his team will be ours, and Senator Kinsey will be satisfied."

"And if they don't come back? What happens to me then?"

She turned away from him to stare back out over the silent fortress of her city. "Do not fear, Ambassador, we have uses for you yet. Our alliance with the Tauri has only just begun."

It was quiet in the ship. The afterglow of escape left Daniel feeling washed out and weary and he sank to the floor of the cargo hold with a grateful sigh. Sam was already there, sitting cross-legged and re-dressing the wound on her shoulder. She was silent and pensive, miles away.

"Hey," he said after a moment. "How are you feeling?"

She glanced up, surprised. "Daniel. Hi. I– I'm just changing the dressing."

He nodded, but resisted asking how she'd been hurt. He had a good idea, born of vivid memories, and thought it better to respect her privacy. So he said nothing more, just unzipped his tac vest and shucked off its weight. It felt good to be free of the damn thing. Folding it up as best he could, he turned it into a makeshift pillow and slid down, stretching out and staring up at the low ceiling. If Sam wanted to talk, here he was. If she didn't, he was content to simply be. For a long time they sat in silence. He heard her fingers rustling in the med-kit, heard the soft swish of a zipper being closed, and was just teetering on the edge of sleep when she spoke.

"Daniel?" She sounded unusually hesitant. "Can I ask you something?"

"Sure." He blinked away weariness and propped himself up on an elbow so he could see her better. "What is it?"

She shook her head slightly, frowning down at the med-kit lying in her hands. For a moment he thought she was going to ask him to help dress her wound. But then she said, "Has the colonel ever told you anything about what happened to him down there? When Baal– you know."

Daniel shrank from the question. "Told? No. He, ah, doesn't want to talk about it."

"It's just…" She looked up. "That day at my house, when you said that Baal still used gravitational technology? How did you know?"

"I–" Damn. He sat up slowly, rubbing a hand over his chin and considered his answer. Did he have the right to tell her, or was this too much part of Jack's private world? Then again, she had firsthand knowledge; he wasn't giving away Jack's secrets. "I, um, I saw."

Her eyes widened. "Saw?"

Gesturing vaguely toward the ceiling, he said, "When I was… ascended."

"Oh God." She closed her eyes, fingers tightening over the med-kit in her lap. "Daniel, I'm so sorry. To have to see that–" Her jaw clamped shut, holding everything in.

Quietly he said, "I'm not the one who deserves your sympathy, Sam."

"Why not?" she asked through veiled lids. "I can't imagine having to watch anyone go through that. Especially not– Especially not a friend."

He was silent for a moment, battling his own demons. They refused to be silenced. "I didn't help him," he confessed. "I didn't stop it."

"Could you have?"

"I could have ended it. Made it so he didn't wake up again."

Her eyes flashed open. "You mean you could have killed him?" She sounded appalled, and he flinched.

"He wanted me to."

She shook her head vehemently. "No. You did the right thing." His astonishment must have shown, because she elaborated instantly. "He survived, Daniel. He's still here. And now that *place*," – she almost spat the word – "has gone. And we've won. *He* won."

You did the right thing. Until she spoke the words, Daniel hadn't known how much he needed to hear them. Heartrending as it had been to refuse to end Jack's suffering, it *had* been the right choice. If he'd given in to Jack's request, then his friend would be dead. Lost forever. Instead, he was still with them – battered and bruised, but still Jack. In the end, he'd won. Daniel opened his mouth to reply, but another voice spoke first.

"Who won what?"

Turning, he saw Jack standing in the doorway, eyeing them both with a look that growled, *Drop it!* He complied, opting for a transparent lie. "Sam was just telling me that Teal'c's been betting again. On the Canucks."

"And he *won*?"

A faint smile brightened Sam's face. "Stranger things have happened, sir."

"They have?" Jack sauntered into the hold. "Such as…?"

She shrugged, considering. "Going back in time to 1969? Being stuck in Groundhog Day for over three months? Oh, and once I think you actually let me finish an entire report before interrupt–"

"Ah!" He stopped her with a wave of his hand and eased himself down onto the floor. "Point taken." His brief smile hid more than it revealed, and he turned to Daniel. "So, any luck?"

He stared, puzzled. "Luck?"

"With the thing."

"What thing?"

"You know."

"I do?"

"I believe," Teal'c's baritone rumbled from where he appeared in the doorway, "that O'Neill is referring to the power unit we sought."

"Oh!" In all the chaos, he'd forgotten to mention that he and Teal'c had found it! Dragging his tac vest onto his lap Daniel unzipped a pocket and pulled out the narrow steel cylinder. It was still glowing with a faint violet light. "This is it," said, holding it up for them to see. "This is what we came for."

Sam's face was suddenly bright and eager. She leaned closer and traced a finger down the smooth metal surface of the device. "Wow, it's so small."

"Well, you know what they say," Jack muttered. "It's how you use it that counts."

A smile and a hint of color touched Sam's face, but she ignored his words. "It's certainly not Goa'uld."

"No," Daniel agreed, "The markings are written in Ancient."

She nodded. "Makes sense. This technology is nothing the Goa'uld could have come up with. It's way too sophisticated."

"Question is, Carter," said Jack, "now we have the battery, do you know where to stick it?"

She smiled. "I shouldn't have too much trouble integrating it into the device, sir." And then an expression of panic touched her face. "You do have it, right? The anti-grav device?"

Jack looked blank, jaw dropping open. What had happened to it after Sam had been taken? They hadn't–

"It is in my pack, Major Carter," Teal'c assured her. "I have guarded it well."

Sam visibly relaxed. "Thanks, Teal'c."

He bowed his head in silent acknowledgement and turned to Jack. "O'Neill, we have left the planet's orbit. However, I require new coordinates. What is our next destination?"

Good question. They weren't exactly in the best shape to go after Henry Boyd and the rest of SG-10. But if they returned to Earth, Kinsey would be waiting to relieve Jack of command and then Boyd would never get home. They were between the proverbial rock and hard place. And they all knew it.

Daniel watched as Jack appraised his beat-up, exhausted team. Teal'c's silent nod spoke his immediate consent from where he stood, hands behind his back, in the doorway. Sam sat up a little straighter when Jack's gaze fell on her, despite her wan face and bloody shoulder. And then his eyes came to rest on Daniel. *You still want to do this?* he asked mutely. *I understand if you don't.* Daniel simply placed the power unit on the floor in front of him like an offering. When he looked up he said, "So?"

"So…" Jack pushed himself to his feet, dropped his hands back into his pockets, and regarded them carefully. The single look encompassed them all; it spoke of his absolute faith in his team, underpinned by a mulish resolve to do the right thing that was inimitably Jack O'Neill. With a determined nod he made the decision.

"Let's go bring Henry Boyd home."

Concluded in
STARGATE SG-1:The Cost of Honor

Available now